<u>Books by Christopher Woods</u>
<u>Soulguard Series</u>

Soulguard
Soullord
Bloodlord
Rash'Tor'Ri

<u>This Fallen World Series</u>

This Fallen World
Broken City
Power Play (Forthcoming)

Copyright©2016 by Christopher Woods

Cover art by
Derrick Gallagher

Acknowledgements:
I'd like to thank all of you readers who have waited, patiently, as I took so long to get this one ready.
And as always, I must thank my loving wife, Wendy, who made it possible for me to live my dream.
And thanks to Tracy Mullins for a little story about a bear.

Rash'Tor'Ri
Christopher Woods

Prologue

Rictor Hughes stood atop one of the enormous buildings in the city of Hub. Beside him crouched Kil'Sin'Deres, one of the strongest Kresh Rictor had ever seen.

"Seems odd to be workin' with you," he said. "Spent years tryin' to kill every one of your race I could find."

"When I decided to have Rash'Tor'Ri place his Mark on me," the giant Kresh rumbled, "I felt the same way. I used your race to push mine to join together and face a common foe. Never did I expect the way things worked out."

"He does that shit," Rictor said. "Just when you think you got it figured out, he changes the whole damn game. Boy's been pushin' folks from the day he was born."

"He would never claim any of the credit for what has occurred," Kil'Sin'Deres said.

"True enough. Can you tell if our target is in there?"

"My sources say he is," the Kresh'Farrara'Ti answered. "There is no true guarantee. I cannot see through the walls as Rash'Tor'Ri does. I find the abilities of my master very intriguing. He truly earns the name that was given to him."

"He always scared the shit out of the people around him. Always doin' something that would kill anyone else. Tryin' new stuff all the time. I'm guessin', considering who I'm about to assault a

Demon Lord with, that he hasn't changed much in my absence."

Kil'Sin'Deres laughed.

"Are you sure this will work?" Rictor asked.

"Yes," Kil'Sin'Deres said. "It would not work on many of the clans but this one was different. There were two Kresh'Farrara'Ti at the head of this clan. One of them had taken the other with his Mark. The secondary is still here and the primary went to your world. The clans fell to the secondary when the primary died. If we do this, we take them all."

"It's a sound plan," Rictor said, "If he's here."

"And that is where we stand. We must find out if my source is correct. If we take him, we end the current war on your world. There will be another, but we can do what we can to help him."

"Agreed."

"Are you leaving your men atop the building?" he asked. "It seems dangerous to depend on a single person to reach him."

"They're good," Rictor said, "but they're not ready for this. They're Guard strength, not Mages, or whatever you'd call what I am now."

Rictor chuckled as he saw the one eye ridge raised by Kil'Sin'Deres.

"Maybe I'll tell you about it someday," he said. "When I first showed up it was in a facility with some sort of technology I've never seen in use by you guys. It healed me and more."

"More?"

"Much more."

Rictor launched himself across the distance between the two buildings to land on the roof of the facility housing the Gateway to the Doran Colony, Earth.

Kil'Sin'Deres landed beside him, and the two of them slipped through the darkness to a doorway. They entered quietly, and descended into the depths of the facility.

"Here's where we part ways," Rictor said.

"Remember, they must see you. It has to be a human."

"Oh, they'll see me," Rictor said, approaching the rail that was mounted to the stairs that wound down to the lower floors. "They'll see more than they want to."

Flames began to roll across his body, and he jumped over the rail to plummet down the central shaft toward the bottom of the facility. He Pulled from the Source of this world's life, and exploded with power that rained down onto the guards below. He landed with a crunch as the ground cracked under his feet.

Then he was moving. Out of the stairwell and into the throngs of Kresh that populated the facility. Most of the first Kresh he encountered were soldiers, and he ripped through them as if they weren't even there. The roars were deafening as the alarms were raised. A Wraith rounded the corner, and Rictor ripped its head completely off as he passed the space where the Wraith had been. The body toppled, and more roars sounded.

He saw more Wraiths to the left, and charged in amongst them. The more powerful would be surrounding the Farrara'Ti. Follow the power. He was Pulling without stopping, and the power was flowing through him. Before his "re-birth", he would never have been able to do this. A Mage is limited to the power his body can handle. Rictor's body had become different after the healing. He could now channel the power through himself, much as he had seen Colin do many times.

This must be what it feels like to him, he thought.

One difference he saw was that he did this with the cold calculating of a man who knows battle. Colin would have been fueled by rage, but Rictor sent the power where it would do the most good for his purpose. If his purpose had been to kill everything, he could have done like the Boss. But he and Kil'Sin'Deres had a plan.

The first Ma'Nar came within view, and Rictor hit it with a Soullance unlike any they used in the Soulguard. It projected from his whole body and just obliterated anything in its path. He was just past the Ma'Nar's charred form, and the Farrara'Ti saw him. This was the goal.

The Farrara'Ti started toward him, and every Kresh in the room staggered. Rictor saw the look of utter surprise in the eyes of the Demon Lord. Kil'Sin'Deres stepped from the darkness and walked through the kneeling Kresh.

"Welcome to the Rash'Tar," he said. "And now there is work to be done."

Rictor nodded to Kil'Sin'Deres.

"I thank you, Rictor Hughes," he said. "They had to see only humans until the end or our secret would be out."

"You're welcome, Kil'Sin'Deres," Rictor said. "If you see him while you're over there, give him my best."

"You could come."

Rictor looked at the platform where the Gates opened with a longing he had felt many times.

"I can't leave 'em behind," he said. "I got too much work to do over here."

"Understood."

Rictor slipped back into the darkness of the facility, and retraced his steps to the stairwell.

He hoped the Marking of the clans would help. There were so many of the bastards, it would take many more of the Kresh joining Kil'Sin'Deres before they could become the army he knew Colin needed. In the meantime, he would build the Guard on Kresh, and prepare them for the war that would come. Perhaps then, he would get to see his friends and family again.

Chapter 1

The C-130 was loud, but I had grown accustomed to the noise after all of the trips we had made in the aircraft over the years, since the first attack in Kansas.

"I still don't see why you have to go alone, Boss," Andrea Prada said. Over the last few years, she had been one of the two "bodyguards" that always accompanied me anywhere.

"They're no danger to me anymore," I said. "Kil'Sin'Deres marked the leader of this clan. They're mine now. The hardest thing is goin to be keepin' everyone from shootin my clans before we can get them back off world."

"I don't understand this Mark," she admitted. "I've seen it in action, though, so I can trust what you say. Many others won't. They killed fifty million humans and, poof, they're no longer the enemy."

"I know," I said, "I've got a lot of explaining to do. I never wanted to use the Mark again on Earth. I thought it wouldn't actually be an issue."

"Should've known better than that."

"True enough," I said. "At least, I have some people in my corner. Paige and Gregor, both, are workin' with their people to get the word out about what's happened."

"We're five minutes from target," the pilot said over the com.

"Roger."

"What?"

I hadn't even noticed who the pilot was. I had met him some time back. He was a copilot on a flight I had taken back then.

"How's it goin, Roger?"

"Fair," he answered, "all things considered."

"Best we can all hope for at the moment," I said.

Prada laughed, "I remember that guy."

I smiled.

"How many of these groups are out here on radio silence?" she asked.

"Four in this area," I said. "I'm gonna hit one and let em signal the others. They have flares for that."

"You see Hicks, tell him I said I can't wait for him to get back so I can f…"

"Too much information," I interrupted her.

"Spoil sport."

"Two minutes," Roger said.

The guy in the back of the plane pressed the open switch and the big door began to drop. The flashing light was red. It would flash green when I was over the target.

I already know I was close. I could feel them all. There were thousands of Kresh down in the jungles below us. Most of our forces had been ordered to cease fire, but there were several that were so close to their targets, they had gone radio silent.

The light turned green. Before I could move, Prada grabbed me. Her laughter rang in my ears, as she threw me out of the plane. I guess I deserved that. I couldn't help but laugh.

I twisted and positioned myself where I could look down, and find the target I wanted. I could see the dark souls of my new clans below, and out at the outskirts, I could see the bright souls of the Marines who were set to attack.

I went into a dive, toward the closest of the Marines. At the last minute I opened the portal to an enormous shield parachute. With a bone jarring jolt, even for a Soulguard, my speed dropped to a manageable speed. I had devised this one for a quick drop.

I still hit the ground with a deep thud, and dirt exploded out from my impact. I landed in the center of a squad of Marines.

One of the snipers had been about to fire his weapon, but he jerked around reaching for his sidearm.

"I'd appreciate it if you didn't take that shot, Corn," I said. "Been a few changes in the last couple of days. We're under a cease fire, now."

I approached another of the squad. He held a source weapon. I pulled an envelope from my shirt, "I brought new orders with me."

He read the orders, "Seems we have a cease fire, Marines. Santos, orange flare."

He turned to me, "Care to explain why my orders also say to report everything you do while in our area?"

"It's a long story, Hicks," I said. "The short version is this. You're familiar with some of the things from my past. I told you about the force on Kresh that's building up."

He nodded.

"My forces on the other side took the clan that was hittin' us. Now they all serve a new master. One who will not allow them to kill humans."

"That Mark you were talkin about?"

"Yes."

An orange flare shot skyward.

"Still hard to believe in somethin' like that," Hicks said.

"Follow me and see it for yourself," I said.

I walked past Corn, who still held his sniper rifle's butt against his shoulder. At least, his finger was off the trigger.

"Form up, Marines," Hicks ordered. "We'll be following Mister Rourke."

I headed down into the valley toward the dark souls that waited below. They knew I was there and dropped to their knees as I came within view. They came out of the shadows from every direction.

"Jesus," Corn muttered. "I thought there were a couple hundred of em down here."

There were thousands. If things had been like before, Corn would have opened fire and they would have been swarmed by a flood of Kresh.

"…bowing to him…"

"...What the hell is goin on?"

"…Who the hell is this guy?"

I heard the whispers that passed between the Marines. They weren't familiar with the boost to the senses that the enlarged Soul stream imparted on me. I was used to it by then. I heard the whispers wherever I went.

I saw the Ma'Nar ahead of us. He was the strongest Ma'Nar I had seen yet. Maybe on the cusp of becoming Farrara'Ti. He stood tall as I approached. I saw his eyes narrow as he sensed the power in me. I could see his confusion.

"How is this Mark so strong? You could not have placed a Mark this powerful."

He spoke in Kresh, but I understood him as if he had spoken English.

"I will show you," I said in his language. Then I pushed outward with one of the info dumps that the Shak'Tar used.

"Son of a…" a voice sounded behind me.

"What the…"

I had sent the info dump to those behind me as well.

"That's the Mark?" Hicks asked.

"That's what it felt like as it happened from my viewpoint," I said. "Probably nowhere near what those around me felt."

"And that would carry over to all the Humans around you?"

"That's why I can't use it here. That would have Marked every man, woman, child, and Kresh within ten miles."

"Damn, Rourke," Hicks said. "Startin' to believe all the hype."

"Gonna be hard to convince a lot of the other folks," I said.

"This is something never heard of for my kind, Rash'Tor'Ri," the big Kresh said. "Perhaps there is something to this feeling that came from the one who passed this Mark to my clan. It passed along with the Mark."

"What feeling?"

"An anticipation of something," the Kresh said, "something better."

"That feeling is called hope, Tor'Vas'Reman," I said.

"It is something I have never felt," he said. "It is hard to grasp, much like a Savakos."

I saw in his mind a slimy reptile that slipped through the hands as if coated with oil.

I laughed, "Sometimes it is. But when you truly grasp it, there is no more powerful emotion in the world. Never let it go once you catch it."

"Savakos taste wonderful," he said. "We will see how this… hope… tastes."

"That we will."

"Rourke," a voice said from behind me, "I got someone on the squawk box for you."

I turned to find the com officer.

"Patch me through."

"Soullord one?" the voice on coms asked. "I have one of your aids, here. They want to know where the gate needs to be opened."

"I'll get the coordinates to you in a sec," I said. "Can you give them the coordinates for that clearing over there?

I was talking to the com officer.

He nodded.

"Coordinates incoming," I said over the link, "Soullord one out."

I nodded toward the man and he rattled off the GPS coordinates.

"Now we wait a while, and send these guys home."

"There's gonna be a lot of people who have a problem with this, Rourke," Hicks said. "I'm havin' trouble with it, and I know some of the back story. Some won't have that advantage."

"I know," I said. "Things are probably gonna get a little interesting for me from this point out."

"They did just kill over fifty million people," he said. "That's almost the same body count of World War Two. That's not gonna be easy for anyone to overlook."

"It's true," I said. "But they aren't the same Kresh they were before. You may not be able to see their Souls, but I can."

"We saw what you saw when you did that thing a few minutes ago," he said. "Which means we saw that Kresh's Soul get slammed by the Mark you blasted him with. We saw the thing's Soul afterwards too. I believe you when you say they're changed, but others won't."

"I know, but I can't let people attack my clan either," I said. "When they're Marked by me, I'm responsible for their safety. They're mine, true. But I'm theirs, just as well."

"I sure as hell don't envy you that position," he said.

"Me either," I said and turned to Tor'Vas'Reman. "I need your help with something."

The Kresh nodded.

"You saw in the info dump how I used the others to make the power of the Mark more powerful?"

He nodded again.

"I want to try to call all of the Kresh in to this place. I need you to lend me your support, and the support of all of the Kresh here."

"I do not understand how you can do this, but I will try."

"Just don't fight when I reach for the power."

I closed my eyes, "When I give the word, I just need all of you to push the message with your will toward me. I will be the antenna."

I concentrated on the message I wanted to send, and let them all hear the words. This would be something grand, or it could be something that would make me look like an idiot. Hard to say which it would be.

"Now."

I felt the mental strength of three thousand, and forty one Kresh pushing a single message at me. I launched it outward with my mind.

COME TO ME CLAN OF RASH'TOR'RI.

Hicks and his Marines staggered as the mental voice boomed through their minds.

"Jesus!" Corporal Santos exclaimed.

"Now we just have to wait and see how far that carried," I said.

I looked back at Tor'Vas'Reman. His Soul rolled with amazement. His race would never have been able to make themselves do something like that before the changes made by my Mark. Whatever happened from this point out, his race would never be the same again. There were too many with the Mark now. There would be no going back to the way it was before.

"This is what hope tastes like," he said.

"Rourke, another call for you."

I nodded.

"Soullord one?"

"Yep."

"My superiors want to know what, exactly, the hell was that?"

I guess it had worked. They heard the call all the way to HQ.

"Sending the Kresh back through a gate. Thought I'd try to get 'em to come here instead of huntin' for 'em, and sendin' 'em home in small groups."

"I am to inform you..."

"Give me the damn mike!" I heard a familiar voice in the background.

"The next time you want to try something like that, you better inform the rest of us!" Paige Turner, Archmage of the Soulguard, yelled at me. "And before you try to say something, smart ass, weigh it very carefully."

"Yes Ma'am," I said with a grin on my face.

"That's what I thought," she said. "Now start explaining! Very respectfully."

Chapter 2

The gate had opened an hour ago, and most of the Kresh in the valley were returned to their world.

"Damn, Rourke," Hicks said, "We thought there was a couple hundred of 'em down here."

"Could have been a mess," I said.

"No doubt."

"They would have left if you had started shootin'," I said. "That's part of the Mark. They knew I wouldn't want 'em killin' any more Humans."

"I'd say there's a lot of that sort of thing happenin'."

"There is," I said. "I can feel it. That's the reason I wanted to call 'em all here. Get them away from the ones doin' the shootin'."

"There's a general cease fire ordered," Hicks said. "But we both know it won't stop some of 'em from tryin'."

"True enough."

Tor'Vas'Reman approached.

"I will remain until all of our people are away from this world," he said in Kresh. "The clan came here afraid of Life ender, we leave as part of his clan. We will be a changed race before this is over. Perhaps you should be called the Change bringer."

He pronounced it as Ska'Vor'Ri. I liked being thought of as something more than the one who ends life. I guess I was growing up a little. There are places where Rash'Tor'Ri is what I should be. Maybe there was a place where I could be this Ska'Vor'Ri, as well.

"Maybe so, Tor'Vas'Reman," I said, "Maybe so."

I sensed more of my new clan closing from the north.

"More, comin' in," I said.

Hicks nodded.

The Kresh slowed as they got near, and walked into the clearing. They didn't say much but, as they passed me, I could see them sizing me up. It was an odd feeling, without a doubt. I could see approval in some, confusion in others. They were still dealing with the changes in themselves.

"They will understand, soon, Rash'Tor'Ri," said Tor'Vas'Reman. "They are not as adept with their minds as a Kresh'Ma'Nar. It will take them a time to adapt to the new Mark."

I guess you really can't have inner thoughts around telepaths. They're just thoughts. Nothing inner about them anymore.

The big Kresh laughed. Hicks looked at him in alarm, Kresh laughter can be a bit unnerving.

"Never really dull around you, Rourke," he said.

"True enough."

We spent two days camped around that clearing before all of the Kresh had gone through the gate. I got to watch the changes in

Tor'Vas'Reman as he grew accustomed to the Mark. I had talked to Lyrica before about the Mark changing a person to be one who would welcome the Mark and the time I spent with the big Kresh made me feel even more strongly that it was enslavement. I hated the whole idea of it, but they would respond to nothing else.

"There was a lot of 'em left," Hicks said.

"Close to a million," I answered.

"I like this a lot better than the work it would have taken to hunt 'em down."

"That many could have caused a lot of damage before they went down," I said. "The way they had scattered would have made it even harder."

"This is a much better solution."

"I agree," I said. "I have misgivings about using the Mark, but it is a strong weapon."

"Can we expect this sort of thing in the future?" he asked.

"It depends on the situation," I said. "The way this clan was built was the only way the Mark could be used like this. We can't depend on it in the future."

"Figured as much," he said.

"I could bring my forces over here, but they could close the gate on that side, and kill 'em all in one move," I said. "I can't risk that. We have to keep the others occupied until Kil'Sin'Deres gets enough forces together over there to take the war to them."

"He had a stroke of luck to be able to do as much as he did with this round. He's risking his whole clan every time he does something like this. Until he has the forces to hold off the others, we're responsible for what happens here."

"That's why we're paid the big bucks," Hicks said.

I laughed, "More like the Corp is a good place to put all the crazy bastards."

"Maybe," he said. "Seems the Soulguard has its own numbers of crazy bastards, though."

"Those are the ones who used to be Marines."

He chuckled, "Could be."

Tor'Vas'Reman approached the gate. He was the last Kresh left of the clan that had come in the latest attack on Earth.

"Rash'Tor'Ri," he said with a nod, "We will join your forces, and stand against your enemies. We owe you much after what we have done to your world. Never have I felt guilt for what I have done until this moment. We will do our best to earn the forgiveness of you and your world."

"You were following the orders of your former leaders, Tor'Vas'Reman," I said. "You don't have to earn forgiveness from me. You are my clan, now. My family. Together we'll change a race. Before I learned anything about Kresh, I would hate you for what's been done. I can see you aren't the same Kresh as you were, I can see into your Soul. Go to Kil'Sin'Deres, help with anything you can. If forgiveness is what you seek, know that I forgive you."

The giant stood taller and I could see the beginning of something inside of him that looked very promising to me. There was a violet color spreading through his Soul that wasn't the harsh purple and black that is usually present in Kresh Souls. It was a streak of beauty where none had been before.

Tor'Vas'Reman strode through the gate with his head held high and the gate closed after a few moments.

"He asked for forgiveness?" Hicks asked. "I never would have expected to see something like that."

"I spent most of my life thinkin' they were evil incarnate," I said. "They're much more than that. You'd be surprised how much like Humans they truly are. We're capable of some evil shit. So are they. But they are capable of good, too, just like us."

"You'll have a hell of a time convincin' people after what's already happened," he said.

"No doubt," I said.

"What say we get the hell out of this jungle?"

"My thoughts, exactly," I said. "Where is your extraction point?"

"North to a small airstrip in Bengassou."

"I'll join you if you don't mind the company."

"Sure you don't want to run it?" he asked. "It'll take a while for us to hoof it."

"Nah, I'm good," I said. "I could use the time to figure out how to handle this whole situation when it all blows up."

He turned to his men, "Let's move out, Marines."

"One thing I've learned over the years," he said to me as he turned back around, "During peace time, they'll drag you over the coals. I hope you got a thick skin. When the Kresh come back, they'll need you again."

"All I can do now is face the music," I said. "I've spent my entire life hiding what I was from most people. Looks like it's out now."

"It's out to the people in charge, Rourke," he said. "That doesn't mean it's out to the public. Leaders and a few soldiers know, at the moment. If you're lucky, you can convince 'em to keep it that way."

"I'm certainly gonna try."

We fell in about the center of the squad, and started the trek toward the north.

"I tell you," Hicks said, "This has been the strangest trip through the jungle I ever took. There's no animals."

"Has to do with the Soulguards you have with you," I said. "Most animals can feel the Source through the shields we craft. They get uncomfortable and get out of the area."

"That's pretty handy," he said.

"It can be," I said. "Never had a problem with mice or anything as I was growin' up."

"That could be a good thing."

"Never got to have a pet, though."

"Overrated."

"I would agree," I said. "Especially after Lyrica managed to get a dog that doesn't run away when we're near. Ugliest damn thing I ever saw."

Hicks laughed.

The sun had nearly set by the time we reached the small airstrip. There was a C-130 waiting to take us back to Cairo. There were some faster versions of this aircraft out with jet engines but I couldn't, for the life of me, remember what they were called. I always seemed to be on one of these though, which I had no problem with. I was in no hurry to get back, and have to go in front of the various world leaders to explain my lineage.

Chapter 3

"That could have gone worse," Paige said. "There were only three of the twenty that refused to speak to you."

"Yeah," I answered. "Those are the good ones. The rest wanted explanations and spent most of the meeting lookin' at me like I was a bug or somethin'."

"Several of them just took it in stride, and seemed appreciative that you could end this round of hostilities without having to go into a jungle, and hunt down over a million Kresh."

"True," I said. "It's interestin' to see which ones those were. Russians, Chinese, and the British. Sadly, the Secretary of Defense looked at me like some sort of abomination. The country I was born in."

"Unexpected."

"Yeah," I said. "Things could change soon, though, if Deacons wins this election comin' up. He's got a strong following with those backing the war."

Samuel Deacons had left the Senate, and was in the midst of a campaign to run for President. So far, things were looking good. I hoped his ties to me wouldn't hurt his chances. I generally hate politics, but I will vote for Deacons when the time comes. His politics were a lot simpler than most I had heard of. He didn't sugar coat anything, and he would do everything in his power to do exactly what he promised. He was whole heartedly behind the military buildup after what had happened in Kansas. And he would push even harder after this round in Africa.

I hoped for the best.

"He's got strong backing for the position," she said. "Not the least of which is the endorsement of the Soulguard. The Soulguard is in pretty good standing at the moment. Everyone can see that they don't have much chance unless we all work together. Your Soul Weapons have made the biggest impact of all I think."

"They really made a difference," I said. "I can't even imagine what the line in Cairo would have looked like without 'em. Not to mention, I and a few more of us would've met our makers down in the city."

"Too true."

"At least we got a grudging agreement to keep the details of what happened classified."

"And, now, I want to know about that telepathic message you sent last week," she said. "How the hell did you get that to reach this far? It's never been that strong before."

"I used the Kresh to amplify it," I said. "I wasn't sure it would work, but I guess it did quite well."

"How did you manage that?"

"Same way I did the Mark on Kil'Sin'Deres," I said. "God help us if the rest of his race learns to do this sort of thing. If they would work together, we'd have already been toast. Or eaten on toast."

"Let's just pray they don't start doing that."

"I don't think they will," I said. "Kil'Sin'Deres is huge leaps ahead of them on the civilized spectrum and he never would have even thought to do it."

"And what happens if you were to get killed in one of these crazy stunts you keep pulling?"

"Maybe that's the key to them actually becoming free. My Mark would be gone but the changes that Mark did would remain. The Mark, itself, may not even be gone since it was placed by so many others at the same time. Who knows? We're in undiscovered country, here."

"You get no argument from me," she said.

"That's new."

She looked at me with the single eyebrow raised. I think it's something all women know, that look.

"You know," I said hurriedly, "I'm supposed to meet Lyrica in a few minutes. See you later."

I took off before she could return some sort of response. I knew where I would find Lyrica. I headed toward the Hospital tents. There were so many injured, they couldn't all fit in the Hospitals in the area. Lyrica spent most of her time in the tents helping any she could, which means she would get the more severe cases. Her skills were so far past what medicine alone could do. She could stabilize patients in need of surgery that, under normal circumstances, wouldn't make it. After surgery she could speed healing to a point where the patients could be moved quickly. She was doing enough that there were support Mages with her all the time.

I felt guilty that I wasn't doing the same thing, except I'm not as skilled as she is in healing. She's a scalpel, I'm a hammer. Sometimes a hammer is just what is needed but, in healing, the scalpel is better.

The hammer is better for smashing things, my specialty.

"It truly is your specialty," Pelin said as I rounded the corner. "It is good that you are our hammer."

I chuckled.

"I have news," she said. "We have approximate coordinates for another Gate. It was known by some of the new additions to your clan."

"That's wonderful news!"

"The Gate is in China."

"I bet we'll have a happy new friend there. If we can give them a spot to defend, they'll be thrilled."

In my mind I saw a map with a small circle near the center of China. That circle would be miles across but we had no clue at all before this. This could change things a great deal. If we knew where the gates were, we could set up defenses like we did in Kansas. I think the Kresh would fail if they tried to come through that particular gate again with all of the defenses in place. Even without my presence or Lyrica's.

With this previous warning, we can begin to fortify that area in China. Perhaps create a second position the Kresh could not penetrate.

"I thought you would be happy, Master," Pelin said.

"Extremely," I said. "Don't call me Master."

She nodded and turned to leave, "Yes, Master."

I could hear her chuckle as she walked away. Sadly, my Mark had done more than just make some of them part of my clan. I think they all received a little of the sense of humor I had learned from Kharl. There's no way I was taking the blame. It was all his fault.

I shook my head, and continued on my way to the Hospital tents. I could see her Soul through the walls. Her Soul is a thing of beauty. It's full of vibrant colors, and shines with the passive power of a Soulstream over twenty inches across. I could never tire of watching her. I stopped and watched, as she Pulled power through a patient's stream. It entered the man's aura and, instead of spreading throughout the body, it all flowed to a spot on the patient's left side. I could see the area was much dimmer than the rest of the man's aura. Wounds create weak spots in us. The power flowed to that spot, and began to circle like a mini hurricane.

This was how she could heal a particular spot much more than if she let the power spread through the body. If she had let it spread, it could still heal, but the tolerance for the Source would keep the body from healing the wound as much, than if she steered the power directly to the spot.

She had much more of the healing process figured out than I ever would have. She still received training from a doctor who had dealt with the Soulguard for years, Terrence Pickney. Whenever she could, between massive Pulls to save the day, she would study anatomy, or spend time in hospitals.

I spent my days learning how to blow stuff up. She loves me anyway, go figure.

I slipped into the tent and watched her as she focused on her patient. The soldier was an Israeli soldier. There had been soldiers from around the world at the Battle of the Delta. I wouldn't have been surprised to see injured from any nation. Most of them still had forces in the area.

"I see you back there," Lyrica said, without turning, "Don't need eyes to see where you are."

"True," I said.

We both are Soullords. Our Inner sight is different than normal sight. I had spent most of my life using them together, but found at the second battle of Kansas that I could close my eyes, and see with my inner sight. I could see all around myself with it.

"How is the healing business?"

"We've done what we can," she said. "I wish we could have done more, but there were so many injured."

There had been hundreds of thousands of injured people, both military and civilian, after the Delta. Two Soullords could only see so many. We saved as many as we could.

"Didn't help that I spent more time in meetings than hospital tents," I said.

"We each have our job to do, honey."

"That we do," I said. "Anything I can help with?"

She finished with the soldier she was working on, and turned around and motioned for me to follow her. I followed her across the tent to find three people with dim Auras.

"They caught some sort of virus while out in the jungle," she said. "Looks like full body Pulls."

"Will do," I said and kissed her.

She smiled, and turned to another group of injured soldiers. These looked like follow ups as well.

I turned back to the three in front of me, and reached through the first one's Soulstream for the Source.

With a gentle Pull, life-force from the Source began to flow through his stream faster, and his aura began to swirl with the extra power. His system began to grow stronger, and the body began to fight the virus. My stream glowed a little brighter as my body began to draw from the

Source in order to power my ability. It wasn't much, but everything I did with the powers unique to Soullords cost something in my own body, even small things.

The tolerance for the Source present in the body of a Soullord is all that makes us able to do what we do. With enough supports, I have no idea what the limits of a Soullord's power would be. Hopefully, we'll never have to find out.

Chapter 4

I sat at my desk looking at list of numbers in front of me. Logistics was definitely not my strong suit. I was just glad it only needed my signature. I tried to read all put in front of me but some of it just made my eyes cross.

I signed the spot I needed to sign. I could do this because the particular group in charge of the logistics were completely trustworthy. Sandy and Randy Quincy, the twins, had done a spectacular job with Knoxville and had been promoted several times. Each job they had done with skill and I had suggested them for the position to Gregor.

Gregor was the one who ultimately made the choice. He was the guy who really performed as the Executive Officer of the Soulguard. I'm the sharp edge of the sword, Gregor is the hilt. Without the hilt the sword would just be a pointy piece of metal. With his guidance, I've learned much about the nuts and bolts of running an organization as large as the Soulguard. When the fighting begins, I am much more useful.

He also gave me more time to work with the other projects I needed to be a part of. Like the trip to China that was scheduled for later that week. We knew where a Gate was located in China, and we intended to reinforce a certain valley with so many guns and Source weapons that the Kresh would never break through. I smiled as I thought of that. It would be glorious.

A knock on my door interrupted my thoughts of dying Kresh.

"Enter."

The man who opened the door and stepped into my office was no stranger, but I had only met him once. Alan Stanbridge was the political campaign advisor of Samuel Deacons.

"Mister Rourke," Alan said, "I thought, perhaps, we should speak."

"You look worried," I said. "What is it?"

I already thought I knew what Alan was here for, and I wasn't wrong.

"I am worried about Sam's personal ties to you," he said. "I mean no offense to you, but recent developments may have repercussions that truly endanger his successful campaign."

"I was worried about that myself," I said. "I got the approval of the representatives to classify the information. Frankly, I'm a little disappointed that you even know about it."

"This is just proof that your secret will not remain secret, Mister Rourke," he said with a frown. "There would have been a chance if this wasn't the year of the Presidential election. They'll dig deeper for anything they can use against him."

"What can I do?"

"Not be offended if we have to distance him from you."

"Whatever you need to do, as long as it doesn't malign the Soulguard," I said. "If you attack the Soulguard when we need to recruit more to face the next wave, I'll be truly offended. You don't want that."

"That, we don't," he said.

"How is he doin'?"

"He's in his element," Alan answered. "He was born to do this. An honest man as Commander In Chief is something America has been needing for years. He pulls no punches. He forbade me to come here and see you. He won't hide behind lies. I came to enlist your aid in this. He may need to do this to win."

"If he needs to distance himself from me, he can do that without lies. But you must know why he and I are friends. We are both believers in truth. My secret has been secret because I don't talk about it. If asked, I won't lie about it either. I doubt you'll succeed in convincing him to lie either," I turned to look at the map on the wall showing the numbers of dead throughout four countries in Africa. "I would suggest a different way to meet this, if you can find one."

"You know him well," he said. "He said much the same to me, but I had hoped you may convince him to change his mind."

"I can talk to him, but I doubt he'll change his mind."

"That's all I can ask, Mister Rourke."

"Maybe we'll get lucky, and the facts will remain classified," I said.

"Perhaps," he said as he stood up. "I have strong doubts about that. It may be even worse if it does."

"How so?"

"Then they can make up what they want. To prove them wrong, you'd have to come clean with a story that may be better than their fabrication. It would still be out. One sure thing, people know something major happened, and they know you were part of it. They'll dig for it."

"It was probably a pipe dream to think I could keep my lineage hidden."

"It was feasible until you took control of a million Kresh with the power of your mind. Probably could have still kept the secret if you hadn't sent them home. Much better to have killed them."

"That's because you don't know what was done to them when they were marked. They became my responsibility. They became my people. Would you go home and kill a million people in America to hide this secret?"

"Of course not…"

"Yet you just suggested I should have done that very thing."

"But they're monsters…"

"They're people," I said. "They look different and they have a completely different society, but they are people. They couldn't help what they had become. Now there are a million of them with a whole different future ahead of them. They will become more like humans and a little less like Kresh."

"Not that being more human is a good thing," I continued. "They're have been some pretty despicable things done by humans to other humans. Some, no worse than what the Kresh had in mind for us."

"They would have killed everyone if they had succeeded."

"Yes," I said. "Some of them are monsters. And many of those monsters are the ones in charge of their society. A percentage of them have changed, and some have even joined our side in this war. Most people don't understand that Earth is just one front of a war involving fifteen worlds. We need allies, not dead Kresh. There will be plenty of those to satisfy the most bloodthirsty. I can't use that Mark on Earth. It had to be used on Kresh."

"Why not?"

"It would Mark human and Kresh alike," I said.

His face slowly changed to one of horror as the words I had said sank in.

"You could…?"

"Yes, I could," I said. "And you wondered why I hid what I am from those around me."

"I see," he said.

"Even if my bloodline becomes public knowledge," I said. "There are things we need to keep secret. If I can go public with part of it before it blows up, what are the odds we could contain the rest?"

He was quiet for a moment, "I think we can make this work for you. There will still be massive blowback from the public, but it wouldn't be as severe as letting the last bit out."

"So we can make a plan for this if the news leaks out?" I asked.

"I think so," he answered. "Do you trust your press liaison?"

"I trust Jennifer Alstead."

"The reporter?"

"Yes."

"She's much higher than I feel comfortable with," he said. "We couldn't pay her enough money to keep this quiet."

Alstead's career had gone stellar after her on the scene coverage of Second Kansas. She had gotten caught in the middle of that one and had the footage from the battlefield. She and her cameraman had been able to name their price for that one. Thus her career had sky rocketed.

"I'm a Soullord, Alan," I said. "I've seen her Soul. I know who to trust. I've seen yours, and if I didn't trust that you had Sam's best interests, you wouldn't be here. You want him to win because you are a patriot, not just because he's your boss. You also know that our interests are aligned with his, so now you know what most don't and never will. If we go public with anything, it will be through Alstead."

"You're sure about this?"

"Definitely," I said. "If we have to do it, I want her. She knows me, she knows the Soulguard, and she knows what's at stake. She was in the middle of it."

"I will set it up as soon as I can, then," he said. "I doubt she would decline something like this."

"I suspect no one would decline to cover this story," I said. "She's the only one I know that would sit on it 'til it was needed though."

"I can probably set something up by the end of the week."

"It'll have to be in China," I said. "I'm leavin' Thursday. We found a Gate and we're gonna set a trap."

"A trap?"

I smiled, "You've seen what's at Kansas?"

"Yes."

"We're gonna put that around the gate in China."

"I see," he said. "I'm glad we talked Mister Rourke. This may not be the tact I would prefer, but it may be the best we can do. I will contact Alstead and see if she is willing."

"Let me know, in case we have to go a different route."

He turned to the door, "I pray we don't have to change our plans. This is the best of the choices available."

"That it is," I agreed.

Chapter 5

It seemed that circumstances were swiftly making things more difficult for me. I had spent the whole day in meetings with people who looked at me as if I had caused the whole war myself. My rage was barely contained under the surface. This didn't bode well for a future where my lineage would be public knowledge.

I needed to tame the rage. While I worked on that, I had to use it when I could. Prada and Rostov had set me up a place to work out. It was an old farm where a battle had gone down. There were ripped hulks of tanks and the terrain was already destroyed.

"This should be interesting," Prada said.

"I'm trying to work the Mage weapons into the Dance," I said.

"That should be interesting indeed," Adaya said. "Will we be joining you?"

"Let me run through what I have, first," I said. "I want you guys to see it before we go into training."

Stepping forward, drawing the pair of swords from the sheaths crossed on my back, I settled into the stance that would begin the Dance. The world seemed to slow as I plunged my awareness into the focus of the Dance of Blades. Focus is the key to everything we Soul-guards can do. Our enhanced speed require enhanced techniques to think as fast as we move.

My movements looked to me as if they were normal speed, but the world had ground to a snails crawl. A bird flew across the field at such a slow pace, I could see every detail of its plumage. The yellow feathers blending with the various other colors.

My swords began the intricate patterns I had trained for from the time I could hold a small practice sword in my hand. Flowing from stance to stance, I released the rage from inside and the flames engulfed my body, burning a deep red.

I leaped forward with an over hand swing of the blade on the right. As the blade descended, I opened the right four disc launchers. Disks of Soulfire slammed into the first tank. My body turned with the Dance as that move was finished. The discs stopped as my body spun to bring the left blade down on a rear stroke. When the right came back up the disks began firing again. Power ripped through the torn hulk in front of me.

I switched to another stance and the power came from the Soullance. I watched with a savage glee as another hulk was ripped apart. Then I bolted forward onto the battlefield, and lost myself for a little while in a dance of rage and destruction.

There were eighty three destroyed tanks. I attacked the hulks with an abandon I rarely get to feel unless we are in the midst of a horde of Kresh. After some time, I stopped. The rage had subsided, somewhat. It was still there, but not as close to the surface as it was before.

I'm not sure if I could do this enough to truly bleed away the rage inside of me. How had Kil'Sin'Deres tamed his rage? It probably had to do with living two thousand years. My paltry thirty years hadn't made a dent in it. It just seemed to get worse.

I saw the others crossing the burnt battlefield toward me. Prada, ever at my side, as she had been since long before Rictor had been taken. Rostov, who had tried to fill Rictor's shoes and done quite a decent job of it. Adaya, still haunted by what occurred in Cairo. Asante Xhosa was the final of my guard today. He remained quiet most of the time but solid as stone. Dependable as they come. The others were off on a rare time off duty. There was so much left to do in Egypt but our time here was almost done. The rest would be by the various governments while we Soulguard would move to places close to the functioning Gates.

Many of us were going to China to begin preparing the defenses around the Valley that the Kresh had revealed as a Gateway.

"That was good, boss," Prada said. "It should be real interesting with the whole squad."

"True," I said. "But for now we need to run it with the five of us for a few hours."

The four of them lined up in formation and we settled into the beginning stance. I turned my

MP3 player on, and the grinding music of Seether boomed in my ears.

"Go."

We began to move.

***

"I felt you blowing up some tanks my love," Lyrica said as I entered the hospital tent. "Did you enjoy yourself?"

"Immensely."

"I'll be done here in a couple of minutes," she said. "They re-opened a few restaurants in Cairo. What do you think of a dinner in the city?"

"That sounds great."

"Gather the normal suspects while I finish up here, and we'll make an event of it. We won't be in the area in a couple of days, we may as well enjoy an evening out."

"I agree," I said with a smile. "We all could use some down time. Especially a certain healer."

"I know, I know."

"I'll gather the troops," I said and slid close to kiss her. "I love you, Little Angel."

"And I love you," she smiled.

I left the tent with a goofy smile on my face. I don't understand how, but she loves me. I'm constantly on the verge of turning into a monster, and she is just the opposite. How someone so good could love something like me will always be a mystery to me. But I can't even imagine my life without her in it.

Opening my inner eye, I scanned the area to locate Prada. I knew she would be close. Hicks was out with his platoon on a mission. Prada spent most of her time, when he was gone, shadowing me.

"We're goin down into Cairo in a little bit for dinner," I said as I approached her. "You wanna gather a few folks and come along?"

"Is that a trick question?" she asked. "Of course I do."

"I know Jacobs is here," I said. "He's in for a few days to work with the planes. Kharl is here somewhere but Kyra is back in Kansas with the new trainees."

"The Kid just flew in," she said. "He's supposed to go with Paige when she goes to Edinburgh."

"I'm not sure we can pry him away from Paige," I said with a chuckle. "Unless we can get them both to come. I'll check with 'em."

"I'll get Jacobs and our squad," she said. "You see if the Archmage is too busy for dinner."

"Sounds like a plan."

We parted ways and I headed for the command building. Paige would be there, she was always there. Some had reservations when Paige became the Archmage of the Soulguard. The Council had made many changes after she was placed in command. There was talk of an election for the position of Archmage early in her tenure. After a while, it just seemed to fade away. She was good at her job. Better than any Archmage that had been in place in any recent times. She took her job seriously and didn't take advantage of the position, as the previous Archmage had done.

It wasn't surprising to find Paige in a C-130 with the troops, flying from one place to another. She could keep the jet for her purposes, but she would send it out if it was needed and ride with the Guards.

She was so different from any previous Archmage, many feared a revolt of the Guard if she was voted out and replaced. Her joining me in the Assault on Cairo just further cemented her into the good graces of the Guard. The greatest thing was the fact that she didn't even know it. She was just doing what she thought was right.

"Sir," the sentry greeted me.

"How are you, David?" I asked.

I could see his surprise as I remembered his name.

"Fine, Sir."

"The Archmage here?"

"Of course she is."

"I know," I smiled. "She's always here."

"That she is, Sir."

"Have a good one, David," I said as I entered the door.

"You too, Sir."

The front office was empty. Most of the personnel were off duty at this time of night. I passed Gregor's empty office while approaching the stairs up to Paige's office.

Greg was back in Kansas. There had been some issues with the training schedules for the newest Mages that he had needed to take care of. He was supposed to meet Paige in Edinburgh later this month.

I climbed the stairs to the next floor. Paige's office was the closest to the head of the stairs. I saw both her and Kevin Graves' auras in the room ahead of me. I knocked and heard Paige answer.

"Enter."

I stepped into the room. The first thing that caught my eyes was the Kid. He'd had a hell of a scrape in Los Angeles and there was a streak of grey where the scar across the right side of his head had been. I was sure it was under there, but the grey streak caught the eye. I could still see the haunted look in his eyes, but it was much less than it had been. His first real command had been LA. He'd lost men and it had plagued him. I understood it. It still plagues me that I lost so many in my command. When the losses don't bother me, I'll be the monster I have always feared I would become.

"Kid," I greeted him with an outstretched hand.

"Colin," he returned the handshake. "It's good to see you again, Boss. It's been too long."

"True enough," I said, turning to the Archmage. "Paige, how's the job treatin' you to-day?"

"As well as could be expected, I suppose," she answered. "All they want to talk about is the classified information we discussed at the last meeting. They talk a lot more when a certain individual isn't anywhere near."

"They still agree to keep the information classified?"

"Yes, but I fear it won't remain so."

"Me too," I said. "I'm taking an action to deal with it if it doesn't."

"Do tell," she said.

"Do I need to leave so you can talk?" Kevin asked.

"Might as well write you into it, anyway, Kid," I said. "Some of this you already know but some will be new to you. I made a trip earlier this year…"

Chapter 6

Lyrica led the way to a restaurant called Tabla Luna. It was supposed to be some sort of authentic Latin cuisine.

"Oh, my," Reyna muttered. "I wonder if they have Ceviche."

"Ceviche?" I asked.

"It's a seafood dish used as an appetizer."

"I like seafood."

"You like any food," Jacobs said from behind me.

"He's right," Lyrica said. "You like anything, as long as it comes in great quantity."

There were people backed up out into the parking lot.

"This may take a while," Paige said. "I'll go put our names in."

Paige made her way through the crowd to the man who was the host. I saw him look out the window at us and he asked her a question. She nodded and he rounded the counter to grasp her hand. I saw the excitement and gratitude rolling through his aura. I saw Paige protesting politely but the man shook his head and motioned for her to stay right there.

He rushed to the back and Paige looked at us with a shrug.

A tall woman and three children almost ran from the back area. All three children, a boy of about eight and two girls that had to be twins a few years younger swamped Paige and hugged her. Surprise rolled through her aura as she hugged the children. The mother stepped in and embraced Paige. She whispered something to her and Paige nodded.

It wasn't very long until we were rushed inside and seated at three tables. Several diners were asked to move to different seats to open up tables that were located together.

As we sat, the man from the front approached with his hand outstretched. I stood back up and shook his hand.

"Mister Rourke," he said with a heavy accent. "It is an honor to welcome you to Tabla Luna. I owe you and yours more than I could ever pay. You brought back my life, my wife and children, when they were lost to me."

He was struggling with the language and Adaya spoke up in Arabic. He nodded and spoke back to her.

"His family was in the group we pulled out of Cairo after Lyrica set the world on fire," she said. "It seems, he wishes to provide a feast to the saviors of his family."

After he had spoken for a moment, Adaya said, "He recognizes many who were there. He has studied the news reports constantly and has seen the footage repeatedly. He is asking if we might tell him of what happened during our assault. He says, if it is classified he won't ask more."

"If you want to, go ahead," I said. "None of it is classified and perhaps it might give a little understanding of what we do."

Adaya began telling him what had happened. People around us dropped into silence to hear. More people had crowded closer as she continued speaking. She pointed toward me and motioned downward as if I was going down into something.

A young boy asked something.

Adaya nodded and said something that drew the child's widened eyes to look at me. She continued and motioned as she told the story of the giant dog pile. I saw her point at me and circled her finger around her ear, which earned a few chuckles. She told of the loss of our friend, Lennox Flynn. There were sad faces around us as she told of all the fallen.

Then she pointed at Lyrica and made huge motions with her arms as she described what some had seen with their own eyes. These few were nodding and looking at Lyrica in amazement.

Some asked questions and she once again pointed to Lyrica. I heard the word "almealij", which I had learned was Arabic for healer. Lyrica was studying a menu, remaining as inconspicuous as possible.

Adaya's story wound down and the owner shook his head in amazement. He turned back to the table after motioning for the gathered crowd to go back to dinner.

"I thank you all."

He said something more to Adaya and left for the kitchen.

"He says our dinner tonight is on the house, and he will accept no arguments on the matter. Enjoy."

"That was unexpected," Kharl said.

"True," I answered. "Thought there would be more fuss about the leveling of a pretty good chunk of the city."

"Ah!" Reyna exclaimed. "They do have Ceviche!"

"I'll try it," I said.

"Of course you will.'

"What are you tryin' to say?" I asked.

"Nothing at all, fearless leader," Reyna returned.

"Perhaps she's saying she should order double if she expects to get any," Paige said.

"Or triple if she insists on sitting beside Kharl," Lyrica said.

She ended up needing the triple serving. It was delicious, as were the other items we ordered. I ordered a dish with many types of meat in a fajita style meal. All in all, it was a great dinner.

"All we need to top off the evening is one of the sordid tales that always spring up around these tables," Jacobs said.

"There's nothing that could top the naked savior of Paris," I said.

"Ahh," Rostov sighed, "Devushka moyey mechty."

"Say What?" Jacobs asked.

"My dream girl," Kharl answered. "Learned some Russian in my time. At least the important stuff."

"Sounds like our Russian friend is smitten," Prada said.

"Perhaps you are not a one to speak of smitten, my friend," Rostov said with a grin. "I have seen a certain Marine many times in your presence."

"I think I've seen all there is to see now," Damaris said, "Andrea Prada just blushed."

"I think that is a blush!" Jacobs exclaimed. "Who's this Marine? I gotta meet the guy that tamed Prada! Just wait 'til I get back home!"

"You keep your mouth shut or you'll lose another appendage!" Prada growled.

"I'm gonna have to risk it! This is too much to keep secret."

Prada scowled.

"Speaking of Marines," Lyrica said, "Prada was just telling me a little story, today, that her beau had told her. What say you tell the others?"

"Sully's gonna kill me if I get him started again," Prada grumbled.

"Sully?" Lyrica queried. "I had no idea his name was Sully."

"Sullivan Hicks," Prada said. "Do you really want me to tell everyone? You know he'll get started again."

"How bad could it be?"

I was watching the two of them. I remembered a particular suspenseful part of a movie I had watched not too long ago, and projected the music that had played while the characters were about to be attacked.

"Aw, Hell," Prada said, "He's already started."

Lyrica giggled.

"I don't know what you're talkin' about," I said.

"This!" Prada exclaimed. "This is what he did to a whole platoon of our brave Marines! For two days!"

"In all honesty," I said, "One of 'em was complaining that they would know when things were gonna happen if they had that suspenseful music before it did."

"So they had to live two days in a jungle, surrounded by Kresh, hearing the Darth Vader song whenever Sully walked up?" she asked. "And poor Corn had to hear the Jaws music every time he refilled the water from the stream?"

"There might have been a shark…"

"How about Corporal Santos, who was already freaked out about you?"

"He asked me to play something scary."

"Carnival music?"

"That stuff is terrifying," I said. "How was I supposed to know he was afraid of clowns? He was convinced I had taken the knowledge from his mind. I didn't, I just hate clowns. Carnival music freaks me out."

"He lined the inside of his helmet with the packaging from the MRE's."

"Don't tell anyone," I said, "but that doesn't really work."

She looked at me with her eyes narrowed. I projected a short tune I had heard in a western when the two gunmen stood facing one another in a dusty street.

She shook her head in defeat.

"I told you," she said to Lyrica, "Don't get him started again."

She laughed that musical laughter I loved to hear. This had turned out to be a much better evening than I had expected. Great food, great friends, great family, and the greatest joy of my life. All together at one time. A wonderful evening.

Chapter 7

After some deliberation, we had decided that Lyrica would go to Edinburgh with Paige and the Kid. There were people still in need of her healing, and I could handle the set-up of the area in China. I would be spending long days building shields and weapons. She could help with those, but her skills lay in the art of healing. She should be using them.

"This gate seems to be out in the middle of an open spot like it is in Kansas," Rostov said.

"True," I answered. "If it was in a deep valley, we could bury it."

"It would certainly be faster," Reyna said.

The plane started its descent.

"Looks like we're here," I said. "There should be quite a few people already here."

When the C-130 rolled to a stop and the door opened they saw how many were truly there. I had seen it with my inner sight. There were hundreds of thousands of soldiers already in the area. I saw a familiar face in the front of the group there to meet us.

Len Yueh had gone ahead of us to meet the officials and tell them the news.

"Good to see you, Len," I said.

"We have much to speak of, Sir."

"I'd say we do. Have the Chinese figured how they want this set up?" I said. "It looks like there's a lot of source weapons out there."

"There are many," he said. "Pon Xiang, the head of the Academy here, is on his way in with all of the support Mages and most of the full strength Mages to handle the guns provided by the government. They will imbue the cannons for the defenses."

"Will they need the Source cannons for Mages to use or do they have enough conventional artillery?" I asked.

"They have thousands of weapons, more than we have Mages to imbue them. This is one less thing you will need to construct. They do want shields around various emplacements."

"I figured they'd need some of that. I was expecting to make some Mage batteries, too, but, what the hell?"

"Do you wish to meet our Military Liaison?"

"Sure thing," I said. "Then we'll get right to work."

***

I stood atop the forty feet tall wall the Chinese had been constructing over the last few months and looked across the bottom of the shallow valley, below. Across the valley the wall was beginning to take shape.

"I see why we started the guns and shields on that side of the valley," Prada said. "At first I was a little confused about it."

"Yeah," I said as I formed the latest piece of the huge shield wall that would project another forty feet higher than the bulwark of concrete and steel where we stood. "We've got, at least, some defense on both sides of the valley this way. The more of the wall they get done, the stronger the bulwark."

"We should have done something like this in Kansas," Adaya said. "It's a good idea. Especially with the shield backed against the concrete. Adds more strength to the whole thing."

"When all is said and done," I said, "We can put this sort of defense at every Gate we locate. The one in Kenya could be built while the Gate is submerged, drain the lake that's formed there, and be ready to blow the Hell out of anything that peeks through."

"I wish we knew where they all were located," Rostov added.

"Man, that would be great," I said. "Can you imagine the welcome we could give the bastards?"

"It would be glorious," he agreed.

"Ok, Alexei, You have the next one."

Rostov began to weave a massive shield across the front of the concrete bulwark. When he was through, there was another section of the shield wall ready for me to work with. I extended a tendril from my Soulstream and connected to the construct. I could feel Rostov on the other end.

"Ok, you can cut."

He severed his connection to the shield wall he had constructed. Then he moved on down the wall to begin constructing another section. I took the section he had built and pushed it into the ground to anchor it. Now the top was even with the previous section. It was rested against the bulwark for the bottom forty feet and stretched into the air above.

Then I began to open the three feet by five feet firing slots in the shield. They aligned with the raised portions of the wall that gave the people who would be standing there cover. All along the wall were raised areas with the firing slits. These holes would be manned with Source weapons. Not just regular Source weapons, either.

Jack the Engineer, as we liked to call him had been busy.

What rested behind the walls, ready to be installed were a large amount of howitzer sized Source weapons that worked much like the personal weapon. A person would sit in the control module and use the massive weapon just like the others. The gun would have a mechanical system to swivel and raise or lower the weapon. The mental Pull would fire the weapon. It was fed by a twelve inch stream, and do a great deal of damage. Each weapon would have a crew. The crew was to replace the barrel when it got too hot. Each weapon would have its own stack of spares.

The barrels would be flaming hot, so the weapon was designed with its own ejection system. The barrel would be ejected from the weapon outside the shield to, hopefully, do more damage to those outside. Then the operator would swivel the gun for the replacement to be attached. It was a hell of a cannon, and the Chinese had bought a lot of them from my company.

I finished the slots and formed a large tendril on the far side of the shield. Slamming it down into the Source I watched the brilliant flow of power as it began to power the shield. Then I pushed my end down into the Source and disconnected. I felt some of the power before I managed to severe my connection and released it skyward in a blast of fire.

"Better start payin' better attention, Boss," Prada admonished.

"Was thinkin' about these new guns," I said. "Got a little distracted."

"I was filmin' it with my phone," she said.

"Why?"

"Just in case you blow yourself up, again," she laughed. "We only have the one time on film and I think the Academy would love to get an updated version."

"Hardy freakin' har."

"It's ok," she said. "I'm patient, I can wait till it happens naturally."

"I'm not sure why my closest friends live to see stuff like that."

"I don't know, perhaps it comes from getting thrown out of a bunch of planes."

"If I remember correctly, you weren't the one thrown out of the last one."

"Don't know what you're talkin' about," she said as she pushed a button on her phone. "Let's go get the next section."

"Really?" I asked. "I thought you said you were patient."

"Oh, I am," she grinned. "But I'm damn sure not gonna miss it when it happens."

I shook my head in resignation. Then I had an idea.

"Prada," I said, "You got the next few."

She shrugged, still grinning, and handed her phone to Adaya. Adaya nodded and turned the camera toward me as Prada walked down the wall chuckling.

"Hmph," I grunted and connected to the section Rostov was finishing.

Prada didn't get to film me getting blown up again that day, I made sure of that. Three days later I let my concentration slip and blew myself off of the top of the wall to land in about a foot of mud where the rains had turned the ground to mush. I was happy to see that Prada was nowhere near when this occurred. Unfortunately, Brighton had caught it on his phone.

***

62

"Keith," I said as I saw the camera man Jennifer had brought with her. "How's the knee?"

"Hurts when it rains," he answered.

"I don't doubt that," I said. His knee had been in pretty rough shape when I had healed him on the battlefield in Kansas. Lyrica would have done much better but I did what I could.

"Colin," Jennifer Alstead greeted me with a smile.

It's hard to believe she doesn't avoid me like the plague after what she saw in Kansas. She had been out in the middle of the battle with Keith protected by a squad of trainees and National Guardsmen. She'd also had a firsthand view of the monster inside me.

"Jennifer," I returned her greeting.

I could see her and Keith's fear, but I looked past it to see the rest of what was underneath. Lyrica had really opened my eyes and my world was so much easier to cope, knowing that there was respect below that fear. I used to see the fear and turn away because I hated that people feared me. Now I don't turn away, and I see the rest of the emotional gamut below that fear I saw at first.

"I understand you're ready to do an exclusive," she said. "I remember asking for this a couple of years ago."

"You saw what I did, then," I said. "You even agreed it would be more damaging to know some things than it would help."

"I did," she said. "What's changed? Alan wouldn't be clear on that point."

"There was something that happened that has been classified," I said. "Too many have been a part of it and I don't think it will remain a secret. Alan and I decided it would be best if we got out in front of it with something solid. I hate politics."

"Give me an idea of what we're working with so we can make a plan."

"You saw what I did in Kansas," I said. "My skills as a Soullord put me in a position to manipulate the life force in all of us. But it wouldn't let me do that with the Kresh. The reason I was able to rip that Kresh's Soul out comes from my DNA. When my mother was pregnant with me, there was an attack on the Soulguard base in New Mexico. My Father had been lured to Denver by the Kresh and he had taken the majority of the Guards from the base......"

Chapter 8

Three months of shield making had gone by quickly. I knew nearly nothing about China and the Gate was out in the middle of nowhere. We spent the majority of our time working on the defenses. I was happy to board the jet and head toward Edinburgh.

I wasn't physically tired, but mentally. The Source keeps me strong but the building of basic shields had been monotonous and mind numbing. I did find that the rage wasn't as high with the monotony as long as I had to concentrate. There were still times I had to go out in the center of the open area and bleed it off with training in both blade and Source.

"I almost woke up this morning wishing for an invasion," Prada said.

"I know the feelin'," I answered. "This has been a long three months."

"Too bloody long," Stone muttered.

"They have a hell of a defense set up," Prada said. "I'd love to see it in action."

"Just the firepower of the single gun was awesome," I said. "I would love to see five hundred of the damn things workin' at the same time."

They had set up the first Source battery. The weapon was impressive, but they didn't need us to install the weapons. We had finished the shields and the Chinese Academy had pretty much relocated to the outskirts of the base constructed around the wall. The whole area was crawling with Soulguards and Chinese military units.

"Wouldn't that be a sight, Mate?" Brighton wondered.

"That it would," I answered. "Warren called earlier this week and told me they shipped another two hundred of 'em to Kansas."

"They found enough space to add more guns?" Adaya asked.

"Bloody Americans never have enough guns, Adaya," Stone chuckled. "I tend to agree with them, these days."

"You can never have enough guns," I said.

"Case in point," he said.

"This jet is so much nicer than our normal mode of transport," Reyna said as she approached from the rear of the jet. I never got to use the Soulguard jet, but I thought it was smaller."

"The jet was damaged, a little while back," Prada said. "They repaired it but the structure was warped a little too much. They bought a new one."

"How was it damaged?" Rostov asked.

"Oh, someone kicked the door off," she answered. "Normally the door would have unlatched but the plane was a couple of miles up. The kick warped the frame around the door and weakened the integrity enough that, after several more flights, they just gave up and spent the money."

"What kind of bloody idiot kicked the door out of a jet, miles in the air?"

"I don't know," she answered Stone and looked at me with one eyebrow raised. "Who would do such a thing?"

"There were good reasons," I said.

"And then got one of your loyal Soulguards thrown out the hole."

"I wasn't even in the plane. You can't blame me for that."

"Rictor's on another planet," she said. "It's your fault he did it."

"I've heard this story," Stone said. "No one said the door was kicked out of the plane."

"Oh yeah, it was," she continued. "One of the pilots actually quit after that. The other one was crazy, anyway. The guy that quit had just hired on as a copilot. He flies for some little place that does charter flights over scenic places like the Grand Canyon."

"And I guess I get blamed for that, too?"

"No, he should have had bigger stones than that."

"I agree," I said.

"They have overrides on the planes to blow the door," Stone said. "Why didn't you use those?"

"I was in a hurry."

"So you're the reason we didn't get our yearly raise in pay this last year?"

"Of course not," I said. "Soulguard is stretched thin with the new recruits coming in."

"Sure, Mate, say what you need to so you can sleep at night. We understand, never mind us battlers tryin' to make enough to survive."

"I'll try to live with the guilt," I said with a grin. "And on that note…"

I lay my seat back and closed my eyes, placing my earbuds in my ears.

"It takes a brave soul to sleep around this group," Rostov said.

"If I stay awake you'll have to hear the music, too," I answered projecting the beginning of the song by Gemini Syndrome that had just begun.

"On second thought, sleep soundly, oh fearless leader," Rostov moved to a seat closer to me. "None shall interrupt your slumber."

I grinned and let the projected music subside. The more time I spent with this group of Mages, the more I liked the way we all worked together. A few are always loud, a few quiet, but all of them dedicated and loyal. I felt at home with them like I did with the group I had spent years with in Knoxville. It's a wonderful feeling to feel comfortable with those around you. I have lost a lot of that with others, but those closest to me… well, they were my family.

***

"Mister Rourke," Jennifer Alstead began, "Thank you for coming."

I nodded. I hated interviews but this was a necessary evil.

"I'm sure there are a million questions the viewers want to ask, but the first in my mind would be this. What, exactly happened after Cairo? There are many rumors."

"The Kresh surrendered to me," I answered.

"To you? You, personally? Why would they not surrender to the forces who were chasing them?"

"This is where some of the rumors would be correct," I said. "They say I am part Kresh. I am. This is where we need to dig up things from my birth."

I went on to tell the story of my birth to the world.

"Why I would keep this secret, you might ask. Wouldn't you?" I asked. "I didn't even know for years. Those years were spent fighting these Kresh in caves. We called them Demons because we had no other name for them. I could feel the effects of the Kresh DNA inside me. I didn't know what caused it, but I knew something was wrong. When I found out what it was, I was devastated. They had taken my mother and father and now this?"

Jennifer nodded, "This DNA has to do with why the Kresh chose you?"

"It has everything to do with it," I answered. "I took a trip through one of the gates to sneak onto their home world a little while back. I learned a few things about the Kresh. They are creations of another race to be super soldiers for some war thousands of years ago. These 'Makers' as the Kresh call them were humans. The Kresh overthrew their masters and it's ingrained in them from the moment they are born that they will never be slaves to the 'Makers' again. They would never surrender to a human."

"What did they do to the 'Makers' when they overthrew them?"

"They ate them," I said. "A few, they sent to the colonies so they could keep a steady supply of slaves to operate the machinery left by the Makers. There are fourteen colonies of humans connected to their world. Ours is the only one with the technology to face them. That and the Soulguard."

"Why did you send them back? Why didn't you imprison them?"

"We learned at First Kansas, and so did they, that without a gate open between our worlds they will die here. You may have noticed at Second Kansas they had many gates open all the time."

"Yes, I noticed there were many."

"I couldn't, with a clear conscience, lock them up so their own people might shut the gates to punish them for surrendering. I want them to go home and tell their people that they can survive if they are captured. Perhaps the next wave of Kresh may give up rather than fight to the death, causing thousands of human deaths that might not be necessary."

"This is the core of the reason," I continued. "A big part of the reason I sent them home was more personal. Am I Human or Kresh? To be the man I aspire to be, I could never kill a million prisoners of war. These Kresh are more like us than I would like to even think about. They have families, children, and homes to return to. We may be at war with them but we don't have to be monsters. Some of them are monsters, some of us are too. I choose not to be."

"I see," she said. "We'll proceed to the next question. What abilities have you gained from the Kresh DNA? There are rumors of all sorts of things."

"The Kresh were built with telepathic abilities," I said. "I found out that I could do a few things. It's gotten stronger as I age. This is how I discovered the history I learned while on the other side of the gate. I mean, really, could you imagine sitting on a rock or something sharing dinner with one of 'em?"

"I think not," she chuckled.

"Me either."

"What about other abilities?" she asked. "I saw what you did at Second Kansas. You can't tell me that's normal."

"It comes from a combination of what I am," I said. "A Soullord can see and manipulate the Source, including the Soul. The Kresh DNA made it where I could do this to them as well.

Unfortunately, when I do this it has a cost. The DNA's effects are stronger after I touch their Source. So I don't do that unless it is necessary."

"You understand that many people are upset by what's happened?"

"There's always going to be someone who isn't happy with the action taken by someone else. The bigger the action the bigger the upset. I've done and will continue to do the best I can."

"Pretty good, Boss," Prada said from behind me as we watched the interview on the television in the cafeteria at the Edinburgh Academy. "You almost convinced me and I know what's goin on."

"I didn't really expect to have to use that this soon," I said.

"I guess we'll just have to see what happens," Lyrica said.

"True."

"Did you see the crap from Samson Forrest?" Prada asked.

"I don't watch his crappy show," I answered.

"Something about you being a weapons dealer and bringing your 'Demons' over to push your sales and get rich." Paige said from behind us as she entered the room. "You were right, he is a sniveling shit."

"Did you just say I was right?"

"I have no idea what you're talking about," she answered and walked away.

Chapter 9

"I can't believe they closed the Checkers down," I said, looking at the former restaurant in Murfreesboro. "It's a damn shame."

"I know," Lyrica returned. "While I don't have an obsession with food, I have to say they were some very good burgers."

"Now what are we gonna do?" I asked. "I guess we may have to go somewhere else. I wonder if Warren would throw a fit if I had him buy it and open it back up."

"That's what I call dedication to a burger," Prada said. "I know they were good but, 'buy the restaurant so it opens back up' seems a little excessive."

"Obsessed with food," Lyrica added. "That's what I'm saying."

"I mean, I guess you two international arms dealers have enough money to do it. But really?"

"There's no 'you two' in this one," Lyrica stated. "I like the burgers, but I'm not buying a restaurant just so I can eat there."

"I don't guess I am either," I said. "At least not fast enough to get lunch there today. Any suggestions, ladies?"

"You've been here more than I have," Lyrica said. "What do they have here?"

"There's a good Chinese buffet just up the street there," I said.

"Mmm, Chinese sounds good."

Lyrica may not be obsessed with food like I am, but Chinese food would always get her attention.

"Sounds fine to me," Prada said.

Prada started the SUV and we pulled back out into crappy traffic. I'd seen some bad traffic before, but Murfreesboro was right up there with the worst. At least considering the size of the city. New York was a hell of a lot worse and Atlanta was awful. Nashville was quite a bit worse, too.

It didn't take long until we found the restaurant on the left. Prada swung in with tires protesting.

"Not sure what I was thinkin', letting Prada drive," I said.

"Better than her," Prada answered. "She tends to just step out of moving vehicles to save animals and stuff."

"It was only once," Lyrica protested. "It was a while ago, too. I was just learning to drive."

"Seems the bad habits started young, then."

"You can't argue the fact that I have the cutest dog in the world, after that."

"Cute?" I asked. "That's the ugliest dog I ever saw."

"It's adorable," Prada said.

"Oh my god, the crazy is just oozing from you two."

"She has a thing for you," Prada said. "Proof enough she's crazy."

"You had a thing for him, too," Lyrica returned. "Proof enough we're both crazy."

"Now wait a minute…" I started.

"You better leave my dog alone or I may come to my senses."

I sighed.

We left the car and went into Chef Wang's restaurant. The food was good, the service was good and Lyrica managed to eat more than I did, which was an achievement all by itself.

The trip down to the factory was uneventful. I just enjoyed getting to spend the time with Lyrica. We had precious little time together since the attack on Africa. The months while I was in China and she in Edinburgh had been rough on us both. Then all of the meetings while I was in Edinburgh ate up so much more of our time. This had been our first chance to get away from it all. We had come to meet with Warren and both of us were owners in the company so we could justify going together.

There had been more building going on since I had been to the plant. We had started with one factory. The security was strong around the five plants we had now. Our IDs were scrutinized and called in to the security department, before we were let through the gate to the second plant we had built. This one held the headquarters of the company, as well as a manufacturing plant. Warren wasn't the type to build corporate headquarters in anything other than another plant.

A familiar form waited outside the entrance to the offices. He had lost some of the weight he had carried back in Knoxville, but Warren Grimes looked much the same as he did when I had opened his Soulstream back up.

"Colin, Lyrica!" he greeted, "It's been too long."

"That it has, Warren," I said, grasping his hand. "How are you doin'?"

"Couldn't be better," he said.

"I'm goin' to check in with the security department," Prada said. "You two stay outta trouble."

"I have no problem with that," Lyrica returned. "But as for him, who knows?"

"You gotta point."

"I have no idea what you're talkin' about," I said, and followed Warren into the building.

Waving at several of the folks working the desk at the entrance, we followed Warren toward the back and into his office. You can tell something about a person while looking at their office. His office was clean and tidy but it also looked well used. My office usually looked like a disaster area.

Lyrica sat across from his desk and I sat in the other chair to the right of them.

"So how's business, Warren?"

"Booming at the moment," he answered. "To be honest, we're actually having a rough time keeping up with orders."

"With five plants?" Lyrica asked.

"It's not the manufacturing end that's holding us up," he shook his head. "It's the shields. We need more Soulguards than we have. It's hard to get extra help in that area when we're in the middle of a war. We have a hundred Soulguards working twelve hour shifts. Fifty per shift and they can't keep up with the production levels. We could use, twice that many, easy."

"We'll talk to Paige," I said. "I'm sure there would be enough volunteers to do it if she'll spare 'em."

"We've got enough injured alone to handle this," Lyrica said.

I hadn't even thought of that, "That's a great idea."

"I know," she said. "It came from me so it has to be great."

"Smart ass."

"Half of that's right," she said.

"Har dee har."

"Another reason for this meeting is that we need to procure some real estate overseas," Warren continued. "If not a manufacturing center, at least a distribution center."

"What do you need?"

"A reinvestment of a great deal of the money you've made over the last year."

"Done," I said.

"You don't even know how much."

"Doesn't matter," I said. "It needs to be done. We need our weapons easy to get to any part of the world. You've got access to my accounts. Use what you need."

"I'm thinking I will follow the same business practice as he has," Lyrica said. "We need whatever paperwork you need to use what I have as well. You've worked miracles with his money since he first met you and I can't think of a better investment than the proven methods you've already shown."

"I can do that," Warren answered.

"And as far as reinvesting in this company, whatever I have is at your service."

"Thanks," he said. "This takes a load off my mind. The payoff should be quite substantial after the initial six months."

"That should be fine," Lyrica said. "I don't even know how much money I have right now. I spend more time at Medical Centers than anywhere else. Haven't had time to spend any."

"I spend some on food but haven't spent much more than that," I added. "Speakin of food, did you know they closed Checkers?"

"I had noticed," Warren said. "It's also opening back up in August."

"Great!" I smiled. "What happened? They remodelin' or something?"

"It will be under new management," he said. "The last owners just didn't do it justice."

"I'm glad it's not out for good, I was worried."

"Since you brought the subject up," he said with a grin, "This is your portfolio for the last year. We may be at war but the country moves on. If you'll notice there were several new acquisitions…"

"Holy shit! I bought Checkers?"

"Told you it was under new management," he laughed. "Owned by someone who can appreciate the place."

"I don't know how to run a restaurant."

"Taken care of," he said. "Found a local guy who is said to be a hell of a manager. He's going to run it and, if his reputation is true, run it well."

"Isn't he awesome, baby?"

"Why do you think I'm putting him in charge of my finances?" she asked. "Unlike this one, I would like to spend some time learning how you do what you do, Warren. I hope to get to spend some time in this area this year. I would love to learn some of your magic."

"I'd be happy to teach you," he said. "Now what say you to a tour of the place? A lot has happened since you left to join the fight in Africa."

"Sounds like a plan," I said.

Chapter 10

I could see the Soul of Pelin coming down the hallway toward my office. We had finally made it back to Kansas. Lyrica was back to work at the hospital with Pickney, the doctor who was training her. I had a great deal of paperwork to work my way through.

"Enter," I said as she reached my door.

"Master, I bring a report from your Clans."

"Don't call me master."

"Yes, Master," she answered with a grin.

I sighed, "How are things over there?"

"Relatively quiet, Sir," she said. "The most recent additions to your Clan are still in the facility at the moment. There has been no attempt, yet, to move another Clan into the facility. I don't know how long it will last before a new Clan makes their move. Most who have been near have seen what happened to the others. They want no part of this world."

"That's a good thing," I said.

"In some ways, maybe. The reputation is spreading of Rash'Tor'Ri, and the world that destroys Kresh of all ranks. There are some truly enormous Clans with powerful Farrara'Ti. This may draw their attention and that could be very bad."

"I see your point. How is Kil'Sin'Deres coming along with allies?"

"He has found several Clans who have similar views as he did when he came to you. There is some hesitation on their part. Kil'Sin'Deres says they will come around."

"Any news from Rictor?"

"The Prophet continues his mission on Kresh. Where he travels, people soon disappear. The Kresh have no idea where he keeps all of these people. To be honest, we don't know where he keeps people before he brings them to the Cerres facility. We could find out if you wish it."

"Leave him be," I said. "If he chooses to share where he's keeping folks, then we'll know."

"You are a strange one, Master. Much trust you put in a being who does not bear your Mark."

"I'd trust him with my life," I said. "In fact, I have. Many times."

"Understood, Master."

"Don't call me master."

"Yes, Master."

I sighed again and she laughed.

"Any word from Gorvelis?"

"The last group of people you sent over made it, safely," she said. "The cadre of teachers and scientists that were sent over have begun to work with Gorvelis and his men to begin modernizing the technology on Cerres. It's amazing how fast those on Cerres learn. They accepted the knowledge easily. As if they had just been waiting for it."

"They may not even know it, but they've been waitin' thousands of years for this."

"You could be correct, Master."

"Just from what we've learned in the last few years, I'd say it's about time for the Human Race to make a comeback. It's our job to make it happen."

"We will change the face of Kresh and the Colonies," Pelin stated with a fervor that, frankly, unnerves me. Those that I mark have a well of faith in me that is quite disturbing.

"We have seen what you have done, Rash'Tor'Ri," Pelin said. "We have seen inside of you at what you are capable of and we know you will succeed."

She had read my mind as I had worried. It was something I didn't think I would ever get completely used to.

"The next group of folks going over to Cerres ready?" I asked, changing the subject.

"They are ready, and will be making the trip in two days."

"Good," I said. "I know Kalib will be glad to see Dreanna and the kids."

"He is a warrior born," Pelin said. "But the girl has him well and truly caught."

I chuckled, "Her and the kids all do. Kalib seems to have a weakness to children."

"He's not the only one," she said.

"You know what would happen if I had children," I frowned. "This DNA is turning me into a monster. How do I curse a child to the same fate?"

"You win this war, and make it where the child doesn't have to do what you have," she answered. "Then he only contends with what any Shak'Tar must."

"That simple, eh?"

"Yes."

"Then let's see about winnin' this damn war."

She nodded.

***

There weren't as many of us sitting at the table at this restaurant as there normally were. Only seven people this time. Lyrica had been working late at the hospital. Paige and the Kid were in Montana. Jacobs had managed to show up with Gina in tow. They sat across from me. Kharl and Kyra were sitting on my right. Reyna and Adaya sat to the left.

"So what've you two been up to?" I asked Kharl.

As soon as I said it I saw a scene flash across his aura and my mouth dropped open.

"You didn't!" I exclaimed. "You didn't invite anybody? Just ran off and got married!"

The table went silent as all eyes turned to the couple.

"We been together for thirty years, boy," Kharl said. "Just decided to make it official."

"Congratulations!" Adaya said.

"Conflatulations!" Jacobs exclaimed. "This is great! Beer's on me tonight!"

"Condolences," Reyna said, sadly, to Kyra.

"I know," Kyra said. "I don't know what came over me."

"I can't believe you guys didn't invite me," I said.

"You were in Scotland."

I just shook my head.

An argument from the back of the store interrupted our moment.

"…not serving that…"

"…alien halfbreed…"

These two fragments of an argument caught my attention.

"We don't get to pick and choose who we serve, here, Ashley. I don't want to serve his kind either but we do our job."

"His aliens killed my brother!"

His kind. The two words were like punches to the stomach.

"What is it, son?" Kyra saw the flush spread across my face.

"We just have to do our job," the other voice continued. "To think he was welcomed here before the truth came out."

Rage began to boil under the surface of my thoughts. I stood up and walked toward the back of the restaurant. The two girls stood at the door to the kitchen.

"Let me relieve you of the burden of serving an alien halfbreed," I said a little more savagely than I intended. Rage was rolling off of me in waves. "Neither of you need worry about serving 'my kind'"

I turned around and strode out of the restaurant that I had spent so many evenings with my friends. The rest of the table followed me out.

"What the hell happened?" Jacobs asked.

I dropped a short replay of the last few minutes into their minds, "I couldn't stay in there."

They were pissed. But none so angry as Kyra. She turned around to go back in but Kharl grabbed her.

"Nothin' to be done about it," he rumbled.

"I'll burn this place to the friggin' ground!" she growled.

"Stop," I said. "I knew this sort of thing was comin'. I've been expectin' it, just wasn't really expectin' it here."

She stopped dragging Kharl toward the restaurant, "I'll leave it be for now. But, mark my words, I am not done here."

"Let's go to Hooters or, better yet, just order take-out from somewhere," I said.

"You guys head back in," Jacobs said. "I'll bring pizza and beer back with me. There's still a marriage to celebrate. Boss, you don't worry about these people. We always got your back."

"Thanks Ivan," I said. "Alright, back to my house for a celebration!"

The rest of the evening went well, but there was something hanging over the celebration. It wasn't just the seething rage inside me. I could see it in Kyra, as well. She had taken the waitress' snubbing of me much worse than even I had.

I had known this was likely coming at some point, but it didn't make it hurt less. People are going to find something or someone to hate. At the moment, I was an easy target. The news hadn't let the issue rest since the information had leaked to the public. I'd discovered that the majority of the Press would always look for the bad in any situation, even make it up if it couldn't find a bad side. They didn't have to make up much to report the bad side of me. The torture of a Kresh Soul was replayed many times, and somehow, a video clip from the soldiers gear in Africa had made its way into the public. The world watched as I, with a smile on my face, sent Kresh after Kresh back home through a portal.

Chapter 11

It was late and I stood in the darkness staring at the spot where the Gateway had opened twice before. I couldn't help but wish it would open again. There was so much firepower on this side of the Gate, the Kresh would be crazy to come through here. I would be foolish to believe they didn't know that. I'm sure there were spies amongst us who served them. There were none close to me, I was certain. There were advantages to being a telepathic Soullord. I could see treachery at a glance and feel it with my mind.

I pulled my MP3 player from a pocket and attached it to my shoulder with a shield. Placing the earbuds in my ears and securing them with small shields of their own, I heard the beginning of another Five Finger Death Punch song begin to pound my ears. I drew the twin swords and began the Dance, my rage release. I had plenty of that built up.

I was hearing more and more about my Kresh DNA from, both, civilians and military. I had spent the day on base because of a situation I had run into in town the day before, similar to the restaurant from the previous week. They didn't even have to say it, I could hear their minds screaming their thoughts out. It was a little better on base, but there were some who hated me with a vehemence I hadn't expected from the soldiers I spent time with. Most weren't soldiers I had physically served with, but it cut me deeper than I would like to admit.

I continued my dance for several hours, with my rage at the world in general feeding the thing inside me. Sometimes I could feel it rumble inside. It wasn't just rage, it was something hard to describe. A well of power I could feel, down deep, power I dared not release. It was fed by the Purple Soulstream that led off to the east. Any time my mind got too close to that Source, I could feel the inhuman parts inside of me twist and turn.

My way of taking out Farrara'Ti didn't help my situation. When I touched one of their Souls, even briefly, the otherness in me gained strength. That cold alien feeling, inside, terrified me. I didn't want to lose who I was to that being of hate, fire, and a coldness that didn't feel human at all.

I stopped the dance with my breath heavy and sweat coating my body. Shaking my head to try to stop the musings inside, I sheathed my swords in the scabbards crossed on my back. It did me no good to wallow in the fear of what is in store for my future.

I turned and walked back toward the base to the south of the enormous clearing where we had destroyed two armies in the last few years. The clearing where I had lost friends, thought I had lost my best friend, and lost a piece of the humanity I held so dear. The very spot I walked across was the spot where I had ripped the Soul out of a Farrara'Ti and tore it in ragged pieces before releasing it back into its own Source. One of my earliest glimpses of that being inside of me.

"Why does he go out there all the time?" I heard one of the National Guardsmen ask his partner from a distance they didn't realize I could hear from.

I toned most of it out.

"…waitin for buddies…"

"…was here last time… damn sure weren't friend…"

"…halfbreed…"

"…screw you…"

I walked out of range of the pieces of conversation. The accusations hurt, but there was something else I saw in the conversation. The other guy defended me. It wasn't everyone who judged me, and it was the ones who defended me that made the others bearable.

I continued back toward the residences. Lyrica should have made it home by then. She had spent a lot of time in the Hospital over the last few weeks. Pickney was accelerating her education during the time while we were at peace. He said there was no telling when the Kresh would hit us again and he wished her to be as prepared as he could make her for it.

I saw the dark Soul approaching out of the night. The Shak'Tar all had Souls with the dark purple and black of the Kresh interlaced with the myriad colors of the Human Soul. I had noticed the changes that were taking place since I had

Marked them. The human side was brighter and the darkness was less than before. They claim the Mark was voluntary to follow but I can see the changes in their Souls. The Mark changed them into someone who would willingly follow the Mark of the one placing it. It had to be the case since they willingly served the Kresh before me. Some, a very few, had broken free of the Mark's changes to initiate their first meeting with me. Gorvelis was unlike most of his cohorts at the time, and his Soul changed the least when my Mark was placed on him. Perhaps, because he was already someone who would be willing to follow me.

The one approaching me was one like Gorvelis had been. Pelin had been one of the few that had overcome those changes her former master had placed with his Mark.

"Pelin," I said in greeting.

"Master," she returned, "I bring word from Gorvelis."

"What's going on over there?"

"The peace continues, for the moment," she said. "He said there are rumors of a Clan from the Western Plateau talking of Doran."

"We knew it couldn't last," I said.

"There is still some time, but if they come, it will be bad."

I sighed, "How bad are we talkin'?"

"He is an Elder Kresh," she said, "One of the first generation. His Clans are enormous. He rules more Kresh than the combined Clans in all of Hub. The last Clan numbered around twelve million, a large Clan. Hal'For'Radolin rules over ten times that many. If he moves into Hub, the rest of the Clans will flee. Kil'Sin'Deres will have to pull all of his forces into the Cerres Facility and Cerres itself. Your forces number around twenty five million at the moment. There are seven Farrara'Ti Kil'Sin'Deres has brought together that are willing to join us. They will bring our numbers almost double what they are now."

"That sounds promising," I said. "What's the catch?"

"They will not accept your Mark as a Proxy. They will not subject themselves to Kil'Sin'Deres rule. They wish to be his equals in your Clan. If Kil'Sin'Deres is the one to place the Mark, they feel they will not be his equals."

"You have no idea how much our races are truly alike," I said. "Even Kresh worry about the appearance of power."

She chuckled as she saw in my mind the politicians I'd seen in the past.

"It seems I'll have to make another trip to Cerres," I said. "Probably pretty soon, if this Hal'For'Radolin is deciding to make a move on Earth."

"Very true, Master."

I sighed again and she chuckled.

"Any news on Ric?"

"Your Prophet has been busy," she said. "He has, your term would be, married."

"Married?" I exclaimed, "When did this come about?"

"He married the daughter of a Chieftain on the world of Parlais."

"I thought he was working on Kresh."

"We did, as well," she said. "You ordered us to leave him be and let him do his thing."

"So how did you find this out?"

"He arrived in Hub, a day before Gorvelis sent his update. Your Prophet is requesting some things from you."

"What's he need?"

"Trainers," she said. "He wishes trainers to return to Parlais and begin building a Soulguard presence there. If you smile any wider, I believe your face might break, Master."

"I've realized somethin'," I said. "Even if we fail, here, the Kresh are doomed. We have Soulguards on three worlds plus their own home world. The knowledge is spreading to the other worlds of how to fight 'em. Especially if I can do this thing on Cerres. Fifty million Kresh will be forever changed. Even more after the Mark is done and they see how it is done. Can you imagine anything standing against that many using their combined might? All we need to do is hold long enough for the changes to take effect. I wish I knew how long until that particular gem will surface. Have any of you seen any of the Kresh combine their power on their own?"

"Not that I have seen, Master."

"This is something I want you all to keep watch for," I said.

"Kresh would never do that," she said.

"Before," I said, "That would be true. I see the changes in their Souls. It's not somethin' I can coach them to do. They'll never change if it's my order to do it. It's gotta be done by them. We've shown some of them the way. If they'll only take the path we marked for them. Gorvelis started this and I'll continue it. Maybe, just maybe, we are accomplishing the impossible."

"You have great dreams, Master," she said. "I find that I wish them to come true. What of those arrayed against us? What if they discover this?"

"They can't, just like those I've marked couldn't before they were marked. The Mark changes them. I just hope it changes them enough."

She nodded.

"I'll see about setting up another expedition," I said. "I'll have to meet with Paige and set this up. She was a little upset with the last trip I made across to the other side of the Gate."

"I heard something about a fiery death."

"I did too," I said. "You don't think she meant me do you?"

Pelin chuckled.

"Send word that we're on it," I said. "We'll send another messenger when we get close to ready for the trip. We need to know if there is anything Gorvelis, Sam, or Darrel need, as well.

This may be the last trip through we get to pull off. Depends on Hal'For'Radolin and whether he's serious or just talkin'."

"Some Kresh are slow to act," Pelin said. "Some are not. I would proceed under the assumption he will not be."

"Probably the best idea."

"I will go prepare the messenger, Master."

"Don't call me Master."

"Yes, Master," she laughed as she walked back into the darkness.

I stood there for a few minutes. Rictor, married? Wow. That had caught me completely by surprise. To a Princess, no less. What the hell was goin' on? Kharl and Kyra, now Rictor.

I continued toward the residence shared by Lyrica and I. Was it a sign? Was it even fair to her? I couldn't give her a child, at least, not yet. But I couldn't even imagine a life without her. I knew she was the only one I wanted or ever would want. Perhaps I should ask her. How would I do it? I realized I had already passed the point where I knew I was going to ask. Do I go all romantic and set up a beautiful evening? Do I do the one knee approach? I would need a ring for certain. I could see myself kneeling and placing a ring on her finger. I could even picture the question I would ask. Lyrica Jayne, will you marry...

The door of the residence I was approaching slammed open, and a blur in a pink t-shirt slammed into my chest, sending me rolling backwards through the yard. Lyrica was squeezing me like a vice, her voice, joyously falling on my ears.

"Yes! Yes! Yes! Yes!"

I never actually got to ask. I guess being a telepath can be a bit awkward. I seemed to have been projecting. I looked up with a huge grin on my face to see several people standing outside their quarters. I think a lot of people had heard that projection.

Chapter 12

"You want to what?" Paige looked at me with eyebrow raised.

"I need to go back to Cerr…"

"I heard you," she glared at me. "I'm just not sure how you have the nerve to even suggest it. You kick started the war back up last time you went over there."

"That wasn't exactly my fault," I returned.

"I'm sure it was your fault. Do you know how I'm sure it's your fault? Because everywhere you go, something always happens. Once or twice, coincidence. But every time?"

"There are lots of places I go where nothing happens."

"Where?"

"I'd have to think a little but I know there's…"

"Nope," she said, "There's nowhere."

"Twenty five million more allies," I changed the subject.

"That many? Really?"

"That's why its somethin' I gotta do, personally."

She rubbed her face with both hands, "Is my hair turning grey? I feel like you've turned my hair grey. Always something with you."

"That's not all," I said with a grin.

"Oh dear," she groaned. "What else?"

"Lyrica is going with me."

"You're shitting me!" she exclaimed. "Look! You've made me curse."

"I told her we could honeymoon anywhere she wanted and she picked Cerres."

"How do you expect me to approve both Soullords going off world at the s... Did you say, honeymoon?"

"Yes, yes I did."

Her eyes lit up and her mouth dropped open.

This was the first time she had stopped talking since I had walked into her office. It lasted almost thirty seconds.

"Oh my god," she finally said. "When did this happen?"

"Last night."

"Congratulations to the both of you. I know she's been planning this for years."

"Years?"

"Years," she nodded. "But I still have an issue with both Soullords off planet at the same time."

"We have people watching the other side. When someone moves, we'll know and get back on the double. That's another thing we need to talk about."

"What?"

"There are rumors of the next to come at us and he's big."

"How big?"

"Over a hundred million."

"We can't stand up to that."

"They're limited to one Gate at a time for large groups but I'm afraid we'll see a lot of random attacks all over the place through smaller gates. He'll be limited by the fact he can only use so many at a time. We can thank Merlin for that. He destroyed the other facility and they are limited to one, now."

"That's still a lot to face."

"It is," I said. "If the rumors are true, this may be the last one, one way or the other."

"We need more Mages."

"That we do," I said. "We're makin' Mageguards as fast as we can. There's another group set to ascend today."

"And what news of the Academy on Cerres?"

"Didn't hear anything from Sam or Darrell," I said. "I did hear from Rictor."

"Do I want to know? He's as crazy as you are."

"It seems he invaded another world and is establishing an Academy there."

"What?"

"He would like some trainers if you please."

"Why didn't you lead with this? This is Soulguard business."

"Where would the fun be in that? I had you convinced we needed another expedition before even hearin' that part," I grinned.

"Sometimes I want to just pick you up and shake you," she mumbled.

"I had an instructor or two at the Academy who told me the same thing."

I saw the flash of sorrow that flowed across her aura as she remembered Nora Kestril. They'd become pretty good friends after I had departed. Her death at First Kansas saddened us both.

"Nora threatened to do it several times, even after you left the Academy for Knoxville. I offered to help."

"Whatever do you mean?"

She leaned back in her chair, "Do you realize that you have more people in service to you than a lot of countries? All sworn to you, alone? You've become more of an ally to the Soulguard than a part of it."

"I've always been Soulguard," I stated in my defense.

"I know," she said, "What I'm trying to say is there will be a day when you may need to be the ruler of your people instead of a Soulguard."

"I don't see where they have to be different things."

"You will," she said with a grim smile, "That's when you know what your future is going to be. Right now, you fight. You're more powerful than anyone I know. What happens when the fighting is done?"

"I never thought that far in advance, Paige," I answered. "I never expected to live through the first part."

"Then you need to start thinking about it," she said. "A soldier may live in the moment but a leader has to plan for the future."

"They'd probably be better off if I don't make it through this war."

"What do you mean by that?"

"I saw the changes in their Souls when they were Marked," I said. "There's no turnin' back from that, now. They're different, changed, and they'll never be the same as they were again. The people they are, now, couldn't accept returning to what they were. And the longer they remain this way, the more the changes take hold."

"And how would it help for you to be removed from the situation?"

"They'd be free."

"My understanding is that they don't even understand what freedom is."

"They do now," I said. "They'll understand it more, the longer this goes on. It's the one good thing to come of this telepathic mark of mine. It shows them everything about me, including a great love of freedom. They'll begin to see it, and then they'll want it. Somehow, I intend to give it to them."

"That could be a dangerous prospect."

"Created as slaves," I said. "Even then they chose to rebel rather than remain slaves. Now they are seeing the same thing in reverse. We fight and die rather than be enslaved. It either becomes a circle and they become slaves again, or they and we become equals. I've hated them my entire life but even I can see where this needs to go."

"Still somewhat uncomfortable about it."
"I am too."

Chapter 13

"How's our little air force?"

"Growin', Boss," Jacobs answered. "They brought in some more planes. Jack's been spendin' a lot of time here workin' on shields."

"What've we got?"

"A whole slew of A-10s," he answered. "They're good with crowd control. More of a straight line crowd control but I'll take what I can get. The AC130s are tried and true crowd pleasers and we got a bunch more of 'em."

"How hard is it to do the shields?"

"Not as hard as you'd think, after Jack finished settin' up the hologram projectors."

"Hologram?"

"It mounts at the same spot on each plane and projects what needs to be made. Then a Mage puts it together. We got some damn good focus Mages workin' the shields and they go fairly quickly. Not as quick as a Soullord who can see it, but a lot quicker than a Mage without the projector."

"You guys are makin' me obsolete."

"Nah, just lettin' you focus on more important things."

"This is pretty high on the importance scale," I said. "You guys are makin' a massive difference on the field, and its high priority to keep your people safe and shootin' Kresh."

"Thanks for the vote of confidence, Boss," Jacobs said with a little surprise flowing through his aura. "The boys and girls will be glad to hear it."

"Your guys are doin' a hell of a job," I said. "We're lucky to have 'em."

"Thanks, Boss," he said. "So how'd the Archmage take the news of where Lyrica wants to honeymoon?"

"How'd you hear about that so fast?"

"Gina's been workin' on Lyrica's detail for the last few weeks. There are a couple of permanent members of the detail. You're probably familiar with 'em. A smart assed ox and a rabid squirrel."

"Yeah, I'm familiar," I laughed. "They've been there so long, I don't think either of 'em would want to be reassigned."

"Anyway, Gina's part of the detail that works with Mattie and Trent."

"Well, Hell," I muttered. "What are your thoughts on your girlfriend travelin' to another world?"

"What?"

"I got Paige to approve the trip but I have to take our security details with us."

"That sucks, Boss," he said. "It means I'm stuck here cause I'm not part of the detail. She'll be thrilled, though."

"That's just it, buddy," I said, "We're also settin' up a cadre of trainers to send to a third planet. Seems Rictor's gone and invaded another world. He requested trainers for a new Soulguard

Academy. I need Mages and Guards for the post and I thought you might be interested."

"Really?"

"I hate to lose you from here but you'd be good at it," I said. "I can get you both on the list if you're interested."

"I'm damn sure interested, Boss," he said. "I'll have to talk with Gina tonight. When is it?"

"That's the other thing," I said. "Less than a month away. Lyrica and I are gettin' married quicker than we would like but we want to do it before we go and take a week on Cerres while the peace lasts."

"We'll talk it out tonight, then."

"If you got any recommendations for me for others, I need 'em as quick as possible. We're sendin' quite a few folks over. If Cerres goes as planned, my bunch will take the Parlais facility and close up the Kresh access to it. I think we'll be able to, even without the other additions to the Clan, but we need to go under the expectations of an underground Academy. We'll know more when we get over there."

"How bad is their tech level?" he asked. "I know the other worlds have been held back."

"Not much past medieval tech," I said. "That starts to change as soon as your group arrives. If it's like Cerres, there's a semi-modern facility at the Gate, but we'll be moving out away from there pretty quickly. Rictor will have much more detail for you when you get there. If we successfully take the Parlais facility in Hub, you'll have a base of operations to work out of there."

"Ok," he said. "There's a guy that got ascended close to the time I did. His name's Alex Campbell. Pretty good with his shield work. Was damn good as a Guard. Might be a good addition."

"I'll check him out."

"Then there's a guy that was here a few months back you might wanna check out too. Was some sort of artist before joinin' the Guard. He's got the sort of imagination for makin' new stuff that reminded me of a certain Soullord. Name was Derrick Gallagher. I think Lyrica was the one to handle his ascension. He's good with detailed stuff. He'd make a good trainer."

I pulled a small notebook from my pocket and started writing names.

"What do you think Gina's reaction to this will be?"

"I think it's a big decision. She's got family here but I think she'll still be willin'. This ain't permanent is it?"

"I surely hope not, Ivan."

"That doesn't sound as sure as I'd like you to be."

"They tell me this next guy that's rumored to be lookin at us is a badass. He's one of the oldest generation and has ten times as many Kresh under his command than the last guy."

"That ain't soundin' good, Boss," he said, worry creeping into his voice.

"The last Clan came over with a fear inside 'em. We exploited that fear and ran 'em up through Africa. I got a feelin' this group won't have that fear ingrained in 'em."

"Then you're just gonna have to put that fear in 'em as fast as you can, Boss."

"We're gonna do our best to do just that, Ivan," I said. "But we have to make plans for the future, whether we make it or not. There are two worlds that will be under the protection of my Clan. I want them trained to do what we have here. I want Soulguards over there, Source weapons, and technology to stand up and fight back. If we fail here, they're the next in line to continue."

"You're really worried about this one?"

"Yeah, there are so many of 'em. We faced the last wave of ten million or so and defeated 'em. But the losses were more than we lost in World War Two. In the span of a few days. If this Hal'For'Radolin comes, he's got a hundred million or more Kresh. This is goin' to get bloody as hell."

"I heard several countries have begun conscription," he said. "Perhaps with good reason."

"There's talk of re-initiating the draft here in the US," I said. "People are freakin' out about it but I think we need it. It's one of the big topics in the Presidential Campaigns."

"Deacons for it or against it?" he asked.

"He's stayed away from the topic, for the most part. But he's for it. It'll hurt him if he comes out and says it. Too many people want to run and hide. They don't understand that if we fall, there's nowhere left to go. The Kresh will roll over them like they aren't even there. Their best chance is to join us and face 'em with a Source weapon in their hands."

"Should've said that in that interview," he said.

"No one wants to hear from me right now," I returned. "Last I heard, the widest spread rumor is they all work for me and I'm the Anti-Christ."

"You're just hearin' pieces, Boss," he said. "You always pick the worst and latch onto that. Lyrica's right on that subject. Look deeper and see the ones who are arguing the other side of it. It wouldn't be an argument if no one was arguing the other side. I've found that the loudest tend to be the smaller group in something like this. You'll see."

"I sure hope so," I said. "At least Deacons hasn't been hit with that one yet."

"Oh, it's comin'," he said. "He'll have to pick a side, just like the subject of the draft. When he does, the fireworks should be quite spectacular."

"Too bad you'll be on another planet."

"Aww, man. I hate to miss that particular moment. You'll send reports?"

"Right up to the moment that Hal'For'Radolin's Kresh hit Hub."

Jacobs started looking around, "Where's Prada? I knew somethin' was missin'"

"Her Marine is in town with his bunch of misfits. Goin' out tonight with some of 'em. Somehow they've decided to prove they can drink as much as I can. Not sure if anyone even told 'em about that."

"Poor bastards," he chuckled. "Where? I might come and join you after they all pass out."

"That new bar just outside of the base."

"I know that one," he said. "I gotta meet this Marine that has Prada so tore up."

"Come on by," I returned. "Lyrica begged off on this one. She said she had no interest in the whole endeavor. She said she's meetin' some friends to discuss the upcoming wedding that she is setting up. She told me to stay out of the way and let her set it up. I'd just mess it up."

"She's probably right."

"How hard could it be?"

"Boy, you're like a babe lost in the woods."

"What?"

"Just stay out of her way, you idget."

"We just gotta find someone to do cere-mony…"

"Just let it go," he said. "You have no idea what's involved."

"You do?"

"I was married, before I became a Guard. She and my career didn't coexist and she went on her way."

"What was the career?"

"I was a bare-knuckle fighter, quite a few years ago. Made some decent money from it till

Demons killed off a whole block. The Guard saved my bacon and I joined right up. But we're off topic. Just show up and do what she directs."

"Ok, that's what I had in mind."

"Good, you'll be much better off. I've known you for years. Frankly, I don't know how you tie your own shoes."

"Jeez, man," I said, "Tell me what you really think."

He chuckled and I turned toward the door.

"Alright, time to go," I said. "I'll send for the guys you told me about and I got a few more here to see about."

"Later, Boss."

I headed for the door, "And for the record, I keep one of those charts by the bed, so I can tie my shoes. Quite handy."

I heard him chuckling as I left the room.

Chapter 14

Marcus Stratton and Seran Polomo just stared at me.

"I'm serious, guys," I said. "We really need this."

"And it has nothing to do with the fact that your future wife wants to go off world for a honeymoon?"

"The wedding is being sped up so we can do that while we're over there," I answered. "I discovered the need for the trip before I even proposed… sort of."

"Yeah, I heard about that," Polo, as I liked to refer to him, said.

"I heard that all of your neighbors heard it, too," Marco chuckled. "Gotta learn to keep your mind muffled."

"It did simplify the actual proposal," I said. "She heard me practicin' enough on the way home."

"I would say that was entertaining enough," Polo said.

"More than likely," I answered.

"The issue is having both Soullords off planet at the same time."

"I know, but if you think I could go over there without her again, you don't know her."

"But it's irresponsible of the two of you to go at the same time. You two are Soulguards.

Doesn't that come into it at some point?" Marco asked.

"Nope," I answered. "What you don't understand is Lyrica isn't Soulguard."

"What?"

"Sure, she's Soulguard at heart. But she never took the oath nor does she receive a paycheck from the Soulguard. She's, technically, a free agent. Up to a point, we'll let the fact that there are only two of us help form our decisions. But my agents say it's peaceful over there at the moment. I intend to take advantage of that fact and acquire some more, much needed, allies. I also intend to spend a wonderful week atop a mountain in a world where people don't hate me with my newlywed wife."

"Well, I guess we can't really argue with that," Marco said with a short grin. "I've heard some of what you're talking about, though, and it's not everyone. You know that, right?"

"I know it's not everyone," I said while shaking my head. "It just seems to be everywhere and it grates on me. I can shake off most of the civilian attitudes. They don't know any better, but it's the people I've fought alongside that cut the deepest. Even worse, I see some of the same thing in Soulguards."

"But there are many who support you," Polo said. "Always remember the quiet support. Those who hate are the loudest. Look to the quiet ones and see if you don't find something different in those Souls. There's no way you can look at those and not see something different."

"It's true," I nodded. "Soldiers have had to deal with this sort of thing for decades. Viet Nam Vets were reviled after going to a country they were ordered to. After the war they came home to hate. I can read this stuff and understand it, but I still feel it when it happens."

"Those soldiers weren't telepathic, and didn't have the ability to reach in, and just change the minds of those people who scream the hatred," Marco said. "Have you been tempted?"

"I hate myself for it, but, yeah," I answered. "I've been tempted."

"Anyone would be," Polo returned, "It's only human. The real thing that speaks about character is the fact you don't reach in and alter them."

"Then I would be what they claim I am."

"You do know the world you want to travel across is populated by millions of aliens who hate you, don't you?" Marco grinned.

"True enough, but they have good reason to hate me," I chuckled.

"That, they do."

"What do your forces say about the other thing we talked about?" Polo asked.

"Not sure if we're ready to move regular soldiers over there, yet," I answered. "Everything is hangin' on the success of keepin' those forces as much of a secret as we can. We've got some big numbers, but they've still got much more. I want things a little more stable before we try to move troops across to Hub."

"You're the boss on that subject," he said.

"What do you mean?"

"We discovered some purchases you've made over the last year," he said. I could tell by his aura that he expected me to admit to something.

"What purchases?" I asked. "I don't mess with the money, Warren does that for me."

"You don't know, do you?" Marco asked and chuckled.

"You don't deserve that guy," Polo said, shaking his head.

"So, enlighten me. What did I buy?"

"Several properties," Marco answered. "Some of them international."

"Where?"

"One of them is just a little north of here, covered in guns and shields."

"What?"

"It appears you own the land which has the Gate to Kresh," he said. "And you own a tract of land in Africa, one in Romania, and another in China."

"You're shittin' me."

"It was kicked around to use imminent domain laws to seize the property until we traced it back to who owned the company that purchased the properties. It seems the higher ups don't want to make the owner mad, after all."

I leaned back in the chair, "Well I'll be damned."

"No one knows whether the Chinese or the Romanians will be of the same mind on the subject. I'm pretty sure the Chinese can seize what they want, if they choose to do so. Same with the Kenyans and the Romanians. But, then it would do no one any good unless we win a war on this world and the other. If this is the case, I'm guessing your forces would be holding the other side, so the point is moot. You're the boss."

"That's crazy," I said. "I'm not sure I'm suited for that. I just blow shit up."

"In all honesty," Polo said, "Blowing shit up is a skill that's needed for the foreseeable future. The rest, you'll have to deal with after we win."

"That's if we win," I said. "That's another reason for this meeting. I got a report about rumors of the next one who may be interested in our little chunk of rock. If this Hal'For'Radolin seriously mobilizes, it's gonna get ugly."

"There's not much more we can do here to prepare, but we need forces built up everywhere," Polo said. "What sort of numbers are we looking at?"

"They tell me he has over a hundred million under his Mark."

"Some of those will be women and children," he said. "That still would leave an army over five times the one that came through in Kenya."

"And these guys aren't afraid of us."

"I'm sure you can remedy that."

"I hope so but I wouldn't depend on it."

"How does something like that even work? You say Hub is huge, but how do you get that many Kresh into the city?"

"The Gateway facilities are the outer ring of the city. The backside opens up, and the Kresh pour through the Gate from the plains outside of Hub. I've seen it in the memories of some of the Shak'Tar."

"The size of the setup over there just amazes me," Marco said. "When you take this trip of yours, I would like some pictures of Hub, if you could manage it."

"Should have done that, already," I said. "I've had Shak'Tar runnin' back and forth for over a year now and never even thought of it."

"It's the little things that trip a person up," Polo laughed.

"True enough."

"Now we need to discuss where the troops should be stationed," Marco said. "We should probably set up a meeting with the Archmage."

"Gregor should be able to take care of that," I said.

"True," he said. "I'll see if we can get a meeting with him."

"In the meantime," I said, "I need to catch up with my gift from God, soon-to-be trophy wife, and see what she's done about our wedding. There's really no telling."

Both men laughed.

"Have fun with that," was Polomo's answer. Stratton just laughed on.

Chapter 15

"We have to invite them early," Lyrica said. "Daphne is in Scotland. Trent's father is probably quite busy, with running for president. The rest are close enough to get here on short notice."

"Samuel may not want to come with the current situation."

"He'll want to," she said. "He's going to have to take a stand on the subject, soon. It will be a good time for it."

"So far, he's managed to avoid the subject," I said. "He sticks to the topics that he's runnin' his campaign on. I expect the other side to throw it out there soon. They've been stokin' the fires for a while. And when did you get all political?"

She laughed, "I'm not. I talked to Alan Stanbridge yesterday and he said it would be a good time since Samuel has been pushing harder to get on with it. He said Samuel's been pissed from the moment Alan started pushing him to sever ties with you."

Honestly, it felt good to know that Deacons wasn't willing to kick me to the curb. It might not bode well for his campaign, though. There were a lot of people screaming about my alien heritage.

"Quit thinking about that," she said. "It just gets you all twisted up inside."

"I know. I just can't help it, sometimes."

She reached across the table, as she stood up, and grabbed the front of my uniform.

"I have something else for you to think about."

As she pulled me around the table, I smiled, "Oh, really? I bet it's somethin' much better."

"Yes," she returned and our lips met.

Our streams merged and I lost all thought of the rest of the world as I just embraced the moment, losing myself in her.

***

"Rourke," Sullivan Hicks nodded as I joined the group around several tables at the rear of the Bar and Grill.

"Hicks," I returned and nodded toward the second Marine I saw. "Corn."

Corn raised his beer in salute and took a huge swallow, "You ready to see how Marines drink, Rourke?"

"You guys don't know what you're gettin' into here."

"Oh, I think you may have chosen the wrong group for a drinking contest."

"If I remember correctly, you guys chose to challenge me. And I'll try my best to make it fair for you. I'll match each of you, drink for drink."

"There's five of us," one of the Marines I hadn't met said.

118

"This is Trip," Corn pointed. "He's one of our star players for the evening. He's drunk almost every person ever challenged under the table. We call him Trip because he was known as Terrax the Terrible in all of the drinking establishments near our base where we do our training. His last name is Terrax. Three T's... Triple T... Trip."

"Makes sense, how did you come to be called Corn?"

"You don't really wanna know," Hicks interrupted.

"I'll take your word on that one."

"And this fellow is Enido Roberto Nucci, just call 'im Bob," Corn said with a smile. "He happens to be the only person to ever out drink Trip."

"I see where this is goin'. Loaded the deck with heavy hitters."

"Then there is little old me," Corn said. "I'm not too shabby as a drinker, myself."

He then pointed at another Marine I had met In Africa, "Simmons is able to hold his own with the best of us. And Gallup, there beside him is a notorious drinker. All in all, I think we got what it takes to take you down."

I looked at Hicks.

"Don't look at me, I date a Soulmage. I told 'em they were gonna regret it."

"I tried to tell 'em," I said. "I can't get drunk."

"They're Marines. You can't just tell 'em anything. It's gotta be pounded into their thick skulls, preferably with a hammer. Speaking of which, when you win, they have to meet you at the break of dawn and run ten miles. If you lose they said you have to pick up the bar tab."

"Done."

"Let the games begin!"

Over the next hours I learned what a Harvey Wallbanger was. Along with Sex on the Beach, Mojito, three different versions of Long Island Ice Tea, a Screwdriver, and a plethora of other drinks. Then it got serious. We drank Scotch, Irish whiskey, Bourbon, and my favorite of these, Cognac.

When Jacobs arrived, Corn, Simmons and Gallup were unconscious. Trip and Bob were the only ones still drinking and I was having a conversation with Hicks.

"Didn't you warn 'em?" Jacobs asked.

"They're Marines."

"Enough said," he returned with a grin.

Trip sagged and toppled from his chair in slow motion and Bob stared at him for a second before face planting on the table.

"I told 'em," Hicks said. "Ten miles with this hangover should be just the hammer to drive it home."

I looked to the other tables where other members of the platoon had been placing bets and cheering their comrades on, "Anyone else wanna give it a shot?"

"Hell no!" Rikkers, another Marine I had met in Africa returned. "How the hell are you still alive after that?"

"I can't get drunk."

"We learned when we became Soulguards that the quicker healing made it near impossible for us to get plastered," Jacobs answered. "We tried and it took some serious drinking to even get a buzz. Once you reach Mage, it's impossible to drink it fast enough."

"That's crazy but I'd say you could win a lot of bets with it," Rikkers said.

"Only with hard headed Marines," I laughed. "Most other folks would have accepted it after I told 'em I couldn't get drunk."

"I told you," Hicks said, "They need a big hammer to drive it in."

"You seriously gonna make 'em run ten miles?"

"Oh yeah, and they'll all five finish the run because they're Marines, and Marines are indestructible."

"They'll get a lot of sleep, if nothing else," I said, looking over the edge of the table at a drooling Corn. "I'll get the bar tab, anyway, but I'd prefer if you waited till after the run before tellin' 'em. Let the thought of the huge chunk of pay they will lose help spur them on."

"I like the way you think, Rourke."

"Special torture," I said.

Hicks laughed and eased his seat back, "All right boys, Get these useless sacks out of here and back to base. They got a long run tomorrow and I want all of you there to cheer 'em on. As a matter of fact, you'll all run with 'em and cheer 'em on!"

"Really?" Rikkers asked.

"They're running because they picked a fight they couldn't win," he said as he pointed at the five fallen men. "You'll be running because you didn't!"

As the rest of the platoon carried out the five drinkers, Hicks was right behind them, "Marines aren't afraid of anything men! I'm sorely disappointed in your lack of support. Surely twenty men could have done it!"

He turned and shot me a grin as he followed his boys out the door.

"That looked like it was fun," Jacobs said, motioning for the waitress.

"I've discovered that there are very few alcoholic drinks I like, and I have to go to the bathroom. I'll be right back. I feel like my eyes are floating in whiskey."

"I'd think so," he said with a grin.

Chapter 16

I sat at my desk looking at the never ending pile of paperwork. Every day I would leave and the pile would be smaller. The next day, it would tower over my workspace. I think Gregor was trying to drive me insane. He'd been doing this sort of stuff for the last year or so and I hadn't needed to worry about it.

Unfortunately, I had opened my big mouth a few weeks before about learning the less exciting side of my job. He had taken it to heart and began sending mounds of paperwork through my office. There were a lot of supply forms that would need approval. The part that made it such a grind was the fact I had to read every form before I signed it. When the paperwork had started coming there were forms slipped into the mix to test me. They were obvious but wouldn't have been seen if I hadn't read the acquisition forms. Three hundred and fifty aluminum containers with "dog food" printed on the side.

So far, there'd been one single dog that would even associate with Soulguards. I'm pretty sure he didn't need three hundred and fifty twenty gallon aluminum cans for his dog food.

There had been an acquisition form for an official hangman's noose. The reason for said form was, "In the event that our illustrious War-master decides to take the easy way out."

There were more and they got more and more devious as the weeks progressed. I missed a few and they would be laying on my desk the next day. The piles of the forms I missed had been getting smaller each day.

I looked up as I felt a familiar presence. I could see Pelin's Soul as she approached my office.

"Enter," I said as she reached the door. Most of the people I do that to get a little weirded out over it but Pelin, like me is telepathic.

"Master," she nodded as she stepped through the door.

"Don't call… ah, Hell… What's up?"

Pelin was the one who always brought me reports. The others hadn't worked with me as much and tended toward the info dump most of the Shak'Tar were used to. I preferred a spoken report unless it was necessary for the info dump.

"We have received news from Cerres."

I could see the consternation in her aura.

"Bad news, I take it?"

"The Ferrara'Ti are all there, but they won't stay more than a week."

"Which pushes up the time table three weeks," I said.

"Yes."

"That means the wedding has to be after I get back from Cerres," I said. "Lyrica's gonna be pissed."

"That is what I expect, Master."

I exhaled and leaned back in my chair, "They won't stay long enough to do it after?"

"Ferrara'Ti have never been known for a great deal of patience. I doubt they will have any patience for what is intended."

"Can't be givin' 'em any reason to back out, I suppose."

"Not if you wish to succeed."

"Ok, so the bad news is taken care of," I said. "How bout some other news?"

"Your Prophet has returned to Parlais to begin setting up the Academy for your Soulguard."

"That's good news, sort of. I was hopin' he'd be there when we came through."

"We can send word…"

"No, I can't interrupt what he's set in motion for personal reasons. Would like to see my friend again but he's doin' important things over there."

"Your subjects on Cerres flood the Soulguard outpost you have established. They embraced their new roles as an army to fight the Masters with a fervor not seen in many humans not from your planet."

"Good, they'll not be victims anymore."

"Gorvelis is pleased with the progress of the scientists and teachers you have sent over to Cerres. Their knowledge has spread much more rapidly than you may think. No one can learn faster than telepaths. And telepaths can teach at an astonishing rate. Just the advancement in metalworking is astounding. It will still take some time to build the industrial infrastructure but the knowledge and will is already there."

"That's great news. I wonder how soon we can set up a weapons plant there."

"Transporting the amounts of materials would be a problem at this time, but at the rate Cerres is advancing, it might be sooner than you may think."

"I certainly hope so."

"That's the extent of the report, Master," she said. "If you wish I will dump the whole report for you."

"Don't worry about it," I said. "Now I just have to go and tell Lyrica what's goin' on."

"Might be dangerous," she said with a crooked grin.

"That, it might."

"You better get back in time for the wedding or she will hurt you."

"What could go wrong?"

Pelin stood, chuckling, and turned to the door.

"Everything's peaceful right now. Right?"

She just shook her head as she left the room, still laughing.

"That's right," I muttered. "You know when I'm right."

Her laughter echoed inside my head. Damn telepaths.

I didn't have much left that I wanted to do, and the report gave me a great excuse to step away from the pile of paperwork, so I left my office to find Lyrica. She would be at the hospital in Wichita, or the medical facility on the base. I opened my sight and looked around.

Souls are a beautiful thing, for the most part, and none more beautiful to my eye than Lyrica's. It burns brighter than the Souls around her, most of the time, because of the huge Soul-stream that feeds it. I picked hers out immediately from the others in the base med facility.

I felt a sense of dread. The last thing I wanted to do was upset her. She'd spent all the time and money on setting up a wedding on short notice. What if I couldn't get back in time? I know Pelin had been joking around but I'd learned something over the years. Things never go as planned.

I saw her flash of joy as she saw me approaching, something I cherish more than anything. Then I saw the flow of suspicion that rolled across as she saw my dread. Then worry. She met me at the door to the facility.

"What is it?"

"I just got another report. The Ferrara'Ti are on Cerres. They won't stay more than a week and I have to push up the trip. I know it's not what we planned but I promise I'll be back for the wedding. Just keep getting' everything ready…"

"No," she answered. "The wedding can wait. I'll be going with you."

"But you've spent so much time and money setting up this…"

"None of that matters," she said placing her hand on my face. "What matters is you and I. The wedding can wait until we get back. Marking these Kresh is more important than the timing of our wedding."

"You amaze me every day, woman."

"Of course I do. That's my job," she said with a grin. "When do we leave?"

"Probably tomorrow. I have to meet with Paige and tell her, then get everyone rounded up early. I may be late tonight."

"I'll pack our things," she said. "Marriage or not, I plan on enjoying the trip to another world."

Chapter 17

As usual, nothing truly follows any plan I lay out. It took two days to get everyone set and ready to go. Lyrica had packed us each a duffle that we had strapped over our shoulders. Each of the training cadre had a duffle. There were none in the group who weren't Soulguard so our trip would be unlike the last trip I had taken to Cerres.

"When we cross, we'll head up through the building to the rooftop," I said. "We'll travel from roof to roof until we reach the Cerres Facility. Those of you who are going to Parlais will leave from the Cerres Facility and travel the same way with new guides."

"Any chance we go through the area where the graffiti is?" Jacobs asked.

"Other direction, but there's a good chance your new boss on Parlais might be able to give you the tour at some point."

"Still hard to believe he survived that damn explosion," Jacobs said.

"I know what you mean," I agreed. "It's a shame he had to return to Parlais before we got there. Would have liked to see him."

"I'll tell 'im when we get there," he said. "I see you found Gallagher and Campbell."

"Them and quite a few more."

I could see the excitement and anticipation in his aura. There was much the same in Gina's, except there was a sadness in hers as she was leaving family behind for an unknown amount of time. I had almost chosen not to ask Jacobs because of Gina's ties to Kansas, but I couldn't pass them by if they wanted it. That's why the whole thing was voluntary.

Soldiers had been going to far places all throughout history. Some had families at home and some didn't but they still went.

Another of the cadre arrived. His duffle carrying what looked like nothing but books. He carried a couple more in his hands.

"Gunsmithing?"

"Yes, Sir."

"Riley, is it?"

"Yes, Sir," he answered. "Riley Carpacci. Been gunsmithing for the last thirty years as a hobby. Might come in useful over there."

"Very much so," I agreed.

"I thought as much," he said. "I also brought some early metallurgy texts, as well."

"Good thinkin', Riley."

"There's a few others, too," he said. "I grabbed anything I could think of that might prove useful. Some basic medicine texts. Hopefully we can get more stuff sent through but you said we might be out of touch for a while if things don't go right with your deal on Cerres."

"Very true," I said. "I never even thought of this stuff. Glad you were part of this."

He nodded and joined the ranks of those crossing.

"Damn, that guy is gonna be useful."

"Yeah," Jacobs agreed. "Hope we didn't double up on our text books."

"You brought some?"

"Yeah, I've got some early aviation stuff and some of the metalworking books."

"Everybody is thinkin' ahead except the one who's supposed to."

"That's why you picked us, Boss."

"Well, true enough."

"The folks on Cerres were Marked weren't they?"

"Yeah, I wish they weren't, but it was done before I even knew it."

"It's been a blessing from what I've heard from your Shak'Tar," he said. "We can't depend on the population of Parlais to just embrace our people like Cerres did. We may need to put our power behind a leader there and work it slow."

"I figured Ric probably has somethin' in mind about it. I've been perfectly fine with backin' his decisions."

"I don't fault that," he said. "Just tryin' to figure as much in advance as I can. God knows, if there's one person you can trust it's Rictor Hughes. The man's been loyal as they come. You know they used to call him the Soullord's Pit Bull? He knows you well enough to know what you want done."

"Definitely trust his judgement," I said. "I haven't had my people dig too deep into his business over there. He knows I trust him."

Jacobs nodded.

"I suppose we're ready to get this show on the road," I said and stepped forward to stand in front of the group of forty Soulguards and five Soulmages.

There were varying amounts of excitement rolling through their auras. This wasn't just an assignment to another post in the US. It wasn't even a post in another country, which many of them had done over the years. This was another planet, something only dreamed of up until the portals became available to sneak our people through. I could see the same excitement in Lyrica, the same excitement I had felt the first time I had traveled through gateway.

At least we didn't have to disguise ourselves this time. My forces held the facility on the other side for the moment. I strode through the Great Gate that was open in the middle of the clearing in Kansas. No need for secrecy this time with my clans on the other side. Travel through the portals is interesting, to say the least. I've seen movies of wormholes and such but it was nothing like that. As you pass the surface of the gate, it is like a curtain. No transition through tunnels or anything, just stepping through a doorway.

The technology was amazing, I had to wonder how they created it. I knew it tapped the Source like my Source weapons. I had learned it needed a person to activate the machinery. But how it worked, I had no idea.

A familiar face awaited us on the other side, several familiar faces. At least familiar to me. Kil'Sin'Deres and Tor'Vas'Reman stood to the left side of the platform. To the right were several Soulguards, Sam Keller and Gorvelis. Touran Gorvelis looked quite different than he had on my first visit. His Soulstream was knotted as a Soulguard. His Soul was brighter and he looked a bit younger.

"Sam, Touran," I nodded to them and looked to my left. "Kil'Sin'Deres , Tor'Vas'Reman."

"Welcome back, Rash'Tor'Ri," Kil'Sin'Deres smiled, which can be a little disconcerting to those that don't know him. He stepped forward and looked at Lyrica, "Greetings. It is an honor to meet the mate of Rash'Tor'Ri. We have heard many things about you after the Clan returned from Doran."

I smiled as I saw the doubt in Kil'Sin'Deres aura.

"Don't doubt it, Kil'Sin'Deres," I said. "She's the one who ended the war over there."

"Then Rash'Tor'Ri has chosen wisely," he said with another of those disconcerting smiles.

He stepped back so I could greet the others.

"Good to see you, Sam," I shook his outstretched hand. "You look like this place is good for you."

"Never been better, Colin," he said. "Who would have thought I would have to leave the planet to find my true element?"

"I'm glad you have," I said. "You never were all that happy back there."

"There was too much history with the former Council."

I nodded. He stepped back and Touran shook my hand.

"Greetings, Rash'Tor'Ri, Miss Jayne," he said. "There is much to talk about, but we can do that on Cerres. Shall we proceed?"

"Let's do it," I turned to the gathered group. "Follow these two, men. When we get to Cerres, we'll get you set up with your guides to Parlais."

The group fell in behind Sam and Gorvelis and moved toward the central stairway that led to the top of the building. Lyrica and I held back just a bit before following the group.

"This place is enormous," she said, looking around in wonder.

"Wait till you get to see the whole city from the rooftop."

"I've seen these in your memories but in person it's so much more real."

"You'll definitely enjoy the view from the top, then."

"I have no doubts," she said and slipped her arm around my waist.

We followed the others and just enjoyed our time together while marveling at the sheer enormity of the building. I had never had the time to just look at Hub on my previous trip. Perhaps we could explore a little as we made our trek back from Cerres.

As we stepped out the door on the upper platform, I heard the gasps of more than just Lyrica. We looked out at a pristine blue sky. Larger cities on Earth had a miasma of smog at the top from the industry and vehicles. Here there was none of that. Just a great big sky and an endless view of these enormous buildings. We turned to look behind us at an enormous plain with vegetation just a little off color. Everything had that feel of "just a little off" about it but it wasn't a bad thing.

Gallagher had come to a dead stop.

"Yo, Derrick!"

He shook his head and started moving again.

"I've got to draw this," he said. "Amazing."

"When things are settled on Parlais, you might get the chance to check it out from the Parlais facility," I said.

"That would be awesome."

"You were right," Lyrica said. "This view is spectacular. Why don't the Kresh use the tops?"

"Their size makes any of the upper floors uncomfortable for 'em. They just stay in the open areas. The majority of 'em don't ever even come to Hub."

"There's so much to learn about them," she returned.

"If we manage to end this war, maybe we can," I said, looking out over Hub. "I learn more and more every time I deal with Kresh. It scares me how much they're like Humans. It was so much easier to see monsters and evil."

"The more that die in this war, the harder it'll be to have a peaceful resolution with them."

"I'm afraid so," I said. "The mark seems to be the only peaceful solution and I don't like it."

We came to the edge of the building and, one by one, the group leaped across the area between the buildings.

"Looks like we're taking the route around the outer ring," I said.

"There may have been some issues in closer to the center last time Rash'Tor'Ri came to visit us," Gorvelis returned.

"Some issues, indeed," Kil'Sin'Deres laughed.

Jacobs was looking askance at the large Kresh.

"It takes gettin' used to," I said.

"I can believe that," he answered.

Chapter 18

Fourteen times we had jumped across the gaps between the buildings before landing on the top of the Cerres facility. There were a number of Soulguards waiting on the rooftop. These were all new people to me but I also knew them all. They carried my Mark and I knew their names as well as my own. It was a bit disconcerting.

"Rash'Tor'Ri," the first of the party stepped forward, "We welcome you to Cerres."

"Thank you Simollin," I returned, using the man's name.

"We are here to escort your party to the Parlais facility," he said.

I nodded, "Alright guys, this is where we part ways for now."

Jacobs stepped closer, "I'm gonna miss you, Boss. Try to get this took care of as quick as possible."

I embraced my friend, "Hate to see you go, buddy. We'll get it done, one way or another. You guys be ready for anything, and be careful."

He nodded and stumped off on his shield prosthesis. I really was going to miss him. Gina stepped close and hugged Lyrica. She nodded toward me and followed Jacobs.

Sending my friends off to another world was harder than I expected but I knew it was a necessary thing. They were well suited for the task ahead of them and I knew Rictor would appreciate a familiar face. He'd had ample opportunity to return to Earth but he'd found people that needed his protection and stayed. I know my friend well enough to know that was what had happened. He'd found a cause that required him to stay and fight.

"We'll end this one day, my love," Lyrica said softly. "Then we can travel all you want to and see them all again."

I smiled at her, "I sure hope so."

We strolled over to the edge of the rooftop that overlooked the plains outside of Hub and stood for a few moments looking at the slightly different landscape before us.

"I can already see the difference in you after crossing to an area where they have your mark."

"I know," I said. "I feel like I belong here."

"You do belong here," she returned. "One day we can come back and be here."

"If we can survive the wave that's comin'."

"We have to," she said. "These people need you. They need you more than our world could ever need you. You're changing a race. Making them into something that can withstand the ages alongside mankind instead of over or under it."

"They may not need me for that anymore."

"They still do," she said. "There may come a time when they don't, but it'll be a while."

"I wish the Mark wasn't necessary to bring the change," I said.

"It is all we know Rash'Tor'Ri," Kil'Sin'Deres rumbled from behind us, "We could never have learned what you have taught us on our own. We didn't have the basis to even comprehend what you have brought us. These that join us don't really have any idea what they are about to do. They think they just bring themselves to join a sort of alliance. They don't really believe a Human can Mark them. They truly came here to watch you fail. They will know better after."

"Their impatience has made you change your schedule and they look at it as a sign that they can steer where this Clan of yours goes from here," he continued.

"And when the Mark hits 'em?" I asked. "Will they submit or do like the former master of the Shak'Tar?"

"The group of Ferrara'Ti that originally decided to do this will submit. A later addition, Jas'Tor'Kalamet, is a mystery to me. He is much stronger than any of us and I cannot read him as I can the others."

"How strong is this, Jas'Tor'Kalamet?"

"He is much older than I, and considerably stronger. If he joins his Clans to yours, it will be a huge victory. He, like the others does not understand what is about to occur. In the end he will have to accept it."

"Or he'll react like the other one."

"Doubtful," Kil'Sin'Deres returned. "He is here knowing that the Mark will be attempted.

Sol'Kor'Vanas was taken by surprise and could not handle the changes. Never in his wildest nightmares had he expected to be Marked by a human."

"I suppose we should get this show on the road," I said. "How long will it take to move all of the ones who don't want to be marked over to here?"

"A day should be sufficient."

"Good," I turned back to Lyrica. "Shall we?"

She slid her hand into mine and smiled. We strolled to the doorway that led to the central stairs. Kil'Sin'Deres ducked and slipped through the opened door and we followed.

"I will take the direct route, Rash'Tor'Ri. It will be much more comfortable for me."

Kil'Sin'Deres slipped over the rail into the center shaft with a grace that would surprise most people, considering his size. I'd seen him in action and his fluid speed was no surprise at all.

"Feels strange not trying to kill them," Lyrica said.

"It felt strange to me, too, up until the Mark. Now they feel like the people in Oklahoma feel to me. They're my family, now, sort of. It's a little different than family but there are similarities. It's hard to explain exactly where they lie in that regard."

"I imagine so," she returned. "His Soul looks much different than those we saw before. The other one that was waiting when we got here has some of the same colors as Kil'Sin'Deres. Is that from your mark?"

"It's part of the change they're goin' through," I said. "Their souls change as soon as the mark hits but they keep changing afterwards, too. The longer they are marked, the more pronounced the change. I think it may make a difference if you embrace the change as Kil'Sin'Deres has done. He wanted the change before he ever had the mark."

"I see the difference in you, too."

"What?"

"The second we stepped through the gate, you were among those you marked. Much of the chaos that's normally there was gone."

"I do feel at peace when I'm around 'em," I agreed. "Like the way I can relax around the folks in Oklahoma."

"That was something I knew about, the ones in Oklahoma, but I've seen how you react to the presence of Kresh in the past. It was very far from peaceful. It was a surprise to see you grow calmer when in a city full of them."

"I still get that other feelin' when I get out away from those I marked. Or if I focus on the Kresh out there instead of the ones below us. I keep my attention on these and I can push the others back. The calm is welcome, I get so very little of it."

"I had noticed," she said as she squeezed my hand.

We left the stairwell and followed a waiting Kil'Sin'Deres down the hallway that led to the huge room that held the Great Gate to Cerres. There was a pretty good sized group of Kresh in the room and they stepped to the sides to leave us a clear path to the Gate. A few continued what they were doing but most turned and watched us walk across the distance to the platform.

"Eerie," Lyrica said.

I chuckled, "Feel like a science experiment?"

"Don't know their emotions as well as you, feel a little like the last shrimp on the buffet."

"They observe you because you are the one rumored to have killed a Clan. They wonder if you are a worthy mate to Rash'Tor'Ri. If the rumors are true, they approve." Kil'Sin'Deres said.

"I'm just a little offended, I think," she said.

"It is not meant to offend," he said. "We can read each other and see if our mates are worthy of us or if we are worthy of our mates. Rash'Tor'Ri has proven to be a warrior, unparalleled. But we cannot read you. There is much fascination with that."

"If it is battle prowess they respect," I said. "They can rest assured, she's done more in moments than I've done in years. But if there are doubts, you'll see. Time will tell."

I turned back to her, "Ready to see Cerres?"

She looked around at the staring Kresh, "Oh yes."

"It'll be just as bad there," I grinned.

She sighed and we stepped through another shimmering curtain into another world.

143

Chapter 19

The enormous crowd of people on the other side wasn't what I expected. A telepath should have gotten more of this from Kil'Sin'Deres throughout the journey. But I hadn't, it was a total surprise. The plaza was lined with Kresh'Ma'Nar and Kresh'Sor'An along the left side. The right side was lined with Shak'Tar, each and every one with Soulguard knots, and Soulguards from Earth.

Directly in front of us at the far end of the Plaza stood Gorvelis, Sam, Darrel, and the few Ferrara'Ti that had been marked by me or my Clan. In a group to their left stood six of the large Kresh and a seventh that was enormous.

"Oh, my," Lyrica muttered.

"Wow," I mumbled back.

As we approached the others, I looked at the new group. Most of them were uncertain about me and it could be seen in their auras. But I saw the bare touches of hope that this could actually work.

Except for the big one. He could hide his mind from all around him but he couldn't disguise that aura filled with the chaos of his deception. He wasn't uncertain and there was no presence of hope. He looked like a great predator poised to attack when the deer steps within range.

He caught my thoughts and things went straight to hell.

He slammed the others aside and charged toward me. The world slowed down as I dropped into focus but he was closing too fast. He was across the distance before I could even begin to react.

Then he slammed to a halt as a shield wall sprang to life feet in front of me. I felt the Source surging through her as Lyrica powered that shield enough to stop the behemoth. He started to back up so he could power forward and Lyrica wrapped the shield around him.

Everyone was just starting to realize something was wrong as the huge Kresh roared. I could feel the power she was using to hold him still and it was substantial. He was a strong bastard. Then I felt his mind reaching for me. I staggered as his mind slammed through my walls. I tried to hold my own but he was a juggernaut.

Then Lyrica's hand landed on my shoulder and power poured up both of our streams. The mental attack stopped with a final mental shriek.

I looked forward as I staggered to my feet, to see a shield ball about the size of a softball, hovering in the air at eye level. Lyrica slammed two tendrils of the shield into the Source and dropped it.

The ball dropped the four feet to the paving with a deep thud. I don't know how much Jas'Tor'Kalamet weighed. Pretty heavy, I imagined.

Lyrica stepped in front of me with flames rolling across her body and her eyes looking like pits to Hell. I know because I could see them through the eyes of those standing in front of her.

"Who's next?" she growled as fire filled her hands inside two launchers she had opened.

She was breathing hard and filled with a rage I hardly ever see in her. She was my Golden Valkyrie for that instant, and I had never seen anything so beautiful. I laid my hand on her shoulder.

"That's enough, baby," I said softly. "They're not gonna do anything."

Everyone was backing from her path. She looked at each and every one of those in front of her with that Hell gaze then released the excess power into the sky. Then she, calmly walked back to her place beside me and placed her hand in mine.

There was complete and utter silence from the crowd that had been loud before. Then from behind me came a rumble I recognized as the laughter of Kil'Sin'Deres.

"There is no doubt of your choice in mates, now, Rash'Tor'Ri!"

His laughter was contagious. I chuckled and the whole plaza erupted in the utterly disconcerting laughter of Kresh.

Gorvelis stepped forward with a grin on his face, "Quite unexpected."

The Shak'Tar from the other side of the plaza had joined in the laughter. The Soulguards were still a little behind the others, lacking the telepathy of their cohorts. But there were several nods and smiles of satisfaction. These were people who already knew of Lyrica Jayne and they had heard the doubts of those who had not. They all now felt a sort of vindication. I'd had no idea there had even been any doubt about my little angel.

"Come, Rash'Tor'Ri, and we will feast!" Gorvelis roared above the din of laughter. He nodded toward Lyrica, "I do not even have the words to thank you, Lyrica Jayne. You stopped Jas'Tor'Kalamet before he could finish his plans."

"No thanks are necessary, Touran," she answered. "He is mine. They have to come through me to get to him."

Gorvelis nodded and led us through the crowds of Kresh and Humans that were now filling the Plaza. I could still feel Lyrica's hand trembling from the adrenaline but she held her poise as we crossed the area in front of the multitude of cheering and laughing people. I glanced back to see several Kresh poking at the softball sized shield. One reached down to pick it up but it slipped from his fingers due to its weight. More laughter erupted from the group around him and he gripped it harder, where he could lift it.

He threw it to one of his companions who tried to catch it but dropped it, not expecting it to weigh so much. It landed with a thud to the laughter of the group.

"How long you reckon they'll be throwin' that around?"

"Probably for hours, Rash'Tor'Ri, if not days," Gorvelis answered. "I hate that we lose the numbers his Clans would have given us and I apologize for allowing an enemy into our midst."

"He was strong enough, you couldn't have known," I answered. "But the real problem is that our secret might be out. This guy found out and decided to do somethin' about it. We can't turn down powerful allies, but there's a point where we can't tell if they're true or not. At least, not unless one of us can see his aura."

"We will keep our forces on alert from this point forward," Gorvelis said, as we followed him into the Citadel, the name given to the facility by the locals.

As we entered several people approached. An older lady was staring at me and I knew her name was Delphin. She nodded and stopped in front of us.

"Rash'Tor'Ri," she greeted. "The feast will begin in several hours. Would you and your lady like to join the young ladies, who will show you to the rooms where you can refresh yourselves and retrieve your clothing for the dinner?"

I glanced at Gorvelis who nodded, "We will catch up after the dinner, Rash'Tor'Ri. Matron

Delphin has spent a great deal of time trying to prepare for your arrival."

"Alrighty, then," I said. "Lead on, Matron."

There had been nothing like this on my last visit, but that had been quite a while back. Humans used to avoid the Citadel like the plague in the times before. It appeared that the place had changed dramatically. A group of young women closed and pulled Lyrica along toward the left side of the hall. She followed, glancing back at me.

"Just go with it, honey," I laughed.

"And you, Sir," Delphin said, "Follow me."

I followed Delphin down a hall and to an elevator, the first I had seen in the buildings of the Makers. Somehow, I hadn't really thought about elevators. I guess I hadn't spent any time to amount to anything exploring the buildings on Hub or Cerres. I had been in a hurry the last time I was here.

We entered the elevator and she pushed the button for the top floor. I could see the excitement in her aura as the elevator moved.

"Not used to this yet?"

"There are many marvels here that the Lords would have killed for a year ago."

"How is it that you work here, Matron? The last time I was here there were just military units, basically."

"The High Lord, Gorvelis came to the keep and offered jobs to those willing to work. Servants to work in the Citadel. He offered gold in payment and we jumped at the opportunity to work for pay doing what we had been doing for our masters."

"You were a slave?" I asked, a touch of rage trying to surface.

"I was a slave until the High Lord marked us all. We know to our core how you feel about slavery, and it was abolished rather quickly. It took some getting used to, our freedom. Then the High Lord came and offered us jobs."

"Interesting," I said. "I'm glad to hear the fact that slavery was abolished. I'm also glad you and yours came here. It seems to make the Citadel, less a fortress, and more a home for those living here."

There was pride rolling through her aura at my words. I would have to be careful with what I said on Cerres when people held me in such high esteem. All through history, people with power could easily say the wrong things and cause all sorts of trouble. I was uncomfortable with the way those with the mark felt about me. Perhaps I could, one day, find a way of removing the mark without the whole dying part. That would be a wonderful thing.

The elevator stopped and we exited into a very large room, furnished with what looked to be very comfortable furniture. I hadn't seen this area the first time I was here. Gorvelis had been staying on the bottom floor and I did, as well.

"The rooms up here were old and filled with dust when I started working here," she said.

"One of the first things I decided to take care of when I was placed in charge of the other servants was to clean and prepare these for you when you are here, Rash'Tor'Ri."

"Wow," I said, looking across the room to see a wide opening with an enormous bath tub.

"I am happy that Rash'Tor'Ri is pleased. If you will give me your clothing, I will see to it they are cleaned. There is clothing fit for some-one of your stature in the wardrobe."

"Will they fit?"

"They were tailored to fit you, as was the clothing to which your Lady is being intro-duced."

"Why was she taken elsewhere?"

"It is a vanity of my own, Rash'Tor'Ri," she said. "I wished you each to have the joy of seeing the final product of what I have prepared for you. We have been waiting for a long time to get the chance to have you in residence."

She held her hands out, "Your clothing, Sir."

"Now?"

"Rest assured, my Lord," she said with a grin, "I have seen it all before."

I peeled out of my uniform and placed it in her hands. She waited until I had completely dis-robed before she turned and exited. I turned to the enormous tub and slid into the steaming hot water.

Chapter 20

The huge banquet hall we had previously used was packed. Much like before, there were Kresh, Shak'Tar, and Humans present. Last time the only Humans were Soulguards. This time there were quite a few regular Humans, things had changed since the people of Cerres were marked.

The clothes that Delphin had left in the wardrobe had been something else. The shirt was hand crafted from a green cloth that felt silky yet didn't retain heat like silk. The pants were of a durable stock similar to black denim, but much softer. There were buttons and laces but no zippers. The boots were leather and fit me better than any shoe I had ever worn. I felt like I was dressed like a pirate.

I was met by Gorvelis as I entered the banquet hall but I almost didn't even notice him. Lyrica entered wearing a dress that matched my shirt in color. My mouth dropped open. I always knew her to be beautiful, but I'd never seen her in a dress like this and she was beaming as her eyes met mine. There's no disguising what you feel from a Soullord, and I could see she felt the same as I.

"Sorry, Touran," I said as I noticed him, patiently waiting. "I'm a little distracted."

"Understandable," he returned. "She is beautiful."

"Thank you."

"And a fitting mate for Rash'Tor'Ri, by anyone's standards."

"I still can't believe what we saw out there," I grinned.

"It was a surprise for all of us except Miss Jayne," he said. "She moved so quickly, she had to have had suspicions."

"She was on guard the second we stepped through the gate. Her Soulstream is much larger than mine and her focus much stronger. She's faster and stronger than me. And the reason I'm still alive, many times over, including today."

My eyes were drawn toward her, brilliant green eyes glowing with life, her light brown hair curled and framing her beautiful face.

"Allow me to show you to your seats," Gorvelis said with a grin. "We'll talk later, when you are less distracted."

I laughed and followed Gorvelis toward my little angel. She fell in to step with us and slipped her arm in mine.

"I'm keeping this dress," she whispered.

"I think you should," I whispered. "You do make it look quite lovely."

"Well said," she returned.

Gorvelis led us to the table at the far end of the Hall. It had a pair of seats that faced toward the Hall where we could see everyone in the room. This was a lot more formal than the last trip had been. We seated ourselves in the pair of large chairs. I'd seen things like this in movies and such, but never expected to be the "Royalty" that I had seen depicted. I never wanted to be either.

"That is why it is easy to follow you, Rash'Tor'Ri," Gorvelis said from my right. I should have known better than to expect a telepath not to "hear" me.

"Still doesn't change it," I said.

"What?" Lyrica asked.

"Havin' a half spoken conversation here," I said. "Gorvelis was pickin' up some thoughts about this whole Royal treatment."

"It does feel a little odd," she returned. "And I swear they're still staring at me."

"If you'll notice," I said. "They all seem to be grinning at you too."

"That's a little disconcerting."

"It does take gettin' used to."

"I suppose it would."

"Oh, my…"

My eyes widened as the Citadel staff approached the table with several enormous platters of meats and vegetables. It took two of them to carry each platter. After ours were placed in the center of the table, all but one of the servants left the table to return to the kitchen. The young man that remained awaited orders with a carving knife in hand.

"Just start carving anywhere, Faarl," I said, seeing the familiar colors of appreciation roll through his aura.

"What would the Lady like to begin with?"

"That bird looks divine," she answered. "And just mix up the vegetables. I don't know what any of them are, so I'd like to try a little of each."

He nodded and carved a breast off of the turkey sized bird on the platter. He stacked her a plate that had me drooling.

"And, the Lord?"

"Just carve any of it, Faarl. I'm a carnivore today. I'd like to try every kind of meat you have there. We can talk vegetables some other time."

I looked around to see similar young men serving the people and Kresh seated at the other tables. Kil'Sin'Deres looked at me and grinned.

"It is a new thing to have humans happily serving food to us, Rash'Tor'Ri," he said. "You have changed things more than you could imagine."

"A good change, I hope."

"A good change, indeed."

✳✳✳

"The scientists that came over last year started a college outside of the Citadel," Sam Keller said. "We all put our heads together and figured it would be the easiest way to spread the knowledge and skills out to all the various holds."

"We also put twenty of the Shak'Tar into the College," Gorvelis added. "None can learn faster than a telepath."

"I'd noticed there weren't any Shak'Tar without knotted Soulstreams. I'm guessin' that's the reason."

"We've been usin' 'em for instructors at the Academy too. You'd be amazed how fast someone can tie their stream when a telepath shows 'em how," Sam added. "There's a sacrifice in focus when we do it this quickly but we need an army, yesterday. And there's no doubt these people are willing. They act a lot like a certain kid I met in Knoxville."

"I have no idea what you're talkin' about."

"Yeah, sure."

"How many do we have so far?"

"A little over twenty thousand with knots," he said. "They're lined up at the doors."

"Is it hurtin' the holds to lose that many?"

Gorvelis smiled, "It speaks well of you to think of the holds, Rash'Tor'Ri. But it is doing them a great service to pull some of the men and women from the holds. They have less to feed. In truth we could take many more but we do not have the numbers to teach so many just yet."

"Then you're probably not gonna like my next suggestion," I said. "We need to send some of the Shak'Tar to Parlais. I sent a group of

Mages to start teaching but we could use some of those rapid teachers there, too."

"Our Kresh forces do not control Parlais," Gorvelis returned.

"That's another thing," I said. "Our new additions will be tasked with that right after the Mark tomorrow. I intend for them to move in and take Parlais."

"If we control both facilities, we can begin work in the open on both," Gorvelis nodded. "Without the Mark, we can't guarantee the same sort of response as there was here."

"No Mark," I said. "I don't intend to mark another human. People want freedom, even if they don't know it yet. Once they taste it, they'll want more."

"I agree," Sam stated. "The mark may well end the war, but it isn't what I or any of my people see as a good thing."

"It is all the Kresh know," Gorvelis said. "It was all the Shak'Tar knew until we met Rourke. It was still what we thought was right until recently. I can see the appeal of freedom to any people now."

"Using the mark may be a peaceful resolution," I said. "But the mark is all that I am and I love freedom. Those that get marked by me will probably feel the same, at some point."

"I can see that," Sam said.

"Have we got everyone ready to move out to Hub tomorrow?" I asked.

"Ready to go," he said.

"Lyrica doesn't like it," I said. "I'd just have Kil'Sin'Deres do it, but the new ones want it done by me. They don't want to be marked by him. If I am involved or the Shak'Tar, then humans get the mark along with the Kresh."

"I'd try not to piss that one off if you can help it, Colin," Sam said. "I still can't believe what she did in the courtyard. Even with my focus I couldn't keep up with that. Just a couple seconds from welcome party to a very heavy softball."

"I'll be the first to admit," I said, "there's no way I could have survived without her quick reaction."

"The Kresh keep playing with it. They've even got some of the Guards out there playin' some hybrid of shuffleboard and soccer."

"It's never boring around the woman."

"I don't doubt that for a second."

Chapter 21

I stood near the gate and watched the line of Soulguards leaving the planet for Hub. We were uncertain how far my mark would cover so we were sending them all. The majority of the planet had my mark so it wasn't going to be a problem but those that came from Earth to start the Academy needed to go to Hub, as well as the folks who had come in with Rictor.

"A lot more people than I expected," I said.

"Your Prophet brought us several thousand of his people to train with your new Academy. They were already past the stage where they tied their knots. They needed instruction in the martial skills. I think he kept the ones who already know how to fight."

"He's a lot closer to the front lines than Cerres," I said. "Probably a good thing to get his new folks some training. I understand these folks here on Cerres already have quite a few who can use a sword."

"The colonies have a lot more people skilled in arms. They aren't directly under the thumbs of the Kresh so they aren't held back as far. Those on Kresh in the many small villages are more restricted. I'm surprised the Prophet found as many as he has with some skill."

"Humans are a tricky bunch, Touran, You'd be surprised what can be done in secret. Shak'Tar had it tougher hidin' anything," I returned. "Look what you managed, even with masters who could read you with telepathy. Imagine what you could have done if they couldn't read you at all."

"True, Rash'Tor'Ri, very true."

Lyrica was the last in the line of folks crossing to Hub.

"I should stay," she said. "In case they get out of hand."

"I won't put this mark on you."

"You marked me years ago."

"Not like this," I said. "I'd let the world burn before I put this on you."

"I don't trust them."

"They don't believe it will work on them," I said. "They'll find out different. Then they'll be no danger."

"What if they do like the other one?"

"They won't, look at their souls."

"I know but I'll still worry about it."

"That's your job baby."

She ran her hand along the side of my face, "Be careful."

"I will," I answered. "Try not to start anything over there while I get this done."

"Make it quick or I might."

"It won't take long."

She nodded and walked through the gate. I turned back to the others left in the plaza.

"Let's get this done," I said.

I walked over to stand, facing the six Farrara'Ti, "I know some of you don't believe this will work. It will, and now is the time to leave if it isn't what you want."

None of them chose to leave but I could still see the disbelief in their auras. I guessed that would change soon enough. Turning back to the others, I faced three Farrara'Ti, thirty eight Ma'Nar, and four hundred Shak'Tar packed into the plaza.

"I am the focus," I said. "On three, we go."

I turned back to face the six Farrara'Ti, "One… Two… Three!"

The mental strength of all of them slammed into me and I focused it all into the Mark, everything that made me who I am. My duty, honor, and loyalty went into the Mark. My joys, my sadness, my love, my hate, and my rage poured into the Mark and blasted forward. Every Kresh has born the Mark, from the day they were born. Even those that grow into Kresh'Farrara'Ti bear the remnants of the Mark from before.

The blast of mental power ripped those remnants away and left my Mark on them. Perhaps the remnants of previous Marks was the reason the Kresh hadn't been able to evolve past the point they seemed to be stuck at. Perhaps something new was what they needed to become more than they were. I had high hopes for the Kresh under my Mark but there were no guarantees, my Mark may not be that different from those before. Only the future would reveal that.

All six of the Farrara'Ti staggered back-wards and two stumbled and fell. Kil'Sin'Deres and Pos'Far'Nadir were there in seconds.

"Welcome," Kil'Sin'Deres rumbled as he pulled Sin'For'Natal back to his feet. I knew the name because he was there in my head.

The link formed by the Mark is a bond like none I have ever found anywhere else. I knew where they were, who they were, and how they felt. Just like every person on this whole planet. If we counted the thirty million people on Cerres, my clan ranked up with the largest clans, in num-ber, on Kresh. This was an enormous step toward ending the war with those clans.

"I will send someone to tell the others to re-turn, Rash'Tor'Ri," Gorvelis said from beside me, as we watched the new members of my clan studying the new Mark that they carried.

"Thank you, Touran."

***

"According to Sam," I said, "Hub is in chaos after the death of Jas'Tor'Kalamet. Appar-ently, his clan is running around, crazed. Any suggestions?"

"There are nine Farrara'Ti, here," Kil'Sin'Deres said. "We can enter Hub and mark as many as we can and pull them off of the streets."

"That's a good idea," I nodded. "But I need a couple of the new guys to do something else. That should leave you seven to round up Jas'Tor'Kalamet's clan."

"What do you wish, Rash'Tor'Ri?" asked Sin'For'Natal.

"The two strongest clans need to move in and take the Parlais facility and the one facility between them and Cerres. I think its name is Krongis. Gorvelis tells me that Krongis is held by a mid-level strength clan. If he can be Marked and taken that way, all the better. I understand that Sin'For'Natal has a large enough clan to take the Krongis facility without bloodshed."

"This can be done," Sin'For'Natal nodded.

"Are you strong enough to Mark him?"

"I am uncertain."

"Don't try unless you're sure," I said. "I'm not sure how you guys do your thing to take a facility but Gorvelis says it is more diplomatic than violent."

"If a clan is stronger, the weaker clan tends to move on."

"The control of the facilities have never been an interest of the elder clans," Gorvelis said. "They always know that they can take it if they want it. That won't hold true for much longer, though."

"Their noninterest or their ability to take it if they want?" I asked with a grin.

"Both," Kil'Sin'Deres said. "This is the most delicate time of our war, Rash'Tor'Ri. The time when an Elder can still take us. They could not Mark any of us with your Mark so powerful upon us, but they could overwhelm us with numbers."

"Not without losing their clan as well," Sin'For'Natal added.

"They would not believe it if it was told to them," Kaz'Kor'Ratin, another of my new Farrarra'Ti added. "I would not have believed what is happening here if I was not part of it."

"What of Hal'For'Radolin?" I asked. "Is there still a danger from that quarter?"

"Yes," Kil'Sin'Deres answered. "He has been stirring and some of his forces have been seen gathering. He will gather the warriors of the clan before moving toward Hub, if that is where he is headed. There are some conflicts on Kresh that do not involve humans. Let us hope this is one."

"I wouldn't hold my breath," I said. "If he comes, pull back into the facilities and worlds we hold and get ready to defend yourselves. Unlike the way things were done before, we don't give up what we hold. We defend it to our last breath, if necessary. He should be focused on Earth, so let him come."

"And if he succeeds?"

"Then you kill what's left of his clans, and continue doing what we're doing here. Build the clan so that none can stand up to it, and then take the war to them. We don't have the numbers yet, but we're close. If you see opportunity to help, do it. Just like you did last time."

"If we combined the forces you have on Earth with what we have here..." started Sin'For'Natal.

"Unfortunately, three quarters of the forces on Earth don't know or give a shit about what happens here. It'll take some time and effort to change that. It's one of the unfortunate side effects of Kil'Sin'Deres letting us grow without the knowledge of Kresh."

"There may be a time in the future when that's a strong possibility," I continued. "Right now? Wouldn't work. Over here there's always been some sort of 'authority' over any human government. There was always the Kresh. Over there, each country is in charge of itself and gettin' those governments to place themselves under a central authority would be impossible at this time."

"It would be easier if you just Marked them all," Kaz'Kor'Ratin said.

"Easier? Yeah, it would be easier. Wouldn't make it right, though."

"It galls me to sit here while you're fighting for your lives back home," Sam said.

"I know," I answered. "But, like Kil'Sin'Deres said, this is a most delicate time for the clan. They could step in and stop Hal'For'Radolin. But we'd lose so many, another clan could walk in and take it all. We have to have enough forces to meet the second clan when it comes, and the third, and the twenty-third."

"Oh, I get it, Boss," he said. "Doesn't mean I'm gonna like it any more than I do now."

"If you have to do somethin'," I said, "send forces to help Ric get Parlais on track, and we'll need some people to approach the leaders on Krongis, as well. The Kresh should be moved out fairly quickly, so you can start somethin' up."

"And if we start up an Academy?"

"Darrel is plenty capable to run this one or a new one and you the other."

He nodded and I turned to Gorvelis, "I'll want some of the Shak'Tar provided for that one too. We need the skills of the Soulguard spread to the other worlds as quickly as possible. If I thought we could do it safely, I'd sneak people into all of the colonies but with Kresh that aren't with us in charge of the places, it would be problematic at best."

"It would spread us thin," Sam returned.

"Keep building here and get a good foothold in Parlais and Krongis," I said. "When we feel solid enough, we'll move on to the others."

There were nods around the table.

Hub was in for something it hadn't seen in millennia. Revolution.

Chapter 22

"I feel like I should be out there with 'em," I said.

"We are on a pre honeymoon," Lyrica answered, kissing my head. She sat behind me in the massive tub, my head resting on her chest. "The others wouldn't let you out to play yet, anyway. Last time, you went on a spree in Hub and killed several Farrara'Ti. Plus you put graffiti on the walls of one of the buildings."

"Don't try to put all of the unrest in Hub off on me. You turned their Farrara'Ti into a soccer ball. I had nothin' to do with it."

"Maybe this time. But only because you hadn't reacted yet. You would have stopped him."

"He was moving too fast."

"Then you need to work on your focusing skills, Love."

"You're probably right there," I agreed. "I never was as good at that as I should have been."

"We don't need it to do what we were taught to do," she said. "But the scope of the things you and I can do need more focus than even the best Mages need. We have to have it or people can die."

"I guess you use it a great deal in healing."

"Terry started me out with some of the focusing exercises he used as a surgeon. They were a lot like the exercises done at the Academy. But you have to continue them instead of just doing it to pass a class."

"Focusing exercises?"

I felt her surprise as she realized what I had said.

"You never got those classes?"

"They were in the early stages of Mage training. I was put in well into the training and missed those. I got some training from Kyra like any Soulguard gets but she didn't even have to go too deeply into it because of my other abilities."

"But you talked about the focus you use, before."

"Oh, it's there. I use focus when I dance the blades. The world seems to slow down but I've only reached that deep focus once. It was at first Kansas. I can usually reach a certain level while in the grips of the rage, but that time was different. It was like I had all the time in the world to make my decisions."

"Can you show me?"

I projected the memory of the run through the horde of Kresh with my group from the battle. It was just when I had seen the group of Wraiths. Time had seemed to almost stop for a moment. But then it was gone again and I was back in the world of slow motion that was my normal level of focus.

"That's crazy," she said. "How did you reach it then?"

"I spend a lot of my attention trying not to let what's inside me out. I can set it loose for short periods, but never really set it free. It's even harder now. It's stronger than it was before. That time I got past the rage for a second and found that focus."

"We need to work on it more," she said. "The first thing we need to do is get you started on the exercises to improve your focus. Then we can worry about the rest."

"Yes, Ma'am."

She pinched my side, then her fingers slipped around my stomach, "First, I have a few other plans for you."

"Oh really? What sort of plans?"

"Really fun plans," she answered. "In this bath tub, right now."

"I like these plans," I returned as I slid forward and turned around to face her.

"I thought you might," she said with a grin as she moved forward to embrace me.

***

"Master!"

The voice came from behind us. Which was understandable. We both sat on the edge of the roof of the Citadel. Our feet dangled over the edge and we were, simply, admiring the view. There wasn't any of the squared landscaping left when man cut into forests and planted crops. It looked pristine. I knew the other direction would look just the opposite. They had built the Academy on the west side of the Citadel. We stared over the wilderness on the east side of the building.

"Master, there is a problem in Hub," Sami said from a bit further away from the edge than we sat.

I hopped to my feet and went to Sami. He was one of the Shak'Tar I had converted in the base we had destroyed in Romania.

"What is it, Sami?"

"Hal'For'Radolin is there!"

"What?" I returned. They had said it would take months for his forces to get there.

"He's in Hub, Master. He's marking the loose clans left from Jas'Tor'Kalamet."

"How did he get his forces here so quickly?"

"He did not bring them. He came and he is taking the clans of Jas'Tor'Kalamet."

"Shit!"

"We have to get back to Earth," Lyrica said from behind me. "We have to leave, now."

"Tell them we're leaving, Sami," I said, then shook my head. "Never mind, we'll tell 'em. Thank you, Sami."

I turned and dove off the top of the Citadel. I could feel his shock as he saw me jump. I watched through his eyes as he saw Lyrica grin and dive off the building right behind me. As the ground neared, I opened the shield chute I had designed after the first time I dived out of a plane. My descent changed from high speed to a near stop with a bone-jarring jerk. Then I cut power to the chute and dropped the last twenty or thirty feet to land at the base of the Citadel. Lyrica landed seconds after me.

"Damn it!" she cursed, "I left my dress up there!"

"You wanna go back and get it?" sarcasm dripped from the words.

She looked back up for a second. I could tell she was thinking about it. Her eyes dropped back to me and narrowed.

"Let's go home," she said, followed by a long sigh.

"Sorry, baby."

"I guess it's ok," she said. "At least I won't have to tell Paige I left my dress uniform and medals on another world."

"Ah, Crap."

Her melodic laugh filled the air as she shot around the edge of the building to reach the plaza. I followed her with a grin on my face.

I entered the plaza and the gate was closed.

"Uh oh."

"Can they open it from this side?" Lyrica asked.

"I have no idea. Give me a second."

Gorvelis! My thought boomed through the plaza.

He was out the door to the Citadel quicker than I expected. With the Soulguard knot, he was a lot faster than before. He had a sword in his hand and I could feel his mind poised to Lash.

He saw us standing in the center of the plaza and no attackers. Sheathing his swords, he looked at us with a quizzical expression that just screamed, 'What the Hell?"

"Master?"

"Sorry 'bout the scream, I guess you'd call it. I assume you heard the news?"

"Yes. I didn't quite expect you to react as quickly," He answered. "They are sending the signal to open the gate as we speak. As for the summons, you could make it a little less…robust."

"Guess I need to work on that."

"Pelin can show you a great deal about control of it, Master."

"I'll get with her about that, and don't call me Master."

"Yes, Master," he said with a smile. Every one of them knows it irks me to be called Master. And the every one still do it. Maybe I shouldn't have included that particular sense of humor in the Mark.

"Perhaps not," Gorvelis returned.

"Now, you guys have to stop doing that," Lyrica said. "I get half or less of a damn conversation around you."

Perhaps we should include you in it? Gorvelis projected.

"Use your words," she said. "That's just weird."

He laughed, "As you wish, Kilnyeri."

"Kilnyeri?"

"There is a creature on Kresh called the Kilnyeri. It has been known to kill other animals that dwarf it in size when it or its own are endangered. Most of the time they are a peaceful creature that would be, in the words of your world, 'Cute and fuzzy'"

"So he gets to be life ender? And I'm one of the cute and fuzzy bunnies?"

"It seems so, Kilnyeri," he said with a grin. "But there is no shame in it. I doubt there is another creature on fifteen worlds as fierce as the Kilnyeri."

She grudgingly accepted his words.

The gate opened behind us.

"Well, my cute and fuzzy bunny, let's be on our way."

"I may stab you."

"Whatever do you mean, Your Cuteness?"

"With a knife."

"But my little Bunny."

"In your sleep."

Gorvelis was laughing loudly behind us as we walked back through the Gate, and I felt the Kresh outside of the facility. They were in chaos, fighting one another as they tried to reestablish their own hierarchy. I felt the familiar presence inside me try to claw its way out. I could feel its longing to Lash out at the chaos and make it his own.

Lyrica's hand landed lightly on my shoulder, "Calm it down, my love. We'll be past this in a few minutes."

"I'm not sure I can ever get past this," I returned. The only place I can find complete peace is among those we're leaving behind us."

"I know, I've seen it over the last few days. When this is over, we'll come back. We'll come back to stay."

Chapter 23

"I can feel him," I said. "He's over there."

I pointed toward a point all the way across Hub.

"His mind is like a damn Behemoth," I continued. "We have to get out of here before he gets close enough to mark me."

"Get a move on then."

"I hear that, Milady,' I returned as I jumped across the span to land on the next to the last building between us and the Doran Facility.

We ran across the roof top to jump again and landed on the next roof.

"I hope they had time to do what I asked 'em to do."

"What's that?"

"When we got to Cerres, I asked Gorvelis to cycle through the gates and find out where they open. He said it takes a bit of time to do a cycle so we may have another location or two."

"It's a good idea."

"I thought it might be good to know."

"Let's hope they got us a few."

"I'm afraid it takes almost a week to do a cycle," I said. "I was hoping we would get enough time to get two cycles but it looks like things got cut short. At least we'll have one maybe."

As we landed on the roof of the Doran Facility, a Shak'Tar exited the door to the stairwell. She came to meet us.

"We have almost finished the cycle, Rash'Tor'Ri," She said. "We haven't had enough time to cycle the gate to any more settings besides this one."

"It's one more we'll have, Saara."

"The gate will be ready in less than one hour."

"Are you the highest ranking Shak'Tar, here?"

"Yes, Master."

"I want you all out of the facility before he gets here. No fightin' this guy. Pull everyone out and get to Cerres or Parlais. But there's somethin' I want done before you leave."

"Yes, Master."

I grinned, "Here's what I want you to do…"

***

"You're lucky you left that phone with the Shak'Tar," Lyrica said, looking over the wooded valley below us. The gate had opened on the valley floor.

"I wonder why they're always in a valley or plain," I said. "Maybe it's just easier to travel through there."

"Could be a little harder on a mountain peak."

"And, as far as the phone goes, Jacobs suggested it when we talked about this little plan that didn't pan all the way out."

"At least we found this one," she said. "According to the GPS, we're in northern Argentina."

"True," I answered. "I suppose we can work on the shields for this while the Mages get here."

"Will ninety of them be enough? The last time we did this, we used over three hundred."

"It should work. It didn't take much to blow me off a mountain. But, in the worst case we have to pull some more from Kansas to do it. We still got time, the gate will be cyclin' for five more days. Then we'll see if the trap gets sprung."

"What makes you think Hal'For'Radolin will fall for it?"

"He's a giant. He's not had any fear in him for a thousand years. That would have to breed arrogance, wouldn't you think?"

"Probably so."

"I'm hopin' he is. Arrogance breeds stupidity. We marked all the clans that came here last time, so he can't read 'em if we pull 'em back to Cerres. We keep all of ours well away from him. Then, either he has to take the time and research what's happened or he charges in blind. If we're right about him, I think his arrogance will push for the latter."

"And that's why you set the cycle to the Kansas gate."

"Exactly," I said. "If he charges through that gate, he'll deserve what he gets."

"Then we need to get this done quickly and get back there. I'm going to need to set up the infirmary, immediately."

"Paige is already gettin' it set up for you. She said she would as soon as I told her what was happenin'."

"She really was a good choice for her position," she said.

"Very true."

"She's still afraid of the amount of power her stream gives her."

"It's understandable. She's got more raw power than anyone on the planet, but if her focus slips for an instant, nuclear meltdown."

"I wish there was something we could do for her."

"We could restrict her stream back down some, but then there's the 'most powerful leads' policy."

"Which is the stupidest way to choose a leader I ever heard of," she shook her head.

"I agree. I have to wonder what they were thinkin' back then."

"They talked of a change to a voting system, but they haven't brought it back up since."

"They're worried about a change in leadership while this is still goin' on. Paige is doin' a great job with the governments, and they don't want to risk that. You can bet they'll bring it up when the war is done. Provided we're still here when it's over."

"We have to be," she said. "I need to go back to Cerres and get my dress."

"I pity the ones who would stand in the way of that, my cute and fuzzy bunny."

"Damn Kresh and their stupid animals," she muttered. "I bet you had a hand in this, didn't you?"

"I have no idea what you're talkin' about."

"You did, didn't you?" her eyes narrowed.

"How could you even think that?"

"It's that damn mark," she said. "It makes them more like you. I knew it was your fault."

"Really?"

I heard the engines of the plane and muttered, "Thank god."

"What was that?"

"Nothin', Honey," I answered. "Just happy the Mages are here so we can get this done."

"I thought so."

I turned toward the incoming aircraft with a grin.

"How do you want to do this?" she asked.

"Just before the shield meets the ground, I'm thinkin' we need to put a rupture point like the fireball launcher they taught us to build at the Academy. We steer the power in and let it build until it bursts and we have more like what we had in Romania."

"That sounds simple enough," she said and began building her shield that would cup the right side of the valley.

I began building mine on the left.

It wasn't long until the Mages arrived. I stopped the construction of my shield and turned toward the forest behind us. The first to exit the canopy was a tiny woman, less than five feet and small. Her Soulstream was at least as big as Lyrica's. She glowed with power.

"Miss Renauld," I nodded, "Welcome to the party."

"It's Zeenia," she answered. "You must be Rourke and this must be Jayne."

"Colin, if you don't mind."

Lyrica finished her shield and turned around, "Call me Lyrica, Zeenia. It's good to meet you. We've heard much but never had the chance to visit the Academy here."

"I wish I had been allowed to come north during the second wave but I was needed here."

"We couldn't afford to pull everybody in and leave the others unprotected," I said. "Lord knows, it had to be frustrating."

"To say the least," she answered. "So, what do you need to close this thing?"

"We'll need half of you to Pull and steer the power above me, the other half to steer the power above her. We'll take it from there and steer it into these shields we're makin'. Then the fireworks begin."

"We'll need several supports apiece, as well," Lyrica added.

"That doesn't sound too complicated."

"It's not. We just need a lot more power than we could Pull on our own."

"Let me know when you are ready, I will get my people settled."

"Great," I said. "I'll finish my shield."

"If someone could focus better they could have finished their shield while talking," Lyrica said.

"Yeah, yeah."

I returned to my shield and continued building the cupped form that rested against the left side of the valley we faced. It resembled a cupped hand. When it was finished I pushed it outward into the valley walls, deep enough to hit the rock underneath. I saw Lyrica do the same.

"Ok, Zeenia, we're ready."

"Pull!" she ordered.

The hair stood up on the back of my neck and the familiar feeling of someone Pulling from the Source came over me. A Pull of this size would be felt from a great distance.

Forty streams of Soulfire poured into the sky above me and I reached out with my mind to seize it. One big gout of power formed and I steered it into the feeder of my shield. The pressure built up inside the feeder.

"Now," I said.

We released the power from the rupture on the other end of the feeder and a massive amount of power surged into the cupped shield. The key to this was the power inside of the shield occupying the same space as the solid rock. As long as a shield is connected to a person or even connected to the Source as a construct, it didn't have this effect. But if you steer the raw power of the Source into the space inside, well, you get a different effect all together.

The ground shook under our feet as the walls of the valley lurched. Then there was a massive explosion as the walls of the valley slammed together.

"Madre de Dios!"

I heard several exclamations behind us.

"Cease!"

The Pull ended and everyone stared at the destruction that used to be a verdant green valley.

"Damn," I heard Zeenia mutter. Then in a louder voice, "Very impressive, Mister Rourke, Miss Jayne. I had heard the descriptions of what you did in Romania but it didn't really do the act justice. How did you even think of something like this?"

Lyrica smiled, "It started when this genius blew himself off a mountain…."

Chapter 24

"I knew it," Paige said. "I told you it would happen when you left."

"It's not my fault," I returned.

"It never is."

"This time it really wasn't me," I said. "I didn't do it. Lyrica did."

Paige turned to Lyrica, who had been quiet up to this point, "Was it his fault?"

"Of course it was. If he'd been training his focus, I wouldn't have had to kill it."

"I told him what would happen," Paige looked at me with narrowed eyes. "Whenever he makes one of these jaunts of his to the other side of the gates, bad things happen soon after."

I sighed and just looked at her.

"Nothing more to say?"

I shrugged, "Not much point in it, now, is there?"

"You're learning."

"I'll pick my battles," I said. "This ain't one of 'em."

"Speaking of battles," Lyrica said. "I'm going to the infirmary and checking it out. I'll see you this evening, Dearest."

"Love you," I returned with a smile.

I turned back to find Paige smiling one of those knowing smiles that women seem to all have when something happens that I have no clue about.

"What?"

She just shook her head with that smile on her face.

"So what do you know about Hal'For'Radolin?" she asked.

"He's supposed to be one of what they call the Elders. They've been around since the beginning and they're stronger than anything we've ever seen before. He has a horde of Kresh under him that dwarfs any of the ones that came before. And he isn't afraid of anything."

"Doesn't sound very good."

"But we have the plan," I said. "If what we have in Kansas can't stop him, we're screwed anyway."

"If he falls for it."

"True," I said. "There are no guarantees. He may just cycle the gate again. If he does we get another week's grace period."

"There is that, anyway. Do you think he'll send forces through small gates like they did before Second Kansas?"

"I don't have a clue," I said. "If he's smart, he will. But who knows how the fact that he doesn't have anything to go on will affect his decisions. The first wave didn't, and they paid for it. I can't really predict what he'll do. I couldn't risk getting near him while he was marking Jas'Por'Kadin's clans. His power would have marked me too. The mark I have on the others was fueled by the power of all of 'em. I just have me in here."

I tapped the side of my head.

"Can't risk him marking me," I continued. "I don't even know what would happen then. Don't know if it would carry down the chain with the way the mark was done."

"That is particularly worrisome," she said.

"Even worse," I said, "If he sends forces through as soon as the gate finishes cycling, they'll be the ones he just marked from Jas'Por'Kadin's clan. We won't even thin the numbers of his original clan with the trap."

"Whatever he sends will thin his numbers."

"I'm just a little disappointed we didn't manage to mark those clans and get 'em back out of the way before he showed up. He's messin' up my plans."

"Gregor is fond of telling me that no plan completely survives contact with the enemy. That's why they're the enemy."

I chuckled, "Rictor always had somethin' like that to say."

"I bet he did," she returned. "Speaking of Rictor, did you get to see him while you were over there?"

"Unfortunately, he had gone back to Parlais. Gorvelis said he was supposed to be back by the time we were supposed to be there. The early trip kind of screwed that one up."

"That's a shame," she said. "I know how much you were looking forward to seeing him again."

"Just knowin' he survived is enough," I returned.

"Still, it would have been nice."

"True enough."

"And how are the others? Jack, Darrell?"

"They're turnin' out Guards at an astonishing speed. Using telepaths to teach is a hell of a boost to that," I said. "I expect Darrell will be movin' to Krongis before long."

"Krongis?"

"I sent the new clans to take the facility that leads there. After that's done, I think they're plannin' to open another Academy there. Or they may move into Parlais first. I left the operations in their hands. I just told my clans to take both worlds' facilities."

"You were busy."

"Actually we spent the week lounging in the penthouse of the Cerres Citadel. We've got good people over there and they don't need much guidance to do what they need to. My part only took a few minutes and Lyrica's took even less, although it was the most important thing done while we were there."

"She stopped Jas'Por'Kadin from killing you."

"No, she showed a telepathic race that couldn't read her that she is worthy of taking over if I fall. She may not be able to mark 'em but they damn sure know she can handle herself. To them, it's one of their founding ideals. The strongest of the Kresh are the ones who lead. She just proved that she could take out one of their most powerful Farrara'Ti, single-handed. It's the first step in the direction I want them to go. I want them free of the Mark at some point in the future. Lyrica gives them an example."

"Lofty goals," she said. "Admirable goals."

"The mark is a form of slavery, and I don't like it in the least. It feels right to me when I'm over there or even when I visit Oklahoma. That's why it scares me. I don't want that power over people, even as it feels so comforting to have them near."

"I'm still not sure what that mark is going to do in the future."

"Me too," I said.

I stood up from the seat across the desk from Paige, "I gotta have a meetin' with Marco and Polo. The new guns arrived today."

"New guns?"

"I had Warren send every one of the guns we already had built out here. I'm hoping to set up a few more before Hal'For'Radolin sends his troops through the gate."

"Very good," she said. "We can use as many as we can fit around it."

"No doubt."

Chapter 25

Hicks pulled the end of the barrel around to line up with the housing. It was heavy but three men could mount it to the source cannon.

"I thought they were jokin' about addin' guns to this place," Corn said as he and Santos maneuvered the other end of the barrel around.

"Hicks' rule thirty two," James returned. "You can never have enough guns or ammo."

"You do have a point," Santos said.

"That's why it's rule thirty two," Hicks said.

"So how come they decided to pick on us poor Marines," Corn complained. "The weekend warriors were doin' just fine."

"Shit, Corn," James returned. "They haven't been weekend warriors in a few years now. They got some real action here now."

"I know, but I just can't bring myself to say it."

"They were all pretty busy with the other emplacements," Hicks said. "Not like I have to explain to you monkeys why you need to follow orders. The time limit on that gate cycle was up three days ago. They could bust right in here any second."

"At least we'd have somethin' to do that a Marine should be doin'"

"Shut up Corn," James shook his head. "What were we doing three days ago?"

"Oh yeah," he answered. "Digging friggin' holes."

"This has got to be better than digging holes."

"Well, yeah."

"Then quit your bitchin'," Hicks said. "Grab that barrel."

Corn and Santos took the end with the flanges and hefted it up to rest on the bracket. Hicks lifted end slammed the barrel home with a crunch.

"That's how we do it!" Corn said with a grin.

"Grab those anchors, Prater!" Hicks ordered. "Now you and Jimmy get your work-out. Corn, Santos, James, Herrod, Culpepper, and Roady, with me. Back to the minefields. Corn wants to dig more holes, so we'll dig more holes."

He turned toward the huge plain where they had been placing land mines for days with a grin.

"Couldn't keep your trap shut, could you?" Santos grumbled as he grabbed his gear and joined Corn behind Hicks.

"Not my fault," Corn muttered.

"Sure it's not," Santos returned as he joined them.

Culpepper and Roady joined them and Herrod was right behind. All three gave Corn the look. The look that says "You'll pay for this."

"What?" Corn muttered.

They headed for the middle of the plain. The mines were scattered throughout the area but the field was disarmed while the men worked on it. It was armed with a wireless controller that was held by one of the staff of Dietrich Jaegher, the man who would be in charge of the battle when the Kresh finally showed up.

"Santos, start markin' holes for Corn to dig."

"With pleasure," Santos returned.

Hicks felt the hair rise on the back of his neck and a strange sensation came over him. He turned around just as the Gate opened in the distance.

"Corn! You son of a bitch!"

"What!? It's not my fault!"

"It's always your fault!"

Everyone was scrambling for their weapons. Hicks turned back to the gate to see the first Kresh step through. It was big. Bigger than the ones they referred to as Soldiers. This was a Wraith. The big one stepped aside and the portal erupted with Kresh.

"Shit," he said. "We ain't got the time to get out of here."

"Not my fault…" Corn was muttering as he loaded a cartridge into his Barrett.

Hicks donned the helmet that would make his Source weapon go live, "Prater! Get into that gun!"

"We didn't get it anchored!"

"Tell that to those bastards!"

"This is all your fault, Corn!" James yelled as the guns on the left and right flanks began to fire. The center couldn't fire with them in the way.

"You know what I gotta do boys!" Hicks yelled over the noise of the guns.

"It's been an honor, Sarge!" Santos returned. "Tell them to give it hell!"

Out of nowhere a form landed in front of the Marines.

"What the hell is she doin'!?" Corn yelled. "She's, like, ninety pounds of nothin'!"

Another form landed with a thud and a plume of dust.

"Oh, crap, it's Rourke!" James exclaimed.

"That means shit just got real!" Corn was grinning from ear to ear.

***

"They got quite a few of the guns set up," I said. "Another shipment came in yesterday and the last of those is going in right now."

"I see," Paige returned. "The whole plain is covered with guns. Do you think we have enough?"

"Hicks let me in on a few of his rules. Thirty one or two is you can never have enough guns or ammo."

"At least the ammo for these guns is pretty plentiful."

"True," I said. "Those guys should be on the last one of the day. Looks like it's Hicks' boys. He's got a few of 'em out doin more mines. Marines really love to blow things up."

"You like them, don't you?"

"Yeah, I do. They'd all make great Guards if we could ever convince 'em to make the move."

"I've heard a few things about Marines."

I chuckled, "Rictor and Prada were both Marines before joining the Guard."

"And you really think that's a good recommendation? Those two are both crazy."

My head jerked around and the beast slammed against the cage in my mind as I felt the gate open.

"Damn!"

ALERT! THEY"RE HERE, boomed across the base.

"That's disturbing," Paige muttered as my mental voice faded.

"Sorry."

Kresh started pouring onto the plains for the third time in Kansas.

"Those men can't get out of there," she said.

I felt the familiar clawing of the beast inside me, "I'm goin' out there and hold 'em off till they're out."

"Not by yourself, you're not."

"You sure?"

She was already air born as she leaped toward the platoon of Marines.

"I guess so," I muttered and launched myself toward them, as well.

Landing beside Paige I heard one of the Marines say, "…shit just got real."

The wave of Kresh were closing in and the flanks were tearing up the sides of the horde, but the center guns couldn't fire as long as we were out here.

"What now?" Paige asked.

"Do you trust me?"

She nodded.

"I want you to open up with everything you've got."

"If I slip…"

"I won't let it past your guns."

She nodded again. I could see her fear in her aura, and feel it from her mind. The power she can wield is terrifying. She'd spent the last years just nudging that huge Soulstream for Pulling power.

The Kresh were closer.

"Hicks! We'll be backin' out of here. It's goin' to take all my concentration to make sure this works."

His hand settled on my combat harness, "I got your back. Let's fall back, Marines!"

"Paige," I said, resting my hand on her shoulder. "Fire!"

There's a great deal of difference between someone like me Pulling power through a Soulstream of about fifteen inches and something like this. Paige has a Soulstream that's more than three feet in diameter. Which, if you were to figure the area of a circle, and compare, would make her available power at least ten times what mine is. A person's will determines how much force can be put on that Pull, and affects the amount of power Pulled forth.

For most things, Paige only needs to nudge that power with her mind. It spoke a great deal of the trust she had placed in me when she Pulled, and opened every weapon she had constructed over the years. Power exploded in front of us unlike anything I had ever seen from a single person. Disk launchers, fire ballers, and no less than four Soullances spewed fire and destruction across the front of the horde of Kresh closing in from the front. I had a mental shield in place to steer power out of another Lance. I felt like I had been kicked in the head when the power slammed against them. The Lance spewed fire and destruction along with the others and I staggered.

I hadn't expected this much force behind it, and this was just the excess that made it past her focus. My body was absorbing power from the Source but there weren't any supports. Without supports, it was much harder to handle the power of others.

She would never have been able to do this for more than a second or she would have been overloaded. The fire continued to pour into the crumbling wave of Kresh in front of us.

"Cease!"

She stopped Pulling and I threw the rest of the power across the field at the others behind the charred remains.

"Get them out of here, Hicks!"

"We can do one, maybe two more blasts like that," Paige said. "I can feel it build inside me. You can't stop it all."

"Then we need to move out," I answered.

The Marines were already charging across the field toward the lines of guns. Except Hicks.

"Can't keep that fire up long, you go with 'em," I said. "We won't be firing as we retreat. We'll stop and do it."

He nodded and took off after his men.

We turned back toward the Kresh who were flooding forward over the charred remains of the ones who had met Paige's first blast.

"Ready?" I asked.

Her face was flushed from the power and her aura shone brighter than normal. With a nod she turned back toward the enemy.

"I swear I'm gettin' you a shirt with 'Point this side toward enemy' on the front of it."

She laughed and Pulled. Like before, the world erupted in fire and she shattered the next wave of Kresh closing on us.

She stopped and I could see she was close to the limits of what she could hold.

"That's it," I said. "Now we catch our Marines and see if we can clear the field."

We both turned and sprinted after the Marines. They had reached a point where a good half of the center guns had a field of fire. They began firing as we caught up with Hicks. There was a section in the center where the Kresh still poured through and it was close enough that the Marines would still be caught if we didn't do something.

"Keep movin'," I said. "I got this one. Paige let me know when everyone's clear."

She nodded.

I turned back toward the Kresh. The beast was clawing at the cage, and the rage was beating at the walls of my mind. The last few months rage had been building inside me, with very little to release it. I had kept it under control for the most part. The Kresh'Far, commonly referred to as Soldiers, were almost upon me and I let the walls fall. The rage came screaming from the darkness but there was something else too. Something cold and alien. I've known the rage for years. This was something more.

I let out a roar that sounded more like one of them than a man, and charged into their midst. Power erupted from my stream, and flowed through me as I ripped the soldiers apart as if they weren't even there. Power filled me and it felt so good. My Soullance ripped across the area in front of me, and I flung waves of the Source from my fists into the packed Kresh. If they got close enough, I would rip them apart. Once again I knew I was where I was created to be. This was what I was born to do.

"Clear!" came over my coms and I reached to beat the beast back down and put it in its cage.

It didn't work. I was still screaming my rage to the world and nothing was going to stop me. I tried to rein the monster back in but I had let it out too far. It was like being tossed around in a maelstrom.

"Soullord One! Marines are clear!"

My roar of inhuman rage was the only answer.

Something grabbed my combat armor and I was tumbling through the air, away from the battle. I could see Paige below facing me after she threw me out of the battle.

My time will come, I heard laughter after these words in my mind and I was, once again in control. Just in time to see the Wraith behind Paige attack.

What had I done?

The clawed arm of the Wraith swept down. Even with the focus that slowed the world to a crawl, the arm was moving so fast. Paige blurred and the arm passed through the spot she had been standing. I saw her open a shield that I'd never seen. It was an anchor with a pivot where she was attached. She grabbed the Wraith by the wrist and the creature screamed as she began to spin around. The wraith collided with the Kresh that were closing, and bodies flew backwards as they were pummeled by the Wraith's body. She made one more spin, and the Wraith was tumbling through the air back toward the gate. Then Paige jumped into the air. All of this had happened so fast, I was still airborne when she jumped.

I landed with a thud, behind the fourth ring of guns.

Chapter 26

Paige landed beside me and she was furious. Her aura rolled with it.

"I'll deal with you later," she said and leapt back into the air.

All of the guns were firing, now and I got back to my feet. I knew I had screwed up. What the hell was that? I'd been able to regain control every time I had tried before. It had been terrifying to have lost complete control of it. They had names for this sort of thing. Schizophrenia, Multiple Identity Disorder, and probably all sorts of other stuff.

I looked up to see a line of AC-130s coming in from the airfield. They formed a circling pattern with the inner sides of the craft angled toward the ground. Then they began unloading with their Soulfire enhanced weaponry. What I could see from where I was looked fabulous.

I moved between the firing guns and jumped into the air toward the command platform. As I landed on the platform, Pelin and six other Shak'Tar mounted the stairs.

"Master?" she asked. "We saw and felt what happened out there. You will need us, now. We will not let that happen again."

"We'll talk later," I returned.

She nodded and the seven of them backed out of the way of anyone on the platform. They didn't go far though. They took up a formation just to the left of the stairs, where they had plain view of me. Pelin stared at one of them and he nodded. He took off down the stairway. Then she turned and watched me. I could see their auras, and they were poised on the edge of action, worry rolling through all of their souls. They had felt all that I had, and they knew something was wrong.

I tried to put thoughts of what had happened on the back burner, and took stock of what was happening on the plains of Kansas. Kresh poured through the gate but they were hitting the lines of fire from the Source weapons, and the Artillery had begun to hit the lines as well. Now the AC-130s were adding their substantial firepower to it.

Jaegher watched the field intently, "Roll fire to Bat-two. Bat-one, barrels."

Dietrich had set the fire pattern so that they could keep steady fire into the plains. There were four batteries, formerly three. The new guns were Bat-four. One battery of cannons were manned at all times. It just so happened that Bat-one had been manned when the attack occurred. It could have been any of the others just as easily. Bat-two had been on alert, already, and all were prepared to hit the field at a moment's notice. It took a lot of men to keep that sort of prepared- ness, but we were banking on Hal'For'Radolin doing what Kresh had done for so many years and just try to plow through us. He wasn't going to disappoint us apparently.

"What's the word, Storm?" I asked as I reached the spot where Zebadiah Storm watched his monitors. Storm was the man who read the data from the observation drones.

"Upwards of a hundred and thirty thousand have come through, Sir," he answered. "The heat and ash is beginning to interfere with the drones' systems."

"Hadn't thought of that," I said.

"The heat from the field is playing hobb with the atmospherics, as well. We may end up with some storms from this. Visibility is definitely going to drop."

"Code Alpha usually brings some rain afterwards," I said.

"Code Alpha is short burst," Storm answered. "This is extended length. You took out close to what has come through at one time with a Code Alpha. This has already done that and it's just warming up. If things start to get too close we can open up a second battery and double the firepower."

"Damned impressive," I said.

I watched the field as the Pull from the Source weapons made my teeth hurt. In Egypt there had been about thirty thousand Source weapons firing into the sky for Lyrica to use for the Omega. They had been hand held weapons. These were to those weapons like a Howitzer compared to a handgun. There were eight and a half thousand of these weapon emplacements. Even with the separating them into four batteries, there were over two thousand guns firing into the Kresh as they tried to spread out into all directions. It was shooting fish in a barrel.

I felt sorry for the Kresh that kept pouring through the gate into that. If Hal'For'Radolin had been, even a day later, they would be safely stationed on Cerres. Instead, they got to die to teach Hal'For'Radolin a cautionary lesson about attacking the Doran Colony. Worse, his clans had not even come into the picture yet.

"Here come the A-10s on a strafing run," Storm said.

"Jacobs would love to see this."

"They have to get the aircraft in early, before the heat causes problems for the planes."

"I'm glad someone had some sort of idea what to expect."

I could feel the winds beginning to pick up. You could see it blowing into the field in front of us and more ash began to launch up in the center. It hadn't occurred to me that the intense heat from the constantly firing soul weapons would do anything like this.

Dietrich shook his head, "Pull the planes back to base. The sky doesn't look like it's going to get any better."

One of the staff surrounding Dietrich tapped his mike and gave the order. Dietrich never let his eyes stray from the battlefield.

"You ok, boy?" he asked without turning away from the view in front of him.

"Yeah," I answered. "For now, at least."

"I want a report on what happened as soon as this is done," I could see how serious he was about what happened. They ones closest to me were familiar with what happens when I let the beast out. He was worried.

"Visibility has gone down the crapper," Dietrich muttered.

"Maybe I can help with that," I said as I opened my inner eye. "I can let you see it from this perspective if it'll help."

I projected what I was seeing to him with my mind. He jerked just a little as the view turned to flows of power.

"Damnit, man."

I stopped projecting.

"Don't stop," he said. "Just takes a few minutes to get the mind wrapped around that. The dark ones are Kresh?"

I opened the link back up and closed my eyes. The Sight is mental. I had just perceived it as visual for most of my life.

"Yep, their Souls are mostly black and purple."

"Wow, you can get a three hundred and sixty degree view."

"I'm the center of the view, so you can figure the placement of troops from my position."

"Then step up here beside me so I can go to work."

I grinned and stepped up to a position right in front of Dietrich. He pulled a chair from one of the desk stations.

"Sit and concentrate, boy," he said. "We got work to do."

Most people would think I might get upset by being called 'boy' when I'm the second in command of the Soulguard, the leader of a complete world of thirty million humans, the head of a clan of Kresh numbering close to sixty million souls. Not likely. Dietrich Jaegher was six hundred and fifty years or so old. He can call anyone he wants a 'boy'.

Pelin snorted from close beside me.

"Very true, Master," she said. I felt the comfort of the Shak'Tar on the platform as their minds settled in around the walls I used to cage the beast inside me. I couldn't feel that clawing I was so familiar with for the moment. "We will help. You concentrate."

"Alright," I returned. "Don't call me master."

"Yes, Master."

Dietrich laughed, "Let's get started."

I concentrated on the area around us and it came into much better focus. Then I worked outward with every bit of focus I could. I could already hear Lyrica giving me a lecture on focus training. Maybe she was right.

"We don't need the area behind us if it makes it any easier," he rumbled.

I let the focus be on the area in front of us and let the rear fade. The battlefield was much more detailed, after that.

The Soul weapons were flowing with bright yellow torrents of power. The humans were multicolored and infinitely different. The Kresh were Black and purple with many other colors interspersed. They were also infinitely different if you looked close enough to tell it. I never would have looked past the surface, if not for Kil'Sin'Deres. He showed me that the Kresh were more like us than I would ever have wanted. He put a face on my enemies. It was much harder to slaughter the enemy, after they were given a face. For most of my life they had been a faceless enemy that I was able to hate without doubt.

But these Kresh, even while I disliked doing it, needed to die. I had wanted to invite them to become so much more, but now I would kill them. My mind hovered over the battlefield, and watched as hundreds of thousands of them burned. Perhaps I might have felt different if these had been the original clans of Hal'For'Radolin. I don't know. The tears I felt on my cheeks told me that I had changed so much from the young man who had sworn to kill them all so many years ago. At least there was no one in front of me to see it. Pelin rested her hand on my shoulder and squeezed gently.

"Bat Three, open fire," Dietrich said. "Bat Two, replace barrels. Bat Four, target the area just inside the gate. There's a few Demon Mages there. Open fire."

He turned to the second of his Staff, "Blow the mines."

Moments later the center ranks of Kresh erupted with fire and death. The ring of mines were about halfway between the first ring of guns and the Gate. They had waited to fire the guns until the Kresh were past the mines. This would make certain the guns wouldn't set off the mines. A ring of Kresh three hundred feet wide were just obliterated. The minefield had been dense. We had planned, if given enough time, to have it mined from there to the gate itself.

Then Bat Four opened up on the Kresh just outside the gate. The shields of the Kresh'Ma'Nar held for a few moments but the sheer volume of fire slammed into and shattered them. The Kresh'Ma'Nar were ash soon after.

Chapter 27

"Just what the hell were you thinking?" Paige's anger was rolling through her aura. "Do you even know how close it came to losing three crews of gunners? They wouldn't open fire with you out there. I will not lose men because of your bloodlust!"

I nodded. There wasn't any use saying anything. She was right. I had watched the memories of what I had almost caused. Because I couldn't put the beast back in the cage, we came damn close to losing those three crews of gunners. They wouldn't fire and they wouldn't leave either. They knew they needed to be there when they needed to fire. And they had been. When Paige threw me clear and jumped clear, herself, they had opened fire with the rest of the gunners.

"Nothing to say?"

"No excuse," I said. "I couldn't stop."

"What the hell does that mean?"

"Never mind," I said and stood up. "The Shak'Tar claim they can help me prevent it from happening again."

Her eyes narrowed, "Prevent what?"

"Nothing," I answered. "It won't happen again. I've taken steps."

"What is going on with you?"

"I don't know, exactly. When I do you'll know."

I stood up and left Paige's office. Pelin, who waited outside the office looked at me for a second, read what had just gone on and walked into Paige's office. I turned to go back in, seeing the anger in her aura. She slammed the door in my face.

You need not be a part of this conversation.

I may be a dumb ass sometimes, but I know when I don't want to be involved in a situation. This was one of those times when I figured I better not get involved. I walked out of the building, and made my way to my own office. There was some paperwork that had to be done. The official report on the Third Battle of Kansas would include the losses we had taken. Forty four dead and three hundred wounded. This was the smallest amount of losses we had taken in any major conflict with the Kresh.

They weren't killed and wounded by the Kresh, but by the effects of the Source weapons on the environment. The heat had created a sort of vortex that circulated the heat upward causing the heavy winds to come in toward the center. All of the turbulence had spawned tornados that had wreaked havoc in some areas. One such had plowed into the ranks and sent Soulguards flying in every direction. Including into the maelstrom of fire inside the center of the battlefield. This is where we lost forty four men and women. Others were injured but would recover. It was a tragedy, but I couldn't see where there was any defense from this sort of thing when we had to use those guns.

Without the intense fire from them, the Kresh would have broken through, and we'd have been fighting hand to hand again. We are made for that, but there would have been so many more casualties if we had to do it.

It troubled me greatly that I couldn't regain control during the fight. It's true my rage had been hovering very close to the surface, since we had returned from Kresh. I could see the accusations in the souls of many. There was no escaping that. It had begun when out in public, but I had seen it on the base as well. And it pissed me off to no end. Fear was something I had seen throughout my life. But this unreasoning hatred was hard to shrug off. It fed that rage. But there was something else going on. I wasn't sure what it was, but I would need to find out.

I had been doing the report for about an hour when Pelin returned.

"We will be bringing the strongest of the Shak'Tar here to work with me," she said. "We will be tying our Soulstreams and you will be ascending us to Mageguard strength. We will accompany you."

"Now, wait a min…"

"This is not negotiable," she said and walked out of my office.

I stared at the door she had just walked through. I saw her Soul as she took up her position outside of the office alongside Andrea Prada and Alex Brighton. I exhaled as I saw the amusement in both of their auras.

Hard to argue with that.

***

"Overall, I'm very satisfied with the defenses," Polomo said.

"Very true," Marcus answered.

We sat in the office of General Marcus Stratton of the Air National Guard.

"The mines were a decent addition, too," I added.

"That idea came from one of yours, by the way," Marco said looking at me. "Your man Jacobs popped that idea on us before he left with you to Kresh."

"Sounds like somethin' he'd come up with."

"I do wish there was something we could do about the heat dispersal that wouldn't jack with the weather like this," Polo said, looking out the window into one of the many thunder storms that had sprung up since Third Kansas.

"Don't think there's anything we can do about that," Marco said. "Controlling the weather is a little out of our reach."

"You're a smart guy, Colin, figure something out," Polo said with a grin.

"Sorry, guys I deal in fire, plus," I shrugged "It's over my pay grade."

"Speaking of fire," Polo returned, "I've noticed a whole new respect for your Archmage after what you two did out there. Especially after she threw you a thousand feet while in crazy mode."

"Crazy mode?"

"I don't know if you've noticed, son, but every so often you go into full throttle ape shit mode and it makes a lot of people nervous."

"Yeah, I've noticed," I grimaced.

"Some of your people tell me you have a lot of shit goin on up there," he tapped the side of his head, "but I'm getting a little worried."

"It's got me worried too," I said. "I've always been able to turn it off when I need to. This time I couldn't. It almost cost those boys who manned the guns their lives. If not for Paige, I don't know what would have happened."

"You'd have gotten control of it is what would have happened. You wouldn't have let those boys die."

"I wish I had the faith in me that you guys have. I don't know if I would have gotten it back under control."

"You would have."

"On a different subject," Marco said, "What are we expecting now, after what happened out there?"

"I have no idea."

"You've been pretty good at figuring the Kresh out, so far."

"I got lucky. I guessed he'd be arrogant, and set a trap for him," I said. "I doubt he would have survived to be thousands of years old if he was stupid. The only thing I expect is that he won't be back in Kansas. I doubt he'll send his clans into this meat grinder again. Other than that, I have no idea what he'll do. He could pause, and study us. He could open another great Gate, and try again with a blitz. He could open hundreds of small gates, and really give us a hard time by scattering troops all over the place. Hell, he could turn around and walk back out of Hub and leave us be, but I doubt that one."

"Wait and watch, then," Marco said with a frown. "The least we can do is keep shipping weapons to all of the units, both here and abroad."

"We've got Soulguards in every major city in the world," I said. "They tend to hit population centers when they send smaller groups. The Source weapons have made so much difference. We can spread out further because the weapons work."

"Speaking of spreading out," he returned, "Are your guys ready to move out to Knoxville?"

"Almost ready. We should be on the airfield Saturday mornin'. I have to do some work with a group of Shak'Tar before we go."

"You're not replacing your personal squadron, are you?"

"No way. There's an opening left from the losses we took in Egypt. I didn't want to think about those losses so I just kept puttin' it off. The Shak'Tar have been staying away from using the Soulguard techniques because they wouldn't be able to take the oath. Now they need to be with me, so they did it anyway. Can't really keep a secret from a telepath."

"I'd say not," Polo said. "Frankly, I'm surprised they hadn't done it after the first time they met your people."

"They know how much the oath means to me."

He nodded.

"But they're needed to help keep what's up here in line," I tapped the side of my head.

"And they can do this?"

"They showed me they could help when I got up on the command deck to help Dietrich."

"Good."

"It's not like they gave me a choice anyway," I laughed. "Pelin and Paige hatched this up and informed me what was goin' to happen."

Marco chuckled, "That sounds about right. I'll have the planes ready for Thursday morning. God knows I hope we don't need any support from Knoxville on the East coast, but I want to be prepared if we do."

"You can say that again," I answered.

Chapter 28

I sat at a table in the same bar where the Marines had tried to out drink me. Hicks had asked me to join him for a drink. I knew there was something he wanted to ask me but we were both mesmerized by the train wreck that was taking place at the bar.

One of the Marines I had never spoken with yet was sitting beside Lee. Lee was one of the Shak'Tar who had come in from off world. How they had gotten by the forces of Hal'For'Radolin was a close kept secret held by the Shak'Tar. Leemukatyaniala was her name but we just called her Lee. Apparently the strongest of the Shak'Tar all came from the same world, Sorost. They all had names that sounded like that.

"Hello, Miss," We heard Trace, "Have you ever been to Canada?"

"No, I have not."

Lee and the others from Sorost had to have been of the same blood as the Native American folk of our world. She was about five feet and six inches tall with dark skin and eyes that were so dark they were almost black. Her black hair was held back in a loose ponytail. She could have been Kyra's sister.

"It's cold there," Trace said. "Sometimes you just have to do stuff to keep from goin' crazy, you know."

Lee just stared at him but he was undaunted.

"We drink a lot up there," he said. "We drink just to pass the time sometimes. By the way, can I buy you a drink?"

"If you wish," she said with a shrug.

"Does he realize every man in this bar has been after her since she came in?" I asked.

"He doesn't care," Hicks chuckled. "Probably doesn't know she's a telepath either."

"Kind of hard to hide your intent if you're hittin' on a telepath."

"Are you a beer drinker or is it whiskey?" he asked.

"Whiskey."

He pointed at the bartender, "Let's get this lady a shot of some fine Irish Whisky."

He turned back to her with a grin, "Speakin' of Whiskey, I had a friend back in Sudbury. He was a real drinker. I ran into him one night at the local bar and he grabbed my arm."

"He said, 'I need a favor, Trace.' So I followed him outside. He had this bottle of Scotch and he took the lid off and threw it over his shoulder. I knew right then this was something big. He handed me the bottle and said, 'Drink' so I took a big swallow and handed it back to him."

"I asked, 'What's this favor?' and he handed me back the bottle with a nod of his head. 'Drink.' So I drank another swallow. 'Come here,' he said and I followed him to his truck. He started to open the camper and stopped. He handed me the bottle with a drunken nod and said, 'Drink.'"

"I drank another swallow as he opened the camper. I looked inside, 'Grady, why the hell do ya have a dead bear in the back of your truck?'. He handed me back the bottle, 'Drink.' He said with a grin."

"So I drank some more. He leaned in and whispered, 'It's not dead. It's sleeping. I found it while I was clearing some brush' I backed away from the truck, 'But how did it get in the truck?' 'I had some plastic and kind of slid it under the bear. Then backed the truck up to the bank and pulled it into the truck.' He answered. I asked 'What the hell are you gonna do with a sleeping bear?' He smiled real big and said, 'I have an idea. Get in the truck.'"

"So I figured what the hell and took a great big swallow of Scotch and got in the passenger side of the truck. We drove thirty minutes or so to his brother-in-law's hunting lodge. Grady hates his brother-in-law. He's an asshole from New Jersey. But Grady has a key to the lodge so we both take a huge drink of Scotch and drag the bear inside the lodge where we removed the plastic and locked the door back behind us."

"He definitely doesn't realize she's a telepath," Hicks said.

"Funny thing is," I said, "I can see if a person is lying by the chaos it causes through their aura. He either, truly, believes it's true or it's true.

I think maybe the use of tranquilizers might be missing but the tale is overall a true story."

"Son of a bitch," Hicks muttered.

"The best part," trace continued, "Was the next spring when we ran into Joey, Grady's brother-in law. He came right up to Grady. 'You won't believe what happened at the lodge! A friggin' bear broke in the front window, tore all the cabinets off the wall, it shit all over the place, and left!' I guess no one noticed the glass from the window was broken outward, not in!"

Trace laughed and Lee joined him. Lee looked at me.

It was a noble attempt, Master, she said in my mind. **What is a bear?**

Better than any of the other attempts, by far, I returned. **Very large, mean, animal.**

"Someone needs to tell that girl to run," Hicks said. "If not, she'll be hearin' Canadian stories all evenin'."

"I'm pretty sure she can handle herself," I said.

"I guess these Shak'Tar are pretty tough," he returned.

"She gets tired of it, she can make you forget she was even here."

"Not much chance she's gonna get drunk either," he said with a laugh.

"True, she's got a Mage strength Soulstream already. Her stream is about twice as powerful as my own. A week ago he wouldn't be hittin' on her at all. She's sixty five years old and looked it.

With the new stream she looks about thirty or so already. Not sure how far that will go."

"Damn, I need to give that some serious thought. I'm gettin' a little old for this shit, my-self."

"You'd be welcome."

"Thanks."

"So what is it that you need to talk about?"

He reached into his pocket and held a ring out to me.

"I'm touched, Sully, but I'm already spoken for."

"Asshole. I've been a Marine for a long time, Rourke, and I never married because it wasn't fair to leave someone back home wonderin' if I'll make it back. Then along comes Andrea. The fact that she's followin' you around always has me wonderin' if she'll come back. Not because of you but where you guys have to go. I'm used to me bein' in the shit all the time."

"What do you wanna know?"

"If I were to ask her, would she be like I was and refuse. If you think she would be prone to run if I ask I won't ask."

"Six years ago, I'd have said she would run. Now, I'm not so sure. I'm probably the last person you should ask. Predicting what a woman will do is not one of my strong suits. I know that in the last twelve years I never saw the woman stay with one person as long as this time. Never seen her act the way she does for any one person. I would say go for it. But if you really want an answer from someone who would probably know, ask Lyrica. She watches everyone and knows a hell of a lot more than people might think."

He nodded, "I'll do that."

"Better do it quick," I said. "We're headin' to Knoxville tomorrow."

"We're goin' with you," he returned. "Got orders to move out a few days ago. We're hitchin' a ride. From there we move out to Europe."

"They say where you'll be?"

"Italy, to begin with. Afterwards, we'll be lookin' at Germany. All subject to change if the Kresh hit."

"Make sure you're on my plane and you'll get a chance to talk to Lyrica. She said she wasn't lettin' me out of her sight. She's comin' too."

"You do tend to get in more trouble when you run off without that girl."

"It just seems that way because she bails me out when she's there to do it," I said. "We still get in the trouble."

Chapter 29

Hicks returned to his seat next to me with a grin on his face. The plane was loud but I didn't need to hear him. He'd been up near the hatch where Lyrica sat with several of the Shak'Tar, Mattie, and Trent. Lyrica grinned as I looked toward her.

"Rourke," I heard over the com, "We need you in the cockpit."

"Roger," I answered and unbuckled. I had felt the gates begin to open a little while back. There wasn't anything to be done until we got some reports. Pelin and her squad had been on the rage that tried to spring forth immediately and I was, actually, in better shape mentally than I had ever been.

"Sir," the copilot said as I entered the cockpit, "they hit Atlanta. We've got some footage if you want to see it."

He held a tablet out to me. I took it and started watching.

Pausing the report, I said, "I need to take this in the back and figure what we're gonna do. Change course toward Atlanta. Have there been any more reports?"

"I heard chatter of Baltimore, New York, and Pittsburgh, but there's no confirmation yet."

"Then Atlanta it is. Patch me in to the other plane."

"Yes sir."

"Get me Rostov."

I started toward the back and paused as Rostov's voice sounded in my earpiece, "Copy Soullord One."

"They hit Atlanta and I'm changing course to support. I need you guys to continue toward Knoxville. There's chatter of New York, Baltimore, and Pittsburgh. As soon as you get a confirmation, change course and use your best judgement as to which target to aim for."

"Most of your squad is over here," he said.

"I know. I have the Marines, Shak'Tar, forty Mages, and Lyrica. We're good. Reinforce where you feel like you're needed the most."

"It will be done."

I continued toward the back of the plane where Hicks was already heading toward me. Lyrica and Pelin joined us. I pointed at Autumn Richarz, the ranking Mage who was on her way to take command of the outpost in Knoxville. She joined us. I placed the tablet on the seat in front of us and started it back up.

The Kresh poured up the interstate system from the South into the center of Atlanta. The first group of cars had plowed into their ranks at nearly a hundred miles per hour. Atlanta drivers were all crazy, anyway. Bumper to bumper traffic running eighty and ninety miles per hour. The Kresh hit the interstate and it hit back. But it ground to a halt pretty quickly. Kresh ripped cars apart and killed any they could reach. The people behind those had vacated their vehicles and ran off the roads toward the buildings. It was ordered pandemonium. Atlanta had been hit when the Kresh were trying to distract us before Second Kansas. They had drummed the emergency plan into everyone from that day on. Get off the roads. Get out of sight.

It was pretty bad. The Kresh kept plowing forward killing where they could. Their goal seemed to be further north. They weren't spreading out in every direction like they had done the last time. The footage we were seeing came from a helicopter that was above the horde of Kresh. The image jerked to the north as a couple of vehicles thundered down the southbound lane through the empty cars. The National Guard had fitted a pair of tractor trailers with armor and a huge wedge shaped guard on the front.

"Holy shit, those are cool," Lyrica said.

Cars flipped sideways from the trucks and left a relatively clear interstate behind them. Armored Humvees with a variety of weapons followed the trucks. Some had Source cannons, some with fifty caliber guns, others just had men with guns. The Northbound lane had more Humvees and a couple of pickups with Source cannons mounted in the back of them.

"Is that friggin' Darth Vader?" Hicks asked.

"Hellboy is on the cannon in the second truck," I said.

"There is a huge Sci-Fi convention going on this weekend," Trent said as he joined us.

"How would you even know that?" I asked. "You always hated Sci-Fi."

"They asked if I would come make an appearance."

"What?"

"A few years ago, we were Sci-Fi, Boss."

"Hmmm… I guess."

"You're just mad they didn't ask you."

"Hmmmpf."

"Told you he'd get mad," Trent said to Lyrica.

She laughed.

My eyes were drawn back to the report. The Trucks had stopped and the tops of the trailers flipped back as Source cannons rose from inside and opened fire. The Humvees spread out and fired, as did the Comic Book Militia.

"We're on approach, Sir." My coms sounded.

"Ok," I answered, "Richarz, take your Mages and Source chute the Marines down on top of these four buildings."

I had paused the display and pointed out the buildings. "Make sure they have enough folks to imbue the guns and then join us."

"I want ten Mages to accompany Lyrica and I. Pelin I want your folks on this building here," I pointed. "I need you guys for the other thing not fighting. Trent, Mattie, you're with us. We're gonna give those bastards a reason to quit pushing our guys north."

"What you have in mind?" Hicks asked.

I smiled and Trent groaned, "Do you really have to ask?"

Hicks grinned back, "Give em hell."

"Lyrica and I are out first. We'll do a combat drop. You others use chutes and join us. Pilot, let those boys down there know they're getting reinforcements."

The door on the back of the plane opened.

I placed the thong on my swords in their scabbards to keep them from falling out, and headed toward the opening ramp, Lyrica by my side.

"Remember to use your shields this time," she said as the light turned green and we dove out.

I closed my eyes and focused on the ground below. Our boys were holding out but they were in some serious trouble. I Pulled and channeled it out a shield conspicuously shaped like a rocket, and with a scream of joy sped downward. There's nothing quite like a combat drop.

Chapter 30

Jinx felt a tap on his shoulder, "Can I get your picture?"

"Sure thing, Kid," he answered in the gruffest voice he could manage.

He turned around and put the unlit half smoked cigar in his mouth and smiled.

"That's the best Hellboy costume I ever saw at a con," the teenager said.

"Thanks, Kid."

The two teenagers continued on their way and PFC Jinx Webb continued toward the spot he'd been angling for from the time he had arrived at the Convention Center. He saw the trucks in the back. One of the more successful writers he had heard of had bought a couple of Source weapons and had them on display. Gary Cortina was leaning against the first truck as a couple of guys took pictures.

"Yo, Dodge!" Jinx yelled as Darth Vader walked out of the row to his left. "Come here!"

Lance Corporal Frank Dodge, AKA Darth Vader, saw him and hurried over.

"Jinx…I am your father…and your mother is so good at this thing we like to do where she uses her tongue…"

"My mom would kick your ass, Dodge."

He paused for a second and nodded, "You're probably right."

"I know I'm right."

"Let's get one of Gary's books so he can sign it," Jinx said. "Plus I'd like to see if these guns Rourke sells to the public are the same as ours."

"I bet they are," Dodge returned.

"I wouldn't doubt it," he said. "Despite what some people think, Rourke always seemed like a straight shooter to me."

"Me, too."

There were several people in line to have books signed and get pictures so the two of them stepped in behind a couple of guys in Mandalorian armor. The line moved slowly but it wasn't a problem. Gary was talking to each person as they came through, which spoke well to his character. He was a friendly guy.

"What can I do for you two?" Gary asked as they stepped forward. "That's a hell of a costume. I don't think I've seen anyone do Hellboy anywhere near that well."

"We have a guy in our squad that used to be one of those body artists," Jinx said. "He designed it for me."

"I thought you two might be Military," he said. "Marines would be my first guess but the National Guards are looking more and more like Marines these days."

"There was a time that would piss a guy off," Dodge said. "But those days left when the Demons hit us on our own soil."

"Off duty Marines, then."

Jinx smiled, "Marines are never off duty."

Gary laughed, "What can I get you fellows?"

"Thought I might get a hardback of your first series signed," Jinx said. "I've read them all but only have paperbacks."

"We can do that," Gary said and reached into a box. "So who do I make it out to?"

"PFC Jinx Webb."

"Bet you catch a lot of grief over that one."

"They're the ones who gave me the nickname."

He laughed again.

"Let me ask you a question," he said. "Are you qualified on the Source weapons?"

"Sure am," Jinx answered. "So is Dodge here."

"The saddest thing I've found is that I'm part of the percentage of people who can't use the things," Gary said. "I bought both of the cannons on the trucks and several of the one man weapons. I love to see them in action, but I can't fire one myself."

"It's a hell of a rush," Jinx said. "Do you mind if we take a look at them? How did you manage to even bring them here?"

"Gun laws are pretty specific about transporting guns and ammo but these don't have ammo, so we can haul them due to a technicality. They aren't enforcing the gun laws as much anymore, anyway."

"That makes sense," Dodge said. "I'd want everyone to be armed, these days. Never know when the Kresh are gonna drop back in on us. After the thing in Kansas last month, there's no telling what they're gonna do."

"True," Gary returned. "Let's go take a look."

Gary stood up and they followed him to the first truck, a newer model GMC. Jinx looked into the bed to see the whole thing was a steel plate.

"I was wondering how you had them mounted," he said. "Looks completely functional."

"Oh, it is. The plate is welded to the frame which has been reinforced. Along with the springs, of course. It's got the Duramax diesel engine and the horsepower to haul the thing. The other truck is a Dodge with the same reinforcements."

"Sweet," Jinx said.

"This is one of Rourke's new models with the three hundred and sixty degree swivel mount."

"Nice," Jinx nodded. "I just tested on one of these last week. Looks like he didn't cut any corners for private buyers either."

"His partner assured me that they shipped the same to everyone."

"Make sure you never use it on a person," Jinx said. "That contract isn't just for show. You target people and the whole thing fries from the inside."

"I remember signing the contract to never use it on Humans."

"It's enforced," Dodge said. "Even if you could get past the programming and do it, you still gotta face Rourke, if he finds out. That's one scary son of a bitch."

"I've seen the footage."

"It doesn't really do him justice, if our Sergeant isn't bullshitting us," Dodge said. "He was in Egypt. He said the guy is something else. He said Rourke's girl, Jayne is even more terrifying. For a Marine Sergeant to say anything is terrifying means something."

"You know this model wasn't made for a vehicle, don't you?" Jinx asked.

"I talked to the engineers when I bought it," Gary answered. "The head engineer said they are a wall mount gun but with the proper weight system it could be mounted in a truck. He started drawing everything out on a napkin. I had to stop him and see if he would get me a schematic on how to do it. Both trucks work well."

Jinx chuckled, "If Rourke ever sees it we'll have 'em all over the place. The guard has some mounted on vehicles but they're smaller."

"Damn, Jinx, I wanna shoot one of these," Dodge laughed.

"Me too."

"Might be able to set that up after the convention," Gary said. "Let me get your information and I'll get in touch."

"That would be awesome," Jinx answered.

One of the other authors ran up to Gary, "You have to see this, Corvina."

He handed him a tablet and Gary's face paled, "They're here. That's I-75."

Then the horns across Atlanta began to scream. They were installed after the first time the Kresh hit Atlanta. Much like air raid sirens, they went off when a definite raid was in progress.

"You guys really want to fire the guns?" Gary turned to Jinx and Dodge. "Here's your chance."

"Hell yeah," Jinx answered.

"If we get to the National Guard base we can follow them out to meet 'em," Dodge said. "Jinx, you're the gunner, I'll drive."

"We have two trucks," Gary said. "I'll drive one. What do you say, John?"

The other author grinned and ran for the Dodge.

"A Dodge deserves a Dodge," Dodge said and jumped up in the back to climb into the operator's chair. The helmet was on the seat and his Darth Vader helmet hit the floor.

Jinx jumped in the back of the Chevy and pulled the horn stubs from his costume off. The gunner's helmet slipped easily onto his head and he strapped it down with the chin strap.

The com system went live as the helmet seated. Corvina slipped a helmet on his head, as did John. Their coms were live as well and they could all hear the military chatter of the Guards as they were loading up for an assault.

"Attention, National Guard units," Corvina said. "I have two Source cannons on trucks coming your direction. Please inform where you want them placed."

"Go to channel twenty three, please." A voice returned, "Terry! Get these guys information and let's figure where to put 'em!"

The trucks fired up and John pointed his at the loading docks. There was one with a ramp but the door was closed.

"Open the damn door!" He yelled at the convention guard near the door.

The guard shook his head and Dodge swiveled the cannon around to point at the door. The guard's eyes widened and he slammed his palm on the button that raised the door.

"Hold on, Marines!" John said over the coms. "This is gonna be a bumpy ride!"

The truck shot down the ramp and turned left. Gary followed right behind him. The roads were crowded with empty cars. One of the first rules when a raid siren goes off is to stop, leave the vehicle and get inside the nearest building. The Kresh focused on the streets last time before attacking buildings and the National Guards and Soulguard would need the streets to meet them in. Most of the roads had a single lane designated for military use after the first attack and John slammed through several empty cars to plow his way to the Military lane. Then he floored it.

"Those steel bumpers make sense now," Dodge said with a grin.

"Part of the counter weight but useful for certain other things as well," Gary said.

Up ahead of them was a car in the lane.

"That's a nice Beemer," Dodge said.

"Be a shame if somethin' were to happen to it," answered John as he plowed through between it and the other lane. The BMW died with a loud crunch sound. They could hear John chuckling as the Dodge kept going.

Surprisingly, there were very few vehicles out in the military lane. They neared the National Guard base just as two armored semi trucks plowed through the empty cars to reach the military lane. Behind them came twenty Humvees with smaller Source cannons mounted in the backs. Several of the Guards did the double take looks as they saw the two wall cannons approaching. Jinx saw the familiar black armor of the Soulguard as a group of them launched themselves over cars and shot down the street at high speed.

The two trucks fell in line behind the Humvees.

Chapter 31

I watched the fight below as Lyrica and I closed in. The first armored truck had been swarmed and the second was in bad shape. It had turned and started rolling but the Kresh were right on top of it. One of the trucks fired across the span between the lanes and cleared a section to give the truck some time to get moving. All of the Humvees were rolling with their guns pointed back into the Kresh. The two trucks were doing the same.

I grinned as they fired. The recoil would slam the trucks which swerved or lurched forward with the shots. Those were the new wall mount guns we had been putting in China. The Humvees were firing into the Kresh but there were a lot of them. The Kresh jumped into the second semi just as I opened fire on the pack closing with the pickups. The recoil slammed me back like getting kicked. I expected that, having done this many times.

Rash'Tor'Ri! Boomed through the minds of the Kresh and Humans alike. I kept firing my disk launchers into the packed numbers of Kresh'Far, or soldiers, as we commonly referred to them.

Lyrica and I both unloaded on the Kresh in front of the semi as it got a little ground covered.

Then I slammed into the ground with a crunch of asphalt.

***

Jinx fired the cannon and the whole back-side of the truck slid sideways. Gary Corvina was laughing like a maniac and cut the wheels into the slide. It lurched forward again.

"I love this thing!" Jinx screamed as he fired again. This time it swept across the Kresh that were trying to pile into the second semi. The first one hadn't gotten turned all the way around before the Kresh reached it. Jinx could say one thing for the National Guardsmen in the guns. They didn't stop firing as the Kresh boarded the trailer. The fired until they were dragged out of the seats by Kresh. They were brutal, these Kresh and Jinx was doing his best to keep the bastards out of the second truck.

"Barrel's getting hot," Dodge said.

"Don't have any extras," Corvina growled. "Fire 'em till they melt."

"Gonna happen sooner than we'd like, Gary," Jinx said.

"Can't let these bastards get any more of those guys," Gary answered.

"I know."

"Rear! Six o'clock!" Dodge yelled. "Incoming!"

Kresh poured up the northbound road and they had no obstructions. Northbound traffic had sped away as the southbound traffic had ground to a halt.

Jinx spun the cannon back to the rear and opened fire as the others in their convoy of Humvees fired with both Source cannons and fifty calibers. The Kresh poured through the fire and kept coming. There were a lot of Kresh killed but there just weren't enough guns.

Jinx's eye twitched as a roar sounded in his mind, **Rash'Tor'Ri!**

"Boys we're on a dead end road!" John yelled. Traffic is covering the interstate ahead and we ain't got an off-ramp!"

"You guys get up there and abandon the vehicles. We're soldiers. You're civilians," came from the coms as the Humvees slowed.

"Oh, hell no!" John and Corvina both returned.

Jinx grinned, and triggered the cannon with a solid burst. The Kresh closed on the vehicles and one grabbed the end of the cannon. Jinx fired right into its face. Another closed from the side and reached for Jinx. Jinx drew the .45 he carried everywhere and dived straight inside the Kresh's reach and pushed the .45 into its mouth. He pulled the trigger three times as he felt a burning pain in his side where the claws ripped deep gashes. He and the Kresh tumbled to the ground but Jinx staggered back to his feet. Gary stepped up beside him and both of them unloaded their pistols in the face of two others.

Jinx growled as two others rushed forward at the pair. He jerked in surprise as both heads exploded, along with a bunch of others. Then there was an explosion of power in front of them and two forms crossed in front of the National Guards. Kresh dropped in pieces as the swords of both Soullords moved like lightning.

Then there were ten more forms slamming through the ranks of Kresh. More fell to the snipers if they got near.

"You said you had some portables?"

"Yeah I do."

"Now would be a good time for one," he said and touched his bloody side. "And some duct tape?"

Gary reached into the truck and pulled one of the one man units with another helmet and a roll of the familiar grey tape. Jinx quickly tore several pieces of tape and taped the wounds closed. Then he swapped helmets and strode forward to open fire with the smaller source weapon.

***

We ran across the front between the Kresh and the soldiers. The snipers were taking out any close in to the men and we cleared a swath with

236

swords and disk launchers. Trent, Mattie, and ten mages hit the field right behind us and cut loose with launchers. Then they followed Lyrica and I right across the front of the army of Kresh.

"Right behind you, Boss."

I grinned and turned to face the Kresh still closing from the south. I felt the beast inside me clawing to get out.

"What's next?"

"Kill them all," I returned and I let the beast out of its cage.

I let out an inhuman roar and the world slowed to a crawl as I charged into the Kresh. The Mages formed a V formation and we ripped them apart. Richarz' Mages arrived and joined the melee. Any that tried to move around our formations were burnt by the National Guard gunners.

The city attacks we had been involved in before were anywhere from five to ten thousand Kresh. This new clan had put close to fifty thousand Kresh into Atlanta. The Soulguard forces had gone south, below them, while the National Guard had met them on the northern front. When the northern Kresh couldn't advance and the southern route was also blocked, they began to spread into the city. It seemed that I wasn't the attraction I had been to those clans that had heard of me.

It took two rough days of hunting after the Main battle to clean Atlanta out. The Kresh stayed to the streets for the most part, but they followed humans into buildings in some places. Those were the worst. We'd find forty or fifty Kresh in a building, still eating what was left of the inhabitants.

Lyrica had stopped fighting and started working on the injured National Guardsmen as soon as Richarz had hit the field with her Mages. The Guards had been torn up pretty bad, as well as a certain Marine in a Hellboy costume. He had refused to stop shooting until Lyrica picked him up and took the helmet off of him. As soon as she had walked away after healing his wounds as much as she dared, he retrieved his helmet and rejoined the effort to clean out the city.

Chapter 32

"We lost a hundred and twenty five thousand people."

I looked at the Major who was speaking. His statement felt like an accusation but his Soul showed none of that. Perhaps it was my own feeling of guilt that we couldn't stop them quickly enough.

"They didn't follow the pattern the others did," I said. "The other clans driving motivation was to kill me. I used myself as bait several times. This time it didn't work."

"That's not something you can blame yourself for, Sir."

"I know but it was much better for others when we could depend on that happening. Before, even the cities I didn't fight in were cleared by others pretending they were me to bait traps."

"Reports say that it was worse in New York and Baltimore. Close to a million dead from the two combined. And Pittsburgh is literally gone. They hit the west coast in Los Angeles, San Francisco, and Seattle. But we had more forces there and took fewer losses. They were hit harder in Europe and China than we were, here, and the death toll in Tokyo was worse than any of the attacks."

"The Kresh were killed in every attack but they are killing a much higher ratio of humans than we are of Kresh."

"And they haven't fielded anything higher than a Wraith," I said. "Not many of those. There was just the one here in Atlanta. You can bet somethin' big is about to happen. I bet he's usin' every small gate they have to flood the cities. But the big gate is still gonna open somewhere and I doubt it will be Kansas. If we're lucky it'll be China. They have more guns now than we have in Kansas. Let the bastards poke their heads out there."

"Very true," Major Branson returned.

"Thank you, Major," I said, taking the paperwork he offered. He turned and strode from the room. I looked down at the pages in my hands. The list of my dead grows and grows. The civilians on the list I kept were just as much my dead as the soldiers.

You cannot blame yourself for all of them, I heard inside my mind. Pelin was never far from me, hardly ever within sight, but always present. She or Lee would shadow me at all times. Sometimes, with one or two of the others.

I could shut the gates to Earth, permanently, I returned. **Yet, I choose not to.**

A necessity for the greater good, Master, she projected. **Can you sacrifice fifteen worlds to close off this one? Without what is happening here, those of yours on these other worlds would not be able to stay unknown. If they are discovered they will be destroyed. Along with any future where the Kresh can be anything but the monsters they are thought to be. We**

must buy them the time needed to survive. Then we can take the war to Kresh and away from Doran.

I know, I sat back in my office chair. **But how do I not blame myself for all of this?**

There is a heavy price to pay to be in command. Sometimes the choices are hard. You will make the right decisions, Master. We can see it when we look inside of us at your Mark. It is who you are.

I wish I could muster the faith in myself that those around me seemed to have. I shook my head. There was no time for self-loathing, I needed to get the troops ready to move to Europe. The Great gate wouldn't be here in America, it would be somewhere over seas. We knew the locations of five gates, leaving two uncharted. Three of those gates were blocked from use. One was Kansas and they'd discovered what would happen if they came through, there.

China had more guns set up already than Kansas had and they were adding to the defenses at an alarming rate. But there were still two unknown gates. I felt that moving to Europe would put us closer to the event when they opened up one of those Gates.

I saw Prada's Soul as she approached the building I was using for a command center. She was grinning as she entered the room.

"You have a visitor, Boss," she said. "Important visitor, at that. Samuel Deacons will be here in less than an hour."

"What's he doin' here?" I wondered aloud.

"He announced he was coming as soon as he heard we were here. The Kresh hadn't even been cleaned out."

"Just odd he would come here when he needs to distance himself from me."

"Do you honestly think he would distance himself from you?" she asked. "His son is directly involved here, not to mention the history you have with the man."

"I figured Alan would do that."

"Not if Deacons knew he was doing it," she said.

"That was the idea. He wasn't supposed to know it."

"Well you're not getting out of it this time," she laughed. "He specifically asked for you to meet with him."

"Well, I guess I better be there, then."

She laughed again, "I also have a little news from Kansas. Do you remember that restaurant we had the little incident at?"

"Yeah, I remember it."

"It seems that it's under new management."

She was enjoying this way too much. There was something she was building up to.

"The name has changed to Nightwing's."

"She didn't," I said. "I knew she was pissed, but I didn't think she was that pissed."

"Oh yes she did. And Soulguards are very welcome at the place."

"Kind of surprised she didn't burn it down when she bought it."

"Oh, she made some changes to the place. First thing she did was vet the staff. Some were sent on their way."

I shook my head, "Gotta love her."

It wasn't much longer before Samuel Deacons entered my office.

"How are you, Colin?"

"Pretty good, Sam," I answered. "How's the campaign?"

"I hate to even say this, but the Kresh hitting again has boosted my polls immensely. The thing that bothered me the most was the fact that my schedule kept having me at the opposite end of the country from where you were at during any given time. Then the old kanuckle head figured out what was up. I'm just a little pissed at Alan for doing it, and a little pissed that you helped."

"I don't know what you're talkin' about," I said.

"Yes, I'm sure," he said. "It seems that Alan has avoided the subject for quite some time, but there will be a time when they'll throw that subject up to try to do what they can to hurt me. The thing is, I don't see our friendship hurting me. And, frankly, don't give a damn if others do. I owe you more than I could ever repay you. This world owes you more than they could ever repay."

"Thank you, Sam. That means more to me than you might think."

"I was in Nashville when this broke loose. I figured I might catch you and clear up the question everyone seems to be dodging. Outside are three news vans. Today I want to show them where I stand with you and where I stand with the Soulguard. Right beside you. I wish I could have done it before the attack but it's too late for that, thanks to you and Alan."

"At least now it shouldn't be as big a problem as it would have been."

"In some ways, true. In other ways it would have been better to do this sooner. Now, some will think it was done because we went back to war. Which is a political move instead of the move of a friend."

"Possibly," I said

"But we'll deal with that when it comes," he said. "So tell me, what's the plan now?"

"My group is about to load out for Romania," I said. "We have to prepare for another Great Gate to open up and I'm thinking it won't be here. The base in Romania is centrally located in case the next gate is over there. If they come back to Kansas, they deserve what happens. If they hit the one in China, they'll have more of the same. The other three we know of are effectively blocked. There are two left unaccounted for."

"Sounds like a good plan," he said. "Will my son be joining you?"

"Yes sir, he will."

"Then I should make time to see him before I go back to Washington."

"I'm sure he'd like to see you."

"What are your opinions on the lady he is seeing, if you don't mind me asking?"

"She's one of my best friends, Sam. She's good people."

"That's what my assessment was but it never hurts to ask someone who can see into Souls."

I chuckled.

"Let's get this photo thing taken care of and we'll see if we can find Trent. Perhaps there is a place we can just sit and talk."

"I'm sure we can find somethin'."

Chapter 33

I felt the Great Gate open and looked to the northwest. I felt the beast inside me clawing to get out. The minds of my Shak'Tar were there in an instant. It was a comforting feeling to not have to fight the darkness inside me alone. I clicked my coms.

"We need to head on a Northwest heading," I said to the pilot. "A gate just opened in that direction. We should hear details fairly soon. How's the fuel situation?"

"We have enough to reach anywhere within another thousand miles. There's a fuel depot in Vaslui, Romania, if we need to go that far."

"I think we'll be going farther than that."

"Then we'll set course for Vaslui for a refuel. Then we have full range again."

"Sounds good," I said. "Notify the other planes and make sure they can all make Vaslui. If so, we're good."

"Yes, Sir."

I turned to Sergeant Hicks, who was seated beside me, "Looks like we have a change in plans."

"We'll fight wherever the fight is, Rourke," he said with a grin.

"We need to work up a plan using both my people and yours," I said.

"True," he said. "I have a couple of suggestions if you don't mind listenin'."

"Lay it on me."

"Ok, here's a mockup of a skirmish," he said and pulled some papers from his pocket. "Say the enemy is here. I would put my guys here and here…"

***

"We can intercept them in Novaya," Rostov said. "They've destroyed Ufa and most of the surrounding area."

His accent was more pronounced with the distress he was feeling. He was born less than a hundred miles from Ufa.

"The largest group of them is working its way west. They overran Avdon and Sanitoriya and continue west. There is no way we can reach them before they take Uzytamak and Arslanovo. Novaya looks to be the soonest we can get there."

I placed my hand on his shoulder, "We'll get there."

He nodded.

It was three hours out and I could feel them all as they spread from Ufa, Russia. The Gate had opened right in the middle of the city and Kresh had poured forth from it. Not just any Kresh. Thousands of Wraiths led the charge and they were damn close to unstoppable. I tried to keep the beast inside calm, and waited for the time when I could let him out. I watched helplessly as the dark souls spread from that gate, and the bright souls in their path were snuffed out like candles. We were the closest force with a chance to do major damage to them. The Russians were closing from the north and more forces from Germany were closing from the west behind us. Our planes would be the first to arrive and it was our job to stall that flood if we could.

"Getting that crazy look in his eyes," I heard Trent. "Thought you guys were helping with that."

"That is just normal crazy," Lee answered. "Worry not, friend, Trent."

Trent chuckled, "I guess we'll know when it goes past that, huh?"

"I'm right here," I said.

"Of course we'd know," Mattie said. "The plane would be crashing, and we'd all suffer a painful fiery death."

"Right here."

"Maybe we should just push him out the back and run."

"All for throwin' him out of the plane," Prada said.

"I heard you got to do that," Trent returned. "I bet that was fun."

I sighed.

"It was great!"

"Coming up on our drop zone, Sir," the pilot informed me through the coms. "Five minutes."

"Thanks," I answered. "We'll be going with the formation Hicks suggested. Once we're on the ground, the snipers will look for high ground and the Marines will begin evacuating anyone who hasn't left already. Soulguards will form on me and we'll head out to meet the Kresh to the east of town. This will give the Marines time to pull as many people out as they can."

Lyrica stepped up in front of me, "You know there are over five hundred people down there. The Marines won't be able to get them out before the Kresh get there. These don't have that hatred of you that will keep them coming at you. They'll go around us while the middle is fighting with us."

I looked at the growing darkness to the east. I wanted to be out there killing them.

"We need to gather those people and shield them," Lyrica said.

I knew she was right and there was a sinking feeling in my stomach. If we went with my plan and she was right, we would lose both the civilians and the Marines. Did I want to kill them so badly that I would do that?

"She's right, Sir," Hicks said. "We've gotten complacent with the Kresh falling for the bait of Rash'Tor'Ri. If they don't turn and face you, there's plenty enough of 'em to go around."

"Ok," I said. "New plan! We hit the ground and gather anyone we can find in this central building."

I pointed at a large storage barn for the farms located around Novaya.

"We get 'em in there and we'll build a shield to protect 'em. Lyrica and I will direct you to the ones hiding. Once that's done, and only after that's done, we'll go meet the Kresh."

The light by the rear door began to flash and the ramp dropped open. I moved to the back of the plane.

Prada and Trent followed. I turned to Trent and grasped his shoulder. "You know what your job is."

He nodded and shoved Prada out of the plane. I laughed at the cursing over the coms. She hadn't turned her coms off and there were things said that should never be repeated. I dove out after her. Close to three hundred forms dropped from the three C-130s into the night sky above Navaya. Two hundred and fifty eight Soulguards, forty two Marines, and eleven Sha-k'Tar. I had asked Hicks about his platoon some time ago and why there wasn't a lieutenant like most Marine platoons. They had chosen to use him as a noncommissioned officer to run it. The Marine Corp was growing as quickly as the Soulguard and there was a lack of commissioned officers.

"Guards take the outside buildings," I said. "Marines take the close ones."

"We need eyes on top of the water tower," Hicks added. "Corn, Santos, and Nucci, that's your position. Trip, your fire team is with me. When you hit the ground, spread out by fire teams and work fast. Listen for direction from the Soullords."

"Rostov," I said as we neared the ground. "I need you with me. I need a translator."

"Affirmative."

We touched down near the central building we would bring the civilians to.

"Go," I said. "Lyrica and I will be on top of this building to steer you toward people. They're concentrated toward the west."

They spread out and disappeared into the night toward the west.

I jumped up onto the roof of the warehouse, Lyrica seconds behind me. Rostov joined us. Lyrica immediately started scanning to the west.

"Fourteen souls in the house to your right, Adaya…"

"Three in the basement of the house on your left, Reyna…"

She continued to direct the others.

"I need you to translate as I use a mental message for the people, here. I need to tell 'em that the soldiers will help them and bring them to a safe zone."

"Da, this I can do."

As he relayed the message to me in Russian, I projected the same out into the darkness. I could feel the confusion from the people who were hiding but I could also feel the relief from many. It was the best I could do. Rostov relayed more of the message and I projected.

It wasn't long before the first of the people of Novaya arrived. They were with a single Mage.

"Get 'em inside and settled," I said. "They'll be here for a while."

"Yes, Sir."

More began to trickle in and then a large group, and another.

I started scanning the town, as well, and helping direct the Marines to various groups of scared humans. Everything unfolded smoothly as people closed on the warehouse. It finally came down to just a few marines and Guards outside of the warehouse.

"All right, guys" I said. "Come back in and we can set up a shield before we go east after the Kresh."

Lyrica was already working on a shield to tie to the Source as I called them in. It was a dome that surrounded the warehouse. She had almost finished it when the last Guard entered the perimeter. Our three lookouts had descended the water tower and I looked past them to the closing darkness with an anticipation that still scares me. What kind of monster loves to do this as much as I do? I could feel the beast inside poised to come forth and wreak havoc on my enemies.

That's when the night lit up bright as day in the east and the blinding light had me holding my hands over my face.

Chapter 34

Shields! Shields! Everyone raise shields! Support the shield! My mental voice boomed outward.

I have to give my Guards credit. Shields slammed out to reinforce the dome Lyrica had created. I could still see the three Marines running toward the dome and I knew they weren't going to make it. I bolted forward and ripped a hole in the layered shields. More shields raised behind me.

Lyrica!

I trusted she would see what I was doing. In a flash, I was right in front of Nucci and Santos. I grabbed both of them by the battle harness each wore and threw them back behind me at the shield. A few steps more and I grabbed Corn. Throwing him at the shield as I turned I could see a massive blast wave rolling toward us. I pulled from the Source as I launched myself back toward the shield. I saw openings as the Marines flew through the shield to be caught by other Mages. Corn passed through and I smiled, reinforcing my personal shield. I was moving fast and the dome was close when

Hell slammed into my back and hurled me forward.

It was like a great fiery hand had swatted me like a bug. I felt the fires burning my back as I slammed into the shield at nearly two hundred miles per hour. It was solid for a bare instant but I felt my left arm break before the shield was out of the way. The fire at my back was suddenly gone and I was Pulling like a mad man. The Source was hitting the far side of the shield as I shot past the front of the warehouse. The power slowed me enough to survive the impact, but I had twisted to protect my left arm only to slam into the shield wall on the right.

More pain shot through me as my right arm took the brunt of it and I felt the shoulder dislocate. I came back to my feet with an inhuman roar as the pain washed over me. My back was on fire and I smelled burnt hair and flesh. I turned back the way I came to find myself staring into emerald green eyes and her hands landed on my chest.

I stopped. The minds of my Shak'Tar settled around me and the beast was shoved back down. Lyrica grimaced as she reached over and popped my shoulder back in place.

"Give me your arm," she growled.

The pain washed over my senses again as she took my left arm and found the break. It spiked again as she set the bone. Then we began to Pull. I could feel the burn in my back begin to recede, as well as both arms.

"There's radiation inside the dome," Adaya said, as she neared us. "People won't last long in this. We can withstand it but the Marines and the town folk can't."

"I'll be done here in a moment," Lyrica snapped.

"I'll survive," I answered. "We need to do somethin' about the others."

"Just what do you think we can do?"

"I don't know but we have to do something."

She took a deep breath and stopped Pulling through me, "Ok, I would ask what the hell you were thinking but I already know the answer."

"Does anyone know how much time we have to come up with something?"

"Ten minutes?" Adaya answered.

"Shit."

"Exactly."

I closed my eyes to think, "Could a regular Guard withstand it?"

"I would think so," Lyrica said. "What are you thinking?"

"The Squirrel King."

Years ago I had found a squirrel in the mountains of Montana that had a Soulguard knot done by a young Soullord who spent a lot of time in the woods as she grew up.

"There's over five hundred people," she returned as she immediately understood what I was talking about. "We don't have time. We may get a hundred done in ten minutes."

"Rostov!"

"Yes?" he returned as he approached.

"I need you translating again," I said. "Hicks!"

"Here," he said from my left.

"Come here," I said. "I need you to do somethin'."

He coughed, "Is it gonna kill me any quicker than this radiation?"

"This could help. Lyrica I need everyone in the shield's streams lit up. Get as many supports as you need."

She nodded and went to the Mages. In moments I felt the streams thrum as she lit up every Soul in the shield and they became visible.

"Rostov, start translating. If you want to live, follow these instructions to the letter."

He translated and I projected it.

What you see is called your Soulstream. This will make you strong enough to survive the radiation if you will follow my direction. I projected.

"We start with you, Hicks. Reach out with your mind and grasp it about two feet out."

"Ok."

"Move it."

The stream moved. I projected what was happening into the minds of everyone.

All of you will follow the instructions as I show them to you.

"Pull it back toward you in a loop to your chest."

Hicks pulled it back to his chest. As it touched his Soul it attached.

"Son of a bitch!" he exclaimed as the Stream fed his Soul from two separate places. He could feel the difference already. I looked back to the Marines to see they had done the same.

"Reach out and grab it again."

Hicks did as instructed.

"Now bring this one around to your shoulder."

One by one we formed the loops that make up a Soulguard knot. I watched as over five hundred people became Soulguards without the Oath, including forty two Marines. The Souls began to strengthen instead of fade. At least the gamble had paid off this time. We had bought us some time. Not much, but some time. Everything outside the dome was radioactive. The air couldn't even be let in. I wasn't sure anything could survive that, maybe not even as Soulguards.

"What's next?" Hicks said and turned. His move wasn't with compensation for the new strength and he lurched sideways. "Damn."

"We need everyone out here," I said. "You need to experiment a little and get used to the difference."

He nodded and staggered back toward his men.

"All Mages," I said on coms. "Bring out all of the civilians. I have a plan."

"Oh dear," Reyna said. "He has a plan."

"Who's plan?" I heard Stone.

"Who do you think?"

"Your mics are on," I said.

"Oh bloody hell, him?"

"Maybe Lyrica helped with it," Adaya added.

"That might even be worse," Prada said.

"Can still hear you," I said.

"I had nothing to do with a plan," Lyrica said. "If I did it would be a wonderful plan."

"Sir," one of the Mages from inside the building spoke, "We have seven people in hear who didn't get the knot."

"Seven, I can handle," Lyrica said and entered the warehouse.

I nodded and turned toward Rostov and Adaya, "Ok, here's what I want…"

Chapter 35

"Does anyone know what happened yet?" Daphne Cavanaugh asked. "Who set off a nuclear bomb in the middle of Russia?"

"They're sayin' a mid level bureaucrat in Ufa did it," Kharl returned, looking out into the wasteland left by the bomb. "But, really, who knows?"

"Has there been any news of whether anyone survived it?"

"Not much news yet."

Daphne rested her hand on the big man's shoulder and squeezed, "If anyone could, it would be those two."

"They were so close to Ufa," Kharl said. "The planes had barely cleared the area when the blast went off."

His head snapped around toward Ufa as the hair stood up on the back of his neck.

"You feel that?" Daphne asked as her head snapped around as well.

"Oh yeah," Kharl said with a grin. "If someone out there is Pulling that hard, it means survivors."

The enhanced sight of a Soulmage allowed them to see far out into the waste. Both saw the plume of dust spurt into the air. Then another a little closer.

"Whatever it is, it's movin' fast," she said.

Kharl finally caught a glimpse of what was causing the plumes as it bounced along the barely discernable road left after the blast.

"That's my boy," he muttered.

Daphne's head cocked to the side as she caught sight of the giant, glowing sled that bounced along the road raising plumes of dust, as it hit the ground and bounced up. On the very front she could see the Russian, Alexei Rostov. He would turn his head and shout something, and a gout of fire would spew from the left or right to steer the behemoth. The rear of the sled was glowing as two forms could be seen standing side by side pouring Soulfire through a port that looked conspicuously like a giant rocket.

"Is he really wearing a red cape?"

Kharl was grinning widely.

"You think he's finally bought into the whole Superhero thing?"

"I don't know, but if he wants to wear a red cape and spandex, I guess we'll have to let him do it."

"Looks like they're gonna hit the safe zone a little north of here," she said.

"What say we go meet 'em?"

"Let's do."

"Your Russian will be glad to see you."

"He's not my Russian."

"He sure wants to be."

"So does half the damn planet, thanks to that damn guy with his camera."

"You could do a lot worse than Rostov, I think."

"Maybe so," she said. "But if he thinks that he wants me just because he's seen my ass, he better get in line. Seems everybody has seen that."

"I think he was much more impressed with the single-handed defense of Paris than the lack of clothing. Of course that was a bit of a bonus."

Even with Kharl's speed the punch to his arm knocked him sideways.

"Keep it up and I'll tell your wife."

Kharl grumbled.

"What was that?"

"You know, I can't believe he made her stream that much bigger than mine," he said. "He's supposed to have my back."

Daphne chuckled and started toward the north where it looked like the giant sled was aiming.

***

The sled slammed into the ground again, and dirt and ash exploded into the air. By then the screaming of the civilians was, for the most part, over. Now they just held on for dear life. At least the lady had given me a blanket to drape over my nearly naked backside. The blast wave had burned most of the clothing from my back. I'm pretty sure the straps of my combat harness was all that held my uniform on.

"Adaya!" Rostov yelled. "Three second burst!"

Adaya Pulled and fired the gout of fire out the left side of the rocket sled, pushing it a small amount toward the right.

Lyrica and I stood side by side and our Soulstreams were twisted together as we Pulled with our combined will. It was something discovered a long time ago. The two of us together could Pull so much more power than the both of us could do apart. Perhaps the combined will pushed deeper into the Source. We were Pulling a massive amount of power and steering it into the rocket. At first the sled had grinded forward but it wasn't long before we gained speed.

We needed to get out far enough that we could let the air flow through the shields.

"How far have we covered?" I asked.

"Maybe ten miles," Trent yelled back to me.

"Minimum safe is twenty out, best guess," Alec Brighton added.

"Do you think we have ten minutes more worth of air?"

"Possibly," he said. "Worse case, we open a little early. I think the new streams should protect the others."

"We'll go as far out as we can before cracking it open," I yelled.

The sled slammed down again and there was a scream as one of the Russians lost their hold on the handles I had crafted with the sled. I glanced back to see a woman bounce toward the edge of the sled. She was interrupted by Corn as he jumped between her and the shield wall. With a few lurches, he returned the woman to her handle and helped her hold on. The Marines had been surprisingly quick to adjust to the difference in strength and speed they attained with the Soulguard knot.

I grinned and poured the power into the rocket drive. I could feel the Source building dangerously high in me so I released an extra burst of power through the rocket from inside myself. I had needed to do that multiple times and Lyrica had done it twice.

"If you'd take the focusing training, you wouldn't have to do that," she said.

"I was just thinkin' about that," I laughed.

I heard Pelin chuckle from my right, **Perhaps, you should listen to her, Master.**

"I don't need any crap from the peanut gallery," I answered. "Don't call me Master."

Yes, Master.

"Use your words," Lyrica said. "That's disturbing."

Pelin laughed again.

"As you wish, Kilnyeri."

"Again with the cute and fuzzy bunny!" she returned. "I'm going to kick Kil'Sin'Deres ass!"

Rostov turned his head, "Reyna! Five second burst!"

Reyna let loose with a gout of fire out of the right side of the sled.

The air was getting quite bad. Some of the Russians were beginning to sag. If they passed out, they would be bouncing all around the inside of the sled.

"Gonna have to crack the shield!" I yelled.

"Agreed," Alec returned.

I opened the top of our sled to the open air. We were close to the boundary we had set for doing it. The air was cool and felt refreshing. Hopefully the radiation levels would be low enough not to hurt us.

"I see people ahead!" Rostov yelled.

I released another gout of fire from inside me that had built up.

I could see the Souls of all the people in the sled begin to perk up when I closed my eyes and looked with my "inner eye". The lack of air had been close. Hopefully not too close.

"Stop acceleration!" Rostov yelled. We stopped Pulling and released a huge gout of Soulfire into the sky.

I looked over at Lyrica who glowed with life. The Source may manifest as a fire, but it is the spark that feeds all life. When you use it, there is a strength of life inside that wasn't as strong before. It is much more visible in us than the typical Mage due to the amount of it that literally travels through our bodies. A Soullord has a much greater tolerance for that fire of life than anyone else.

We turned to watch as people lurched out of the sled. Some of them trying to step forward only to spring ten or more feet.

"I'm guessing the Archmage is going to be angry with you again," Daphne Cavanaugh said from my left just before I was jerked completely off of my feet by a bear.

Well, maybe not a bear, but two huge arms encircled both Lyrica and me and lifted us into an embrace.

"God, I thought I had lost you two," Kharl said as he squeezed us hard enough to kill a large horse. "Who smells like burnt hair?"

"That would be the idiot who had to go out in a nuclear blast."

"What the hell did he do that for?"

"Wanted to work on my tan…" I started.

"To save my sorry ass," a voice came from our backs.

Corn staggered forward toward us, "I never got to thank you, Rourke. I was about to be popped Corn, out there."

"Glad to see you made it through it ok, buddy," I said as Kharl reluctantly released us. "Was hopin' I hadn't broken anything when I threw you. Besides, who would I have to drink with if I let you stay out there?"

"Just so you know," he said. "You'll never have to buy a drink again if one of us is anywhere near."

I shook hands with the Marine, "Watch that grip, you'd break someone's hand with it."

"You aren't gonna remove that?"

"Wouldn't do any good," I shook my head. "You remember how you did it, don't you?"

"Yeah, but…"

"Doesn't matter if you can't see it, It's still there," I said. "Be honest. You'd play around with it till you got it back, wouldn't you?"

He grinned.

"That's what I'm sayin'. It wouldn't do any good."

"What about them?" he asked, turning to the crowd of Russians that had gathered around Alexei Rostov.

"That's gonna be a whole other bag of worms," I said with a sigh.

He chuckled and turned to return to his platoon, "Thanks again."

I nodded.

"So what's up with this cape?" Daphne asked and lifted it to see my naked backside underneath.

"Hmmm," she muttered, "Never mind."

Lyrica's melodic laughter filled the air.

Chapter 36

"At least we found what he'll run from," Paige said.

"Blessed few things to fit in that category," Gregor returned.

"Why does everyone always do that?" I asked. "I'm sittin' right here."

She turned to look at me with one eyebrow raised, "You just sit there and shut your pie hole for a minute."

"We both know that only pie shuts my pie hole."

She held up one finger in warning and opened a drawer. I may have giggled a little when she threw an object to me.

It was a package containing an apple fruit pie.

She looked at me for a minute with the "and you were going to say?" look on her face.

I shrugged and unwrapped the pie.

Gregor was trying his best not to laugh but it couldn't be helped.

"As we were saying," she said, "What are we going to do about the others?"

"There's nothing we can really do about it," he answered. "Just as Colin pointed out, earlier, they know how to do it now. We can offer them positions with the Soulguard, but I'm fairly certain all of them won't accept. Some will but not all."

"The Marines are sworn to the protection of America," I said. "They've already given their oath to the Marine Corp. Once their enlistments are up, they may consider the Soulguard. But in the meantime, there is a full platoon of Marines who know how to tie the Soulguard knot. There will be more. We can count on that."

"I know," she said. "Wasn't there any other way…"

I interrupted, "We had ten minutes and five hundred and forty or so people in the shield that were dying from radiation. We thought of tying the knots ourselves but there was no time. It was the only solution we could come up with."

She sighed, "And now I have to handle the repercussions from it."

"That's why you get paid the big bucks," I said.

She glared at me.

"Don't look at me like that," I said. "These people have just lost everything. Offer them something and they may surprise you. Give them jobs. Give them educations if they don't have one."

"That might just work. Employment, education, and housing if need be."

"Can't hurt to try."

"If they're anything like where I grew up, most of the people hadn't even been to another state. Give them somewhere to belong."

"Every now and then, he makes sense," Paige said.

"Occasionally," Gregor returned.

"Ok," she turned back to me. "I want you to do what you can to reign in the Marines from sharing what they learned out there."

"I doubt I can do that," I said. "But I will relay the concerns you have about it."

"You really don't even want to do that, do you?"

"If it was up to me the whole human race would be taught how to do it."

"Some wouldn't be able to focus enough and the others would be free to take advantage of them."

"It wouldn't be a perfect system," I said. "But the victim pool for the Kresh would be a lot smaller. It would put the Human Race at a more equal footing with 'em, at the least."

"I'll bring your ideas to the Council," she said. "But I have serious reservations about something like that. It's a decision I wouldn't make on my own."

"If we don't think about it, Earth is going to be at quite a disadvantage compared to the other worlds on the other side of the Gate."

"Three worlds are turning out soldiers with the knot. They are training to take the home world back from the Kresh. Some are swearing the Oath to the Soulguard, some are already sworn to others."

"Others, meaning you?"

"Some have sworn to the Prophet. A lot of them don't even know what the Soulguard is. Right now, the knowledge is passed through the Soulguard. It won't always remain so."

Her eyes narrowed, "You did this on purpose."

"Not really," I answered. "It happened and I didn't see any reason to change it."

"Remember when I told you there would come a time when your duties as a Soulguard would clash with your duties as this world leader you've become? This is one of those times. As a Soulguard, you're pushing the limits with this."

"Right now, those sworn to others are sworn to people who are sworn to the Soulguard," I said.

"That's why I say you are pushing the limits. How long until that changes?"

"It changed two days ago," Gregor said. "If we wish to put any sort of control over the spread of the knowledge, it must be now."

Paige sighed, "Nothing is ever simple with you."

"Not all that complicated," I said. "Spread the knowledge. Make them more than victims for the Kresh. What happened in Pittsburgh can be avoided. Think of what would have happened if the Kresh had met the whole population of Pittsburgh with Soulguard knots."

"A thousand years we've kept the secret," she muttered.

"Should have spread the knowledge after the first attack in Kansas," I said. "But that's just me."

"What do you think would be the most efficient way to spread the knowledge, Gregor?" she asked. "Television?"

I noticed she had gone past the question of would it be done to how it can be done in the most efficient way.

"That would be good for those who have television, but we need to get them all."

"Telepathy would be the best way but I would need a lot of Kresh to power something that powerful."

"I don't think that is going to be an option," she said.

"Probably not."

"Then we will approach the Council and see where this takes us. You go get some rest. You've earned it. Not everyone can say they've been blown up by a nuclear weapon and survived."

I probably should have done what she said but there were a truckload of reports left to look through, including our losses on the northern front when the bomb had been set off. The Russian Academy had sent in everything they could muster and they had been within the blast zone. We had lost thousands to the blast. Some Mages had gotten shields up in time but they were blessed few in number.

There had been thirteen thousand who had gone in and less than a thousand made it out. Those thousand were all Mages and they would be in need of help. They had just watched as all those around them had been incinerated. None of the Mages had been close enough to shield much more than themselves. It would have been Hell on Earth to watch that happen.

We had been luckier than we deserved.

Chapter 37

"You keep this up and you're going to be one big scar," Lyrica said as her fingers traced the outline of scar tissue on my back. "Lucky I could start healing immediately."

"Yea, but chicks dig scars," I laughed.

She pinched me, "Maybe I don't like scars."

"You seemed to like them just fine a few minutes ago."

"I may have been a little distracted," she returned.

"I had a lot of these before."

I rolled over to face her. Her fingers traced the scar across my eye.

"Some of them are rather dashing," she said with a grin.

"I bet you say that to all the guys."

"Yea, all my boyfriends are dashing," her melodic laughter flowed over me. "I won't accept any less."

"A girl has to have standards."

"Of course," she returned. "So what are your plans for the day?"

"More of the same," I said. "Reports keep comin' in. The Kresh were obliterated by the blast. They were close in to the center of it. There's no tellin' if the damage carried into the gate to Hub. I haven't heard anything from that side."

"I have some radiation sickness cases coming through," she said. "I'll probably be late getting back, tonight."

"I'm sure I'll be late, too," I answered. "I have to start writing letters today to families."

"You know they aren't all your fault."

She knew how this part of my job affected me. I could delegate the job to others but I feel a need to keep doing it. I had to always remember the cost of the war I had chosen to fight. Every loss we take because I hadn't closed the gate, permanently, was because of my choice and part of the cost. The least I could do is acknowledge that responsibility. I would be days writing the letters to their next of kin.

"I know the stakes of what we are fighting for," I returned. "I chose to place the good of the other worlds over the good of this world. I chose to do that. It is my fault."

"You carry too much, my love." She said. "All of us chose to agree with your choice. It's not just you. For that matter, I could close these gates just as you could. I will not carry the guilt because I choose to leave access to the other worlds. They need what we have to be released from their fate. Your Kresh need you to change their race into something that we can coexist with. There are much larger issues than our one planet."

"I know this up here," I said, tapping my head with a finger. I pointed to my heart, "Here, I feel every single one."

"I know you do," she said and nestled into my chest. "It's what makes you who you are and the man I love."

I held her for a few moments but I knew I had to get to work. With a sigh, I let her go and slid out of the bed.

"No rest for the wicked," I said.

She sighed in return and sat up in the bed, "I hate it when you're right, but you're right."

She stood and began straightening the bed-covers.

"Why do you do that? We'll just mess it up tonight."

She looked up at me with one eyebrow raised, "Until then, it will look nice."

"I always thought it was a waste of time. Ky used to give me a hard time for it."

"Unlike you, I listened to her and made my bed."

I chuckled as I buttoned the last button on my black uniform. We had come out into the open but our uniforms remained the black we had used when we operated at night.

She stepped up and kissed me then traced the scar across my eye with a finger, "Dashing."

I grinned, "I'll see you tonight."

She turned to go toward the bathroom, "It's a date."

Stepping outside into the chill morning, my breath fogged. The cold doesn't affect us much with the fires of the Source flowing through us. A Soulguard feels it a bit more than a Mage, but much less than the normal person.

I hoped the releasing of the ability to the public would happen and I hoped it would happen soon. If I had been the one to make the decision, it would have been done years ago.

As I made my way from the small house that we were using, thanks to a family that had relocated out of the area, I saw the familiar dark soul of Pelin waiting for me.

"Master," she greeted.

"Don't call me Master."

"Yes Master."

We always went through the formula. It was our own form of friendly banter. I knew I would never convince her to stop and she knew I wouldn't stop trying.

"We would like to speak to you about something."

I could see her hesitation, "Just spit it out, Pel."

"Better if we are all there," she answered. "Please come with me, Master."

I followed her to another small house. I could see the souls of the Shak'Tar Mages.

"Master," Lee greeted me. "I want to share something with you about the one you call the 'Beast'. I am older than most of the surviving

Shak'Tar. We never had much chance of a long lifespan under the rule of our former Master."

I nodded.

"I have seen something similar to what you have done, before, Master. My understanding is that you believe you are imprisoning the persona that is created by the Kresh DNA?"

"Yes."

"Master, this persona we feel in you is of your own creation. I have seen this before and it is dangerous. In the beginning, perhaps you just tried to cage that rage we all have inside of us, we of the Blood. This DNA you carry is stronger in you than us because of your ability to touch the Source of the Kresh, but I have seen the persona inside of you. You have pushed many of the things you consider… unsavory, from your own persona into this one. The more you do this the stronger the second persona becomes. You are experiencing this now. It is harder to hold it back than before because you have made it stronger. Your only way to be at peace is to accept that it is you just as the persona you keep in the forefront is you."

"You want me to accept that I am a rage-filled, hateful beast?" I asked. "That I long to be out in a battlefield, surrounded by those I can kill at my leisure? That the joy I felt when I tortured that Ma'Nar's soul in Kansas was truly who I am? If that is me… I could never accept that."

"Master, that is not you," she said and laid a hand on my shoulder. "That is a part of you.

278

Everyone is capable of dark deeds. We all know this as fact, considering the deeds we have done. That capability is part of us, part of who we are. Just as it is part of you. You must accept that it is so, or I fear we may not be strong enough to protect you from yourself. We will never cease to try, we would die for you, Master. But we would prefer not to, if you don't mind."

She pushed me toward the door, "Now, go. Do what duties you have set for yourself. Just put thought in what I have told you. If you need our strength when you do what needs done, we are always with you."

Chapter 38

I looked up from the letter I was writing to Anya Triveka, the mother of Iosif Triveka. The door to the small classroom I was using for an office opened and four people entered. Rostov, Prada, Adaya, and Brighton. They didn't say a word, but each took a page from my list of fallen from our Russian forces we had lost to the nuclear blast.

"But…"

"No arguments," Rostov said in his thick Russian accent.

"Thank you," I answered.

They all had brought the electronic notebooks and took seats in the desks that were scattered throughout the room.

I felt an overwhelming sense of pride as they all began typing at the keyboards in front of them so I returned to the letter I was working on. It was a new thing to be sending letters to mothers of Soulguards. This war had changed so many things. The larger percentage of Soulguards were now younger than I was. Before, these letters would be going to children or grandchildren. I found the change to be depressing.

I finished that letter and hit enter to send it through the channels to be mailed. I tried for quite some time to inform families in person but there were so many that I couldn't feasibly do so any more. I still tried to find something of a personal nature to say about each person, when I could.

Three more letters were finished when the door opened, again. Another group entered and took pages from my list. Galen, Reyna, Cristof, and Asante. There was only one other of my lieutenants and he was on his way back to China at the moment.

"Thank you," I said as they took seats with their notebooks.

I watched them for a moment with a small smile on my face and continued. Kharl joined us after a bit with Daphne Cavanaugh. Kyra would have been present, as well but she was back in Kansas working with a new set of recruits. Gregor and Paige spent several hours at a pair of the desks, too. Everyone was familiar with my ritual and they were there to support me.

After Cairo we had been doing this for weeks. Those are the hardest times to be one of the leaders. All of these people died under your command and it becomes harder as the numbers increased. Third Kansas had been the smallest amount of deaths from a battle in years and they had come from a tornado.

I looked back up to see a smile on Prada's face even as her eyes glistened with her tears. She looked up to see me staring.

"I just found Frank Gildan's name," she said.

"I haven't heard anything from Frank for years," I said. "I wondered where he had got off to."

"Do you remember the first day in Knoxville?"

I chuckled as I thought back.

"What was that he said to you?" she asked.

"He said, Boy, never fight until you have to. But when it's time to fight, you fight like you're the third monkey on the ramp to Noah's Ark… and brother, it's startin' to rain."

She grinned, "That's it. You even got the voice right."

We were both quiet for a minute.

"I'm gonna miss the old son of a bitch," she muttered.

I sat back in the chair, "I think we should find a couple bottles of vodka and toss a couple back for old Frank."

"I would like to 'toss one back' as you say, for Dimitri Kaskof," Rostov said with a nod. "He was one of the Guards in my second command. Always the happiest man in the room."

Most of us had seen a name or two that we recognized from our past and Rostov located a bottle of Vodka. We spent the next hour talking about Frank, Dimitri, and many more. It was a short time of memories and tears. We talked of Lennox Flynn, Luis Ramirez, and Nora Kestril. I told them of Tien Yueh and Jack Riordan, Jenna Seymore and Patrick Shoffner. They told stories of friends that had fallen and of times before the Kresh had declared an all-out war on our world.

Our lists were finished after two days of letters and we all retired to our various duties even closer than we had been before. I had come to rely on these people to a great extent. Rostov was a rock, dependable and solid. Reyna, the same. Adaya, always trying to overcome what had happened in Cairo, being buried alive by bodies. Galen Stone and Alec Brighton nerves of steel and humor in any situation. Cristof and Asante, almost never heard but always there, a pair who would never falter. Andrea Prada, my friend from the day I reached Knoxville what seemed like a century ago. Gregor Kerkhov, a mentor when I first came to the Academy, and Paige Turner, the first girl I ever loved. Always has she been my friend.

I returned to the house to find Lyrica sitting in front of the couch with a dread rolling through her aura.

"What?" I asked as she held her hands against her abdomen as if to hide something. When my sight discerned what it was, a whole gamut of emotion surged through my aura to end in a feeling of mixed fear, happiness, and anticipation. I was holding her before she could even react.

"Oh my God," I muttered into her hair as her head rested against my chest.

I felt the wetness of tears on my chest.

"You're not angry," she mumbled in wonder.

Even as I had gone through the gamut of emotions, anger had never been one of them.

"A father?" I said softly. "I get to be a father?"

The rest of the evening was a bit of a blur as we just held each other and fell asleep in one another's arms.

I felt the Great Gate in China open at midnight that night. I didn't know it was China until I felt the Source weapons open fire. The Pull could be felt from across the continent.

By the time I reached the HQ, they had video footage coming through. The Gate had opened inside the walled area but not in the center. It was much closer to one side. The distance from the other wall's guns didn't save them. The Chinese had the wall guns and guns mounted on the valley floor. A lot of guns on the valley floor. When they opened fire on the Kresh the atmospherics were almost immediate. The plume of heat in the center looked a great deal like the mushroom cloud that we'd seen over Ufa.

The attack lasted three hours. Kresh poured through the gate and died. Three tornados spawned from the heat effect on the atmospherics. One of these hit the wall directly across from the main push by the Kresh, who tried to force their way through the hole only to be met by a hundred thousand Source Gunners on the other side. It was bloody for the Chinese but nowhere near as bloody as it was for the Kresh. I winced as Gunners fell but there were more behind them. They closed the gap in the wall with Source Gunners.

The video was steadily getting worse as ash was blown inward toward the plume that had shot into the sky. We watched, mesmerized, until the video went out completely.

"They damn sure fight like that third monkey," Prada said.

"Right, that, Mate" Alec returned. "Wait till it bloody rains."

"Those Source weapons have made us obsolete," Reyna added.

"They'll always need us for the up close and personal approach," Prada said.

"It'll be a wonderful day when we're obsolete," I said. "We can retire."

"Where is the boss? Who is this?" Rostov asked. "Some dvoynik, what is the word? Doppelganger. Our illustrious leader would never speak of retiring."

"I don't know," I said. "A father should maybe think about it."

Rostov looked at me with narrowed eyes for a moment. I could see the second he realized what I said. Then he had me in a bear hug.

"Congratulations!" he set me back down as the others closed in.

It was one memorable day. The Kresh took one of their largest defeats, while Lyrica and I got to celebrate our coming parenthood.

Six days later the Kresh hit Australia. It took four days to even locate where the gate I sensed had opened. Four days of Kresh pouring through into our world. Then the first reports of the devastation began to come in.

There were nearly thirty million Kresh on our planet before the Australians and Soulguard found them. The slaughter of our forces started the Kresh on their terrible march across the continent. Where there were cities, they left death and destruction in their wake. The first report we even saw was when the Guard launched their attack.

Chapter 39

"How much longer?" I asked the pilot.

"Ten hours, Sir," he said.

"Damn it," I muttered.

"Reports look bad, Sir," the copilot added. "Not much left. The Kresh just hit Sydney. That's where we were plotted to land."

"We still are," I said. "We'll have to do a hot landing."

"With seventy planes?"

"Yes," I said. "They're goin' to be occupied. I'm taking a force in on a combat drop into Sydney. You guys should be clear to land out at the airfield we originally planned."

"Yes, Sir."

I nodded to him and headed back toward my seat. Lyrica sat where I had left her. She was talking to Prada and I stopped for a moment. The tiny spark I saw in her abdomen sent a feeling of awe through me. I worried about bringing a life into the world with my particular genetics, but the thought that I would be a father was a completely new feeling for me.

I smiled and continued toward them.

"Ten hours out," I said. "They've overrun Sydney but the plan should still be salvageable. There's a couple of hundred thousand Kresh in Sydney and we have seven thousand in the planes. The second wave should be coming in about four hours. I'm taking a hundred Mages into Sydney and get their attention. While this is going on, the rest of you will be setting up the base at the airstrip we decided on before."

"Why only a hundred?" Lyrica asked.

"I want to give you time to land and set up a shield while the others get set for one hell of a Code Alpha."

"I'm going with…"

"No, you're not."

Her left eyebrow rose.

"You are going to set up a shield and start readying an extraction area for any people we find. Not in combat."

There are times when a person has to pick their battles. This was one I would not budge on and she could see that in my Soul. She knew part of my reasoning was for the child but the plan was sound, regardless of that.

"You can set up a shield with little help from others. The Mages would have to do it the hard way."

She grudgingly accepted it.

"I will be taking the strongest Mages, and only those with the Juggernaut armor. I intend to spend a lot of time running through the streets, pissing of as many Kresh as we can. When we exit the city, there should be plenty of Kresh to do a Code Alpha."

"Here's a list of Mages I want on this," I handed Prada a list. "Contact them and tell them the plan. We jump out before the planes pass over Sydney, then we cause a ruckus."

Prada nodded and left her seat to get the ones on my list that were on our plane. She would contact the rest of them with the com system.

I did not see any of our names on that list, Pelin projected.

No, you aren't, I answered. **You guys are the most powerful telepaths but far from the most powerful Mages. I may need you to help calm me down when I get out of there.**

She grudgingly accepted the orders, much like Lyrica.

Until then, protect her.

We will, Master. She is carrying a precious cargo.

Don't ever actually tell her that. No comparisons to cargo vessels.

Pelin laughed.

I sat down and leaned back, strapping the belts across my chest. Ten more hours. I could feel the beast, inside, aching to claw its way out. Could Lee be right? Was what's inside me be a creation of my own? Did I shove all the traits I didn't like into that persona? It used to be rage, now it felt like something else. And if so, what the hell could I do about it? Had I worried about what I was becoming so much that I created this inside of my own mind? There would be a child brought into this world with the same DNA as mine. The same power as a

Soullord, or Bloodlord, whatever name we would consider it. I needed to do something to show that child how to survive. This thing that I have done is not the answer.

The comfort of my Shak'Tar telepaths settled over my mind as they helped hold that inner persona down to let me doze off. I had done little sleeping in the last weeks. Lyrica reached over and placed her hand on my leg. My head nodded forward as I fell asleep.

Hicks had told me some time back that one of his rules was to eat and sleep when you can there may not be time later.

I woke differently than my norm as we neared Kresh. My Shak'Tar were keeping me from feeling the beast's reaction to the enemy that I was used to.

I worry about you going without us, Master, Pelin projected.

I can't take you into that yet, Pelin, I answered. **Not enough training and not strong enough. We lost good people in Cairo because the shields weren't strong enough. Can't risk that, here. If they do the same thing here, we'll have stronger Mages to hold longer.**

Understood, Master.

Don't call me Master.

Yes, Master.

I could see the grin on her face where she sat across from Lyrica and me.

"Almost time," Prada said as she approached from the rear of the plane. "I noticed I'm not included on this list."

"At least you don't have to jump out of a plane," I said. "You'll be landing at the airport."

"I guess there is that," she grinned. "I see that Reyna's on the list."

"Her stream is no bigger than yours but her shields are as good as the Jaeghernauts'. As are Rostov's."

She nodded. She had been in Cairo with us and knew what I feared.

"There's not as many here," she said.

"I don't expect 'em to do what they did in Cairo. But we have to be prepared if they do. You're tasked with working under Lyrica. She doesn't have any official rank so you're the liaison between her and the others."

"Like anyone isn't gonna do what she orders."

"You're my second and they know it. Better safe than sorry."

"I doubt I'll be ordering the Soulguard around," Lyrica said.

"This is more for when the other forces get here," I said. "But it won't hurt to have that established from the beginning."

I began scanning with my Sight toward the coast. The dark souls were scattered throughout the city of Sydney. There were still some of the multi-colored souls of humans throughout the city. As my eyes scanned across the city, they snapped back to a point just inside Sydney. The image of what I saw would forever be imprinted on my mind and Rage washed over me.

"God, no…"

Pelin and the others reached out and I slapped their probes back. They may be the strongest telepaths the Shak'Tar had but there was a reason I was able to Mark others.

I was on my feet with flames rolling across my body. The straps that had held me in my seat were snapped, behind me as I turned toward the rear of the plane.

"Tell them to follow when they can," I said to Prada and Lyrica.

"What is it?"

I projected what I had seen, "Open the door."

The airman who manned the door said, "We're not over the target."

"Now."

He saw the flames growing from inside me and when he looked into my eyes I saw a wave of terror cross his Aura.

He slammed his hand down on the button.

Chapter 40

I was out the door as soon as it had opened over a couple of feet and tumbling through the air. I pulled from the Source and opened a shield Lyrica and I had built. In moments I was under controlled flight and the Source jetted out the rear of the shield that looked like a small jet. I blasted forward past the C-130 I had just vacated.

Rage was flooding across me as I focused on what was occurring in the city of Sydney, Australia. There was around thirty Kresh Soldiers surrounding a small group of Souls. These were children. What I had seen from the plane was one of those tiny Souls sail up into the sky above the Kresh. Terror filled the child as he fell and was caught by another Kresh.

A chill rolled through me as the child, a small boy, was thrown again.

"Nooo!!" I screamed as the Kresh stepped back to let him hit the ground.

Something snapped inside me and a white hot rage filled me. My shield shut down as I plummeted toward Sydney. I couldn't land in the middle of them because of the children but I opened up my weapons to brake my speed and slammed to the ground a couple of hundred feet away from them.

Another form tumbled into the sky with a shriek.

I leaped into the middle of the crowd and released an arc of power to each side about six feet from the ground to avoid hitting the kids. Then I jumped straight into the air and caught the girl who must have been five or six years old.

"I've got you," I said.

When I landed I turned to the still form of the little boy. His Soul slipped from his body and I caught it with my mind. In an instant I was next to him placing the Soul back into his body and the boy jerked under my hand. I Pulled through his stream but it wouldn't work. The Soul slipped back out of his body.

They found me holding the Soul gently in my hands, tears streamed down my cheeks.

"I tried to put it back but it won't stay," I said to my dad as his huge hand settled on my shoulder. Looking at that tiny shattered body, I asked, "Why couldn't I save him?"

"Let him go, Son," he rumbled. "There are things even you can't do."

His hand squeezed my shoulder and I let the boy's tiny Soul slip away to be drawn into the Source.

When I stood back up, my eyes were burning with a brilliant white fire. I know this because I could see it in the minds of those around me. The little girl who I had caught was right there and she latched onto my arm. I picked her up and slid her around to my back.

"Everyone, grab a kid," Kharl said and followed my example. He slid the boy around to be hanging on his back. The boy's arms barely reached around his neck. "Alright, Son. How do you wanna play this?"

"Get the children to safety," I growled and turned toward the Kresh. "Then we kill every last one of these murdering bastards."

The Kresh had sensed the death of their soldiers and I could see the dark souls closing from various points in the city.

"Juggernaut up and follow me."

He nodded.

I turned my head to the side and said, "Honey, you close your eyes. You don't want to see what I'm about to do."

"Yes, sir," she said in a tiny voice.

I turned to the others who had kids with them, "I'm going to add a little reinforcement in your shields for the kids."

Kharl nodded and I, quickly added supports for the kid to be safe. I did the same for each of the fifteen other Mages who had passengers as well as for the girl on my back.

We looked up the street ahead of us and the Kresh pouring down that avenue toward us.

"Let's do this," I said and began running up the street at seventy miles per hour.

My shields impacted the Kresh in an explosion of blood and I felt warmness on my back.

"I thought I said close your eyes," I said.

"I looked… I'm sorry."

"It's ok," I said. "But you may not want to see the rest of this."

My shield is designed with bladed edges that cut their way through packed crowds, and I was pouring on the speed. Normally a battle cry of Rash'Tor'Ri would thunder over them, but rather than booming sound that could hurt the child's ears, I used my mind.

Rash'Tor'Ri! boomed through the minds of the Kresh. The rage inside me was seething but it was different. It didn't seem to be the dark rage of the beast I had been used to. They were killing children in some sick game. My Kresh would never even dream of doing such a thing, which spoke toward the vile character of Hal'For'Radolin.

The Kresh started pouring into the street behind us. This would be the point where we succeed or fail. The next street had the fewest Kresh and I turned left, the Mages right behind me. In moments we burst through the masses of Kresh between us and the outskirts of Sydney where the other Mages should be preparing to drop hell on top of them.

A few moments more and we could have been swamped like we had been in Cairo. But now we had a clean run out of Sydney. Accelerating, the Kresh were left behind.

I saw the groups of Mages preparing to greet the Kresh as we ran past, heading toward the glowing soul of Lyrica Jayne. I stopped in front of her and slid the little girl around to set her on the ground.

"Come here, sweetie," Lyrica said.

The girl was embraced as soon as she was within reach.

"Protect them," I said as white flame rolled across my body again and the rage began to build.

I felt the probing touch of Pelin as she looked into my mind to see if I was in control. This rage was different than what I feel when the beast is let out of its cage. I looked at Lyrica and I knew what that difference was. I could see the same righteous fury in her soul. Perhaps it was the fact that we were to become parents soon. Maybe it would have always been there after seeing what the Kresh had done. All I knew was what I could see and what I heard when I looked into her burning gaze.

"Do it."

I turned with a savage anticipation I am very familiar with to return to the lines before the Kresh could arrive.

"Where is he going?" I heard the girl's voice.

"He's going to kill them all, Sweetie."

"Everyone prepare for Code Alpha," I ordered. "Fifty supports."

The horde of Kresh poured across the open area toward us. I felt the supports link up.

"Code Alpha. Now."

My teeth hurt as twenty five hundred Mages Pulled from the Source at the same time and poured it into the sky. I closed my eyes and reached out to grasp all of that power. It began to spin in the sky, a swirling vortex of fire. I felt the power flowing through me from my supports and I looked out with the Sight that allowed me to see the flows of the world. The dark souls were closing and I pulled that writhing vortex straight down onto their heads.

"Cease!" I ordered as I watched the last of those dark souls leave their bodies to be pulled toward the west.

I turned my gaze toward Sydney and the pockets of Kresh that hadn't come out after us. The seething rage within me hadn't diminished in the least and I strode toward the city. This time I would not be running through or from Kresh. I was going to destroy them, all of them.

"Form up on Soullord One," I heard Prada order as she fell in at my side. Rostov took his place at my other side. "Patrol Three, Ten, and Twenty join Soullord Two and welcome guests as they are brought in."

Chapter 41

Paige looked down at the latest reports and back up at Gregor, "Another three thousand survivors just got off in Greymouth."

"That's better than we expected so far," Gregor replied. "So far there are two hundred and eighty thousand survivors they've managed to pull out of the country."

"Out of what? Twenty seven million?"

"There's not much more we can do. We have as many forces down there as we can put there without taking from Kansas or China where we have to keep them."

"I know," she sighed. "It's so hard to see what happened. Every time they hit before we stopped them in days. They've been there for a month."

"Going by the number of wounded in Lyrica's base camp, he's fighting one hell of a war."

"True," she replied. "Both Soulguard and regular military."

"At least we should hear something soon from the lines," he said. "The jet just landed and we have someone from First Battalion."

"We've heard precious little from him up until now."

"Maybe we can get some answers."

There was a knock on the door.

"Enter," she said.

The man who entered looked worn. It was something unfamiliar in a Mage. The amount of the Source that enters a Mage, even on a passive level, should prevent that.

Paige pointed to a seat, "Sit."

"Ma'am," the man answered and sat down.

"What's your name, Son?" Gregor asked.

"Jason Hobb, Sir."

"What has our errant Soullord been up to?" Paige asked.

"Ma'am, I was at First Kansas, Second Kansas, and several others. I saw what he did at all those places, but something happened in Sydney. He came out of that city with some kids they'd saved. He left them with Miss Jayne and went back into Sydney. When he came back out of there, not a single Kresh was living and they brought out another group of survivors."

"That tracks with what we've heard," Gregor said. "After that things get a little fuzzy."

"That's because we barely had time to keep up with him," Jason said. "He left orders for the next wave to report to Jaegher and he went south down the coast. A small force stayed with Jaegher to meet the next wave of our forces. As they landed, Jaegher formed a second force and sent it north. I didn't see that part, I was following Rourke. We hit a sizeable group of Kresh down around Melbourne and he didn't even

300

slow down. When we came out of Melbourne the Kresh were dead and four Mages escorted the survivors back to Sydney."

"Ok," Gregor returned.

"He didn't stop, Sir. He just kept going with those freaky white flames in his eyes. We went north and met another force. He did a Code Alpha on them and just kept going."

"How long had this been?"

"Three days, Sir," Jason answered. "The Soulguards began to lag behind about the time we met the second battalion that Jaegher had sent north. They'd turned west to meet us. They joined our force and we camped in a town for a couple of days. We needed the rest but I don't think he did. He ate and spent hours with the wounded, healing the worst of them and seeing them loaded in trucks back to the original landing zone. The morning we left he was found pacing along the edge of the camp looking west like some caged animal."

Jason shook his head, "I understand the need to stop the Kresh, but he was driven by something. Those telepaths got there right before we moved out and from that point forward, there was always one or two of them with him."

Paige nodded.

"We spent the month like that," he said. "We'd fight and search for the next Kresh. They were scattered all over the country and we went from town to town, city to city. Where we found them, we fought. The Navy had warships off the coast when we were close enough to the coast to use their help. The planes started to arrive and we welcomed the support from the gunships."

"When we camped in a town or city, we'd take food from grocery stores to feed the men and rest while we could. I never saw Rourke stop. He fought, healed, and paced circles around our forces. I did see him eat but I never saw him sleep. I did sleep, myself, but I never saw him do so."

"Didn't the Kresh empty the grocery stores?"

"No Ma'am," he answered. "The Kresh ate people."

Paige winced.

"And where is he, now?"

"He's closing on the Gate, Ma'am," Jason said. "They've pulled everything together to assault the Kresh at the Gate. There are millions of them waiting for him. He's got the gunships ready to support him, and they are close enough to have missile support from the ships off the coast. There's about to be one hell of a fight and I'm half the world away."

"After such a month, I'd think you'd be happy to get away from the lines for a bit," Paige said.

"No Ma'am," he returned. "He's going to need everyone he can get to go after the gate."

***

I stared into the darkness to the west. I could see the twisted power of the Great Gate and the dark Souls that surrounded it.

"What do you see out there?" asked Alec Brighton.

"A lot of damn Kresh," I answered. "They're waitin' out there at the Gate. I'm so used to 'em chargin' at us."

"I know," he said. "They've taken a lot of losses, but they've never just camped in one spot and waited for us."

"Even in the cities we cleaned out they've came at us in numbers."

"What are they doing?"

I stared toward that darkness with spots of bright scattered throughout them, "They're holdin' prisoners scattered through their ranks."

"They're using human shields?"

"Probably to keep us from usin' a Code Alpha on 'em."

"So they have us outnumbered and we can't use our biggest weapon?"

"Seems so," I answered. "It'll interfere with the planes and the ships throwin' down fire into 'em, too."

"This just gets better and better," he said. "After what they did in Melbourne…"

Alec Brighton was born and raised in Melbourne. He'd been right there at my side when we cleaned it out. I'd been with him when he found his home destroyed and his family dead. He didn't have much family left before this and none left after.

"It's goin' to get bloody," I said.

"So be it," he said. I could see the turmoil in his aura, the hate, pain, and loss. "They want it bloody? Bloody they'll have it."

"Let's go tell the others what we have waitin' for us and get this party started."

He nodded and we turned back toward the small town in the distance where our forces awaited.

Chapter 42

"I don't see how we can save all of the prisoners," Reyna said. "We can't be sure where they are."

"That's gonna be part of my job," I answered. "I can see 'em. I want five squads to work the southern flank, and five to do the northern flank with me. The majority of the rest will hit the center. I need two squads of Mages ready for an Alpha if I can find an opening. How do you want to deploy your forces General Halifax?"

Halifax had been the highest ranking officer of all the myriad troops sent to reinforce our ranks from the nations of the world.

"We can't move as close to their ranks as you but we can offer a hell of a lot of supporting fire. We have ninety eight hundred Source gunners ready and waiting. I'd like to follow your men in and support."

"Sounds good," I said. "I'm going to depend on you and yours to handle coordinates for the naval units and when I clear an area of prisoners."

"I'll have my best on that, Mister Rourke."

"Thank you, General."

Halifax made his way to the leaders of seven different armies that had joined us in our assault on the Kresh in Australia to start making plans.

"We'll be moving out in four hours," I said. "Get some rest if you can."

I turned and left the building toward the Infirmary which had been set up in a small hospital.

"You should rest," Pelin said from my right. "You didn't even notice my approach, Master."

"The wounded have been tended to, Master," Lee said from my left. I hadn't heard either approach.

"Two hours, no more," I said and changed my route toward a small house.

I entered the small dwelling. The Shak'Tar had cleaned the blood off the walls and floor for me sometime during the last day.

I eased myself back into the bed in the smallest bedroom.

"Two hours," I said.

They had joined me after the first week and they forced me to start sleeping a couple of hours each night we were camped. The body could handle as much as I could give it but the mind begins to weaken after so much time awake. Sleep is the time a person can rest his mind to keep from going crazy. May have been a little late for that, already.

Not crazy, Master. What you have done is capable of being fixed if you will do it, Lee projected. **You must accept that you are capable of good and evil. You can't cage one with the other.**

Maybe they were right about it but I found it impossible to think that what I keep locked up inside me is really not caused by my Kresh DNA, but something I have done to myself.

I was asleep before I could even argue my point.

Time to move out, Master.

I came awake instantly, as the beast clawed at his cage. I looked at my watch, shaking my head. They'd let me sleep three and a half hours.

You needed it, Master, Lee projected.

Don't call me Master.

"Yes, Master," she said from the chair beside the bed.

I shook my head again as I sat up. There was no use arguing with any of them. I don't know whether it was because they were telepaths or because they were women. Honestly, it could be either.

I reached down and picked up my harness that held the twin swords of the Soulguard. Strapping it on and placing the coms in my ear, I was ready to go. Probably wasn't a bad thing they'd let me sleep a little longer. There wasn't much I could do with the wounded and it made everyone nervous when I paced back and forth impatiently.

"Boss," I heard a thick Russian accent as I stepped out of the house. "What a way to greet your comrades. We wait out in the heat and behold, our benevolent leader comes out of a house with ten women."

I laughed, something I had done precious few times in the last month.

"Ten telepathic women," I said.

He frowned, "There is that."

There was one hell of an army massed just outside of the town. I followed Rostov to the group of five hundred on the north side of the army. I had three hundred Mages and two hundred Mageguards in Division One. Division Two had similar numbers. Division Three had fourteen hundred Mages and twenty five hundred Mageguards backed by twelve thousand Soulguards. Halifax's Battalion would follow up with his ninety eight hundred Source Gunners. All of the air support was ready and waiting the order to enter the fray. There were ten destroyers off of the coast ready for coordinates.

We were as ready as we could be and the beast was clawing to get out. I felt the minds of my Shak'Tar as they helped me keep it caged.

"Let's move out," I said. "Halifax will direct from HQ on movements. I will call for support or Alpha if they give me an opening. You've all got the standard operating procedure for either of those events."

Division One moved to the north with me in the lead.

"Division One, closing on target," I reported.

"Division Two, ETA five minutes."

"Division Three, point squads will hit in five."

"Understood," I said. "Good luck and watch yourselves. Turning over movement command to HQ."

"HQ has control."

I focused on the Kresh that waited ahead of us and the bright Souls that would be my target.

"Aiming for the first group of prisoners," I said. "When we reach them, there are twenty, Squad One will grab 'em. Up until then we will be in personal shields. Each of the Mages that have a human will then Juggernaut and take them out. There are five groups of twenty or so on the northern flank, so we're going to lose a whole squad to moving them out."

"Will do, Boss," I heard Reyna answer. She was the Captain of Squad One.

"Keep ranks close and let's try not to get covered up like Cairo. We have to keep moving." I drew my swords and the white flames of Soulfire began rolling across my body.

The Kresh ahead of us charged forward as they saw us. I Pulled from the Source and lashed outward with an arc of power that slammed the first ranks of Kresh backwards.

Then we were amongst them and I fell into the Dance of Blades with an ease of long practice. My blades blurred and Kresh died. Those Mages ranked in a deadly wedge to my left and right hit the Kresh, and in moments, we were all synchronized in the Dance. I left my Sight open and focused around me on the Souls, both Kresh and Human.

Dark souls slipped from bodies and were pulled back toward the gate while the more colorful souls of my allies slipped back down into the Earth. I felt every one of our losses as we closed with the first group of prisoners. We lost three Mages on the first charge.

I used the disk launcher to remove the head of the Kresh that was closest to the prisoners and we surrounded them long enough for Reyna's people to pick up a prisoner apiece. They raised Juggernaut armor and ran at full speed back the way we had come.

"Move out!" I ordered and attacked once again.

Kresh fell to my blades and the beast pounded at the cage. I needed to keep my wits so I held the beast in check with the help of my Shak'Tar. We changed our trajectory and aimed toward the next group of prisoners.

Four times we slipped away with the groups of Humans before the Kresh changed tactics. Rather than let us close and free prisoners, they would slaughter the Humans when we got close. The other Divisions were having the same reaction from the Kresh.

"Sir," Halifax said over the coms. "I know you don't want to kill people but their dying anytime we get near. You need to start dropping Code Alphas."

"An Alpha won't clear the field but it will help," I said as I severed the head of a Wraith that closed with me. "Start calling in the guns and the planes. They've left us no choice."

"Sorry, Sir," Halifax returned. "We have a communication for you from Lifeline."

Lifeline is the name we gave the operation in Sydney to get the refugees out of Australia.

"Put it through."

Chapter 43

Lyrica Jayne pulled through the woman's stream and steered that power toward her left arm. It had been broken and Lyrica had reset it. She could see the colors of the woman's Soul begin to glow a much more healthy shade.

"That will hold you until you reach safety," she said with a squeeze to her right shoulder.

"How did you do that?" the woman asked in amazement.

"It's just what I do ma'am."

"You are an angel, dear girl."

That word reminded her of Colin and she smiled. She missed him but she knew it was necessary. What he was doing was the reason she could do her job, heal these people and make sure they reach safety. Her smile slipped away as she thought of what he was facing at the gate. Reports had been that they were holding prisoners to keep him from using the Alpha. Worry squirmed its way into her thoughts.

"Thank you," she returned and made her way to the next patient. This was the last for the day and she would welcome some rest where she wouldn't have to concentrate for a small time.

Everyone could feel the Kresh to the northwest. There were so many it couldn't be helped. Soulguards are taught from the beginning that this feeling of wrongness that anyone can sense is the presence of Kresh. Up until this war began, it had always been small spots that you had to get near to feel it. The numbers at the gate could be felt from across the continent.

She looked to the northwest with her Sight, as Colin called it, and a cold chill ran down her spine. She could see the darkness in the distance, at the gate. The chill came from the other spot of darkness she saw toward the west. This one wasn't as large as the group at the gate but it was closer. Much closer.

"Oh no," she muttered and ran from the tent toward the control center for the airport that they were using for a command center.

She glanced out at the newest group of refugees numbering in the thousands that were camped outside of the shields.

"We have a problem," she said as she entered the command room.

"Don't like the sound of that," Kharl answered.

"Get everyone," she said. "There's a force of Kresh about an hour out and heading this way."

"How big?"

"Very."

"We have fourteen thousand people still outside the shields."

"I know and the ships are still four hours away."

"Shit."

"Exactly," she said. "We'll have to go out and meet them."

Kharl nodded, "I'll get them all together."

"We've still got some of the drones," she said. "We should send them out to get accurate numbers."

"Already working on it," he answered as he punched buttons on the keyboard. "Need to get Ky in here. She's better with the drone than I am."

"I'll get her," she said. "Get the drone prepped and ready."

"Will do."

She could see the worry in his aura, and the dread. Kharl had been a Soulguard for a long time. He knew what they would have to do, as did Lyrica. There were fifty Mages left in Lifeline and close to a hundred Soulguards. Nowhere near enough for the numbers she could see in the distance.

Lyrica hit the alarm that would call the forces in the base to readiness and left the room to find Kyra. She would be sleeping in the bottom floor of the control tower.

"What is it?" Kyra asked as Lyrica met her half way down the steps.

"We need you to run the probe," she answered. "We have an incoming force of indeterminate size. I know it's large."

"Damn," Kyra muttered as she rushed up the stairs.

Kharl moved from the seat as Kyra slid into his spot.

"It's prepped and ready, darlin'."

"Let's see what we have," she returned and launched the drone.

They watched the camera as it flew over the refugees to the west. It began to cover ground quickly but still met the incoming Kresh all too soon.

"Son of a bitch," Kharl muttered. "I'll gather the troops."

"Mages only," Lyrica said.

"What?"

"We'll need the Guards to mop up what is left," she said.

"Just what the hell are you planning on do-ing?"

Lyrica turned toward the door, "Whatever I have to, Mom. Whatever I have to. I need you to stay here and bring the Guards in to clean up what we can't."

"Hell, no," Kyra answered. If you think I'll stand by as you go out there to face that, you're mistaken."

"But we need…"

"As I said, hell no."

She put the drone on autopilot with a cir-cling pattern and stood up.

"We all go."

Lyrica could see it in her Soul. There was no way she would convince her to stay behind.

Kharl had stopped to hear this argument, "My guess is that you will find it impossible to get the Guards to stay behind, as well."

Lyrica sighed.

"It is what it is, Honey," Kyra said. "We all go."

Lyrica nodded and the three of them exited the control building with no illusions about where this was going to take them. They'd all seen the numbers the drone had picked up. Well over a half million Kresh were barreling down on them and they had no reinforcements within range.

The alarm had brought the base to life and they were met by the others on the tarmac.

"What is it?" Trent asked.

"We have an army incoming," Kharl answered. "Close to a million."

Trent looked toward the forces they had to defend Lifeline and nodded.

Lyrica saw the cascade of emotions that ran through his aura, ultimately ending with an acceptance of the situation. Over and over she saw this play through the auras around her and her own aura rolled with a pride she had seen in Colin's aura when he looked at his Soulguards.

"We move out in ten minutes," Kharl said. He turned to Lyrica, "What do you have in mind, girl?"

"It has to be something big," she said. "I need to speak with the prisoner."

"I'll get him," he rumbled.

"He can hear what I have to say where he is," she said and walked toward the shield close to the control tower that wrapped around a Kresh captive. They used to be one of the most fearsome beings any Soulguard would see in the caverns.

The Wraith was held immobile by a shield that wrapped closely around him. They'd captured the Kresh some time back in the field. Colin had sent it back to camp for them to interrogate and learn as much as they could from it.

The Wraith stared at them as they approached.

"I know you understand us, so I'll make this short," Lyrica said. "Can you reach the force that is coming with your telepathy?"

"I have no need to help you, meat," the Kresh answered with a deep guttural voice.

"I'll take that as a yes," she said. "Relay a message to the leader of this group."

"You wish to beg for his mercy?"

"I give him fair warning, Kresh," Lyrica had moved so fast the Wraith couldn't even follow. She was inches from him, "Turn around and leave. If he does this I will let him live."

The Wraith was silent for a moment before he began to laugh, "Tor'Dun'Velamas says that he will eat the flesh from your bones. Then he will carry your head back to the others and place it beside the head of Rash..."

His head snapped sideways with a crack. Lyrica hadn't touched him, she didn't need to.

She had caused the shield holding the Kresh to twist.

"Figured that was useless," she said. "So be it."

"We're ready when you are," Kharl rumbled.

"I need a minute," she answered. "I have to leave him a message."

"Talk to him," Kharl said.

"I can't," she returned. "If I hear his voice… I just can't. I'll lose my resolve."

Kharl placed his hand on her shoulder and squeezed.

She entered the control tower to find Grady, the wounded Army lieutenant that would be manning the com system. He was at the console watching the image from the drone.

"Please record a message for me, Grady. I need you to send it to him after we are gone."

"Yes, Ma'am."

Lyrica walked out of the control tower with red eyes but she held her head high. He would never forgive her for what she was about to do. She thought of how fragile he truly was. Everyone would scoff if they heard her say that. Him? Fragile? But she had always seen what was inside Colin Rourke. Everyone saw the exterior, the man who had killed more Kresh than anyone in history. The man who chased the Kresh clan from Kenya to Cairo. The man who had devastated the Kresh at Second Kansas. They saw Life Ender, Rash'Tor'Ri, Bloodlord, and many other names they had given him. She feared for him but there was no other option.

"Move out," she ordered and opened the door to the shield. She could see the fear in them all but they were Soulguards and they wouldn't have stayed behind if she had ordered it. They were all needed to do what she had in mind. She wasn't even sure it was possible, but that had never stopped her before.

She launched herself forward toward the west and the growing darkness followed by Kharl and Kyra, Mattie and Trent, Andrea Prada, and forty five more Mages. She could name them all, as well as name the ninety four Soulguards who followed behind them.

They covered almost three miles before she stopped.

"This will do," she said. "All Mages will be Supports."

"What are you planning?" Prada asked with eyes narrowed.

Lyrica looked forward as the Kresh poured across the huge plain in front of them, her eyes blazing with Soulfire.

"This!" She reached into the Source and power surged through all of the Mages in torrents. Everyone staggered as the whole plain erupted in fire.

Lyrica crumpled and everything faded into darkness.

Chapter 44

"Sir, they came out of nowhere," Lieutenant Grady said. "Close to a million of them. Miss Jayne took every Mage out to meet them, Sir. She left a message for me to play for you."

I had stopped right in the middle of the battle. There was a hollow pit in my stomach. They had just sent the majority of their forces to join us in this last push to the gate. The Mages had reacted quickly and surrounded me.

"Play it," I said with a hollow voice.

"I know I'm a coward for doing this, my love," Lyrica's voice began and I groaned. "I couldn't tell you face to face what is about to happen. There are too many and we are too few, but we can't stand idle while they kill thousands of people that have been through so much."

I could see her face in my mind as she explained, "I will try to keep as many of ours safe as I can, my love, but you know I couldn't get them to stay behind. If what I intend to do works, the Kresh will be stopped here. I'm so sorry for not facing you in person and I hope that, someday you can forgive me. Just know that I will always love you."

"Oh my God…" came lieutenant Grady's voice just before the static as the com system shut down.

The world seemed to lurch to the side as I felt the Source scream as if in agony. That's what it felt like to me. I had people linked to me back at Lifeline and could always feel them if I tried but now there was nothing except the chaos of the Source.

I dropped to my knees, "No, no, no."

Something broke inside of me. They'd taken everything from me. My mother, my father, and then all of the friends who had fallen throughout this bloody war. Now they had taken the rest, Mom, Dad, my friends, my family…my angel and my child.

I slammed my fist into the ground as the darkness inside of me came rushing to the surface. They had taken my little angel! There was nothing left. Nothing but my rage, my hate, and my vengeance.

The beast came screaming out of the darkness of my mind and swatted the Shak'Tar's mental reinforcements aside. They are strong but they were never more than reinforcement to my own mind. And I had stepped aside.

I let the darkness take over. I left one thing and one thing, only. One dread purpose.

Kill them all!

I had wondered what would turn a soul black from the moment that I had met Jim Duke, the man known only as the "Whisper in the Night" to his enemies. It seems that it takes the loss of everything, because when I stood back up, my Soul burned with black flames.

"Support." I ordered.

"How many?" asked Reyna.

"Everyone."

"Dios Mia," she muttered

The dark side of me was not what I expected. It seethed with rage and hatred, but it wasn't like the many times I had let it out before. Perhaps I had never really let it all the way out before this.

I walked forward into the ranks of Kresh and ripped a thousand souls from their bodies. Then a wave of black flame swept the dead from my path.

I heard the coms, "Reinforce southern flank!"

My Sight was open and I saw the whole division that had taken the southern flank overrun by Kresh.

Power thrummed through the streams of close to two hundred Mages as I reached out to snatch another thousand souls from the Kresh. Then I Pulled from that dark stream that fed my Kresh side and lashed out with a black lightning that crossed the area in front of me, incinerating more of them.

I felt the power do things to me with the Kresh DNA. The pain rolled through me but I ignored it

I saw a Kresh'Ma'Nar ahead of me, and reached out with my mind to pull an image. He dreamed of standing before his own clan as a

Farrara'Ti. I twisted that image to show him before his clan but they were all twisted and burnt laying in a wasteland. Then I slammed that image outward with my mind

TAKING EVERYTHING! My mental voice boomed.

I leapt into the air toward the center of their army. As I arced downward, I tore the souls from those below me and landed in the center of thousands of dead Kresh. More pain rolled through me as the Kresh DNA twisted inside of me.

I latched onto another Kresh mind, a Wraith. His fondest memory was of a coliseum in Hub. They had watched as Humans fought various beasts or other Humans in their "Gladiator" style games for their amusement. I shattered that image with all of the Kresh around the coliseum dead and burned while the Humans stood unharmed in the arena. I slammed that image out into those Kresh around me.

LEAVING NOTHING! My voice boomed once again, louder in the minds around me than before.

Black lightning rolled through the Kresh once more, leaving charred remains. The Kresh turned away from the forces they were facing to come toward me.

COME, THEN. COME AND DIE! They charged toward me only to fall as their souls were ripped free to be sucked back into the gateway in the distance. I Pulled from both Sources and Lashed with my mind. Taking a view I had seen personally from the rooftop of the Doran Facility of the open plains around Hub, I twisted it to be littered with burned and dead Kresh in a charred wasteland. That vision rolled across the Kresh.

THIS DAY YOUR WORLD BURNS!

I leapt toward the gate and removed the souls from the Kresh below me.

There is no army, whether it be Human or savage alien that can take the continual losses the clan of Hal'For'Radolin had taken on our world without psychological damage. These clans may have been savage, fearless monsters when they attacked Earth, but they broke that day in front of a gateway in Australia. They ran from me. I chased them, killing any I could reach.

They call me Rash'Tor'Ri, Life Ender. I owned that name on a barren plain in Australia, as I tore through their terrified numbers fleeing for their lives. I was a ruthless killing machine and there was no stopping me.

As I closed with the gateway to Hub I reached out once again for power, Pulling twenty huge tendrils of power from the Source out of the ground. A Kresh'Ma'Nar was just inside the portal and he turned back with a fear that had spread from those before me. In seconds, the gate closed, severing the Soulstreams of millions of their own clan.

My rage was pouring forth and my roars were more like the Kresh than Human, as I thrashed those huge tendrils around, killing the dying Kresh. They were cut off from their Source, but it wasn't enough. I wanted to kill them all.

The Kresh had shut, not only the gate in front of us, but all of them. Every gate on the planet closed at the same time.

"…these damn coms back up or I'll rip your friggin' arm off!"

It took a few moments while I thrashed those tentacles around before I realized the voice was Kyra's.

Chapter 45

"They're up?" she asked through the static. "Colin, if you can hear me, we need you now. Lyrica is alive but we don't know how long we can last. The Kresh, the ones that survived, just died right in front of us. We will hold her here as long as we can, Son, but she needs you."

The second I heard she was alive, I charged back up out of the darkness I had sunk into. Surprisingly, the beast stepped aside, just as I had. There is a reason I don't have to fight with the beast as much when she is with me. I love her with all of my being, whether it be dark or light.

I could feel the changes the Kresh DNA had wrought in my body. My center of gravity was higher, so I was taller. My telepathy was stronger than I could have imagined. I felt the Shak'Tar back in Lifeline, even through the chaos of the Source. I reached out to find myself looking out of the eyes of a terrified Shak'Tar. He was staring at twenty huge tendrils of power hovering above him.

They had followed my mind across the continent. With a surge of power from my supports, I slammed the tendrils down into the Source. The Shak'Tar turned and I could see what Lyrica had done. Across the plain, the Source was no longer below the surface of the world. The whole plain was covered in twenty feet of roiling chaos.

My mind sprang back to my body.

"Boss?" Rostov was right behind me. "What is that?"

We were staring at where the tendrils had closed together. There was a small spot in between the edges that did not close. Through that space I was looking into the eyes of Kren Logis, the Shak'Tar I had been connected with on the other side of the continent.

I was still connected to two hundred Mages but I didn't know how many were close to their limits.

"More supports," I ordered.

I felt others open the support tendrils. Then I reached out with my mind and pushed the tendrils apart. Power surged up the streams of over a thousand Mages as the tendrils spread wider. They reached about three feet.

"Go," Rostov said. "She needs you. We will clean up here."

I dove through the hole that snapped closed behind me. I was standing in front of an amazed Kren.

I AM HERE, my mental voice rolled across the base.

"Where is she?" I asked Kren.

He pointed toward the west where the Source was boiling above the ground.

I looked closely to see a small cluster of souls almost hidden by the Source behind them.

Then I was airborne. I landed in a cloud of dust and launched myself again.

I saw them surrounding her. She was down and a ring if Mages surrounded her. Another ring of Guards surrounded them and a piled ring of dead Kresh encircled the whole group. I landed in the center of that ring.

The Mages were glowing as their Streams flowed forcefully through them into her. Some had already fallen as my supports in Kansas had done, some of those souls were very dim. I reached her side and pulled her to me.

The second I touched her, my stream erupted with power that flowed into her as well. I looked up to see the astonished faces that stared back at me. I had changed, physically from the connection to the Kresh Source. I was me but I was different.

"How?" Prada muttered.

Kyra stepped forward, glowing with the power being drawn through her, to stare closely at me.

"Oh, my son," she said. "What have you done to yourself?"

"Not important," I returned in a deeper voice than before. I looked down at the still form in my arms and reached inside of her mind to do what she had once done for me.

All was black except a small circle of light in the distance. I began to run toward that light at an astonishing speed. The power of the mind was what fueled anything I could do here. Due to my recent changes, that was powerful, indeed.

I was there in an instant. A small patch of light surrounded by the glowing forms of those who supported her. I stepped past them into the circle to find the six year old girl I had saved in Tennessee. She was huddled in the center of the circle of light, looking fearfully out into the darkness that tried to push its way in to take her. In her arms was a small baby doll that carried the same glow as those in the circle. I pulled them close and heard her tiny voice.

"My Angel?"

Then she was back to the form I knew and loved. I could still see the frightened child inside of her, the one afraid of the darkness that would come for her.

"How are you here? Who is that with you?"

I looked sideways to see another form, burning with a dark red flame, just as I was burning with the brilliant flame that lit up the circle. I knew exactly who it was and I nodded to that dark and violent side of myself. Somehow I knew it would take all of us to Pull enough to fulfil whatever "balance" the Source required.

We turned, my dark side and I, to face the darkness as another of the Souls surrounding us faded and the circle grew a little smaller.

YOU WILL NOT HAVE THEM!

I felt Lyrica step up to stand between us. Her hands slid into ours. The baby doll was gone but there was a presence of someone with a psyche yet unformed. I knew this was our child in the womb of my beloved.

IF POWER IS WHAT YOU MUST HAVE, THEN POWER IT SHALL BE!

We Pulled, together, from deep inside of the Source. I felt Lyrica's will join with my own as well as the dark will of my other self. The power Paige had drawn from the Source was miniscule in comparison to what came ripping through our streams to be absorbed.

No one knows exactly what a Source Coma truly is. No one had lived long enough to even find out until I had survived. My best guess is that it is a balance of the power a person has used that is taken back. Most who have ever fallen into the coma burned out in seconds. A Soullord is different. Our bodies were created to withstand the Source.

I still would have died if my friends had not connected as supports to keep me alive long enough for Lyrica to step in. My Source Coma had been small compared to the power required to do what she had done. Fifty Mages were linked to her and she still fell. Those fifty refused to disconnect and many had fallen. She had pulled through our streams for hours when she saved me.

We were out on that plain for two days, but when I walked into Lifeline, I carried the sleeping form of my Little Angel in my arms. Thirty two Mages followed me carrying another eighteen. Twenty eight Soulguards followed. Seventy two men and women had died holding that circle around the Mages. They had killed four thousand Kresh before the gates had closed, killing the other forty thousand that had survived the inferno Lyrica had created.

People crowded forward as we entered to retreat at the sight of what I had become.

I was six feet tall, after the changes that had occurred and my uniform was noticeably tighter than it had been in the shoulders and legs. My nails weren't fingernails anymore, they were talons. The biggest thing that sent people backing away from me were my eyes. They were dark, almost black, instead of the white of the Human eye. The Iris was red and the pupils like pits of black. I saw them through the eyes of those around me and it was disconcerting.

I only hoped my Little Angel would forgive me for what I had done. I may never forgive myself.

Chapter 46

I sat by the hospital bed and looked over at my oldest friend. His Aura glowed but his mind didn't. On the bed to my left lay my second oldest friend.

I had pieced together what my friends had done. They were the reason I was able to save my angel's life. The Source requires a balance, I suppose. When Lyrica had fallen, Trent Deacons had seen four Mages fall down almost immediately. Another fell in seconds. One after another, they were falling. He and Mattie had been there when Lyrica brought me back and neither were stupid. They'd figured out the need for power that Lyrica's body was under.

I saw my two oldest friends embrace through the eyes of the Mages around them No one else realized what they had done but I knew immediately. They had, not only let the power surge through them, but Pulled with their combined will. They fell, but they were the last to fall. The others were enough to hold whatever this need for power was for a longer time.

Everyone had awoken except these two. Whatever the Source had done, I couldn't feel anything from their minds. Their bodies lived but their minds? I could find nothing when I felt for them.

"I'll find a way," I muttered as I squeezed Trent's shoulder.

I had placed them in the position to protect my Little Angel and they had done so. I stood up and brushed the hair from the face of Mattie Riordan with a finger.

"Thank you, my friends," I muttered.

Lyrica was sleeping again. I would have to tell her when she woke this time what had happened. There was much more I would have to explain than the loss of our friends.

What I'd done at the gate plagued me. If I hadn't released that which I carry inside would we have been able to save Division Two which had been swamped on our southern flank? Could I have done a Code Alpha and saved the lives of all of those Mages? Could I have stopped the deaths of Alec Brighton and Adaya Tovah?

Adaya Tovah, who Mage Bombed herself before she would let them bury her alive again. Alec had followed suit after his Division had fallen.

Mages that had followed me had died because of the power I Pulled through them. Not the power itself but they had fallen as they reached their limits. Three of them were taken by the Kresh before the others just stopped and shielded while I rampaged.

I had ripped Souls from Kresh and Human alike when they were held prisoner among the Kresh I would attack. The decision had already been made to use the Code Alpha but what I had done was done with no emotion except for the rage and desire to kill the enemy.

I am a monster, yet they all call me the hero. I had saved the day. They saw what I did but they don't understand why. Perhaps it's something they shouldn't know.

One thing was certain. The war on Earth had changed. We knew where all of the gates were located and they would be reinforced. I looked toward the airport as I stepped outside of the Hospital in Sydney. I could see the glimmer of one good thing I had learned.

Beside the tarmac was a gleaming portal that led to the gateway. With the Source and a lot of support Mages, I had opened the portal I had created to a width of about thirty feet.

I wasn't sure how far I could make one of these things but it seemed to require my telepathy and my abilities as a Soullord. Who knew what the future would hold for that particular skill?

"Your car is here, Boss," Prada said from the left side of the door I had exited.

"Thanks, Andrea."

I slid into the back seat as Prada opened the other door to join me. Alexei was at the wheel.

"You sure he's the one you want drivin'?" I asked. "I seem to remember the last time he drove. Just remember, Alexei, it's a car, not a tank."

"Car… tank… not much difference. Just less armor."

I buckled my seat belt.

The airport was a short distance and I could have done it faster if I just ran. They started using the car after I had been swamped by people the last time I had made the trip to the hospital.

Most of the refugees had been moved out but there were still some that waited for ships. They weren't near the problem as some of the forces that had been at the Gate. The telepathy I had used crossed both races and there were a lot of people who looked at me as some sort of freak. Others as some sort of Messiah.

Both versions of what they thought of me were hard to take. The ones who think I'm some sort of savior actually bother me more than the ones who think I'm a monster. I happen to agree with the latter. What did I really do? I killed my way across a continent ending in a rampage with the sole intent to exterminate a race. My harshest judge would always be myself.

"You're getting lost in there again," Prada said.

"I can't help it," I returned. "I keep thinkin' of what I could have done. Maybe I could have…"

"No," she interrupted. "You couldn't have stopped what happened to Adaya or Alec. The Kresh had some heavy hitters on the southern flank and there wasn't enough time to stop it."

"I didn't even try," I muttered.

"You ended the damn war," she said. "It took a few lives to do it. It's a harsh truth and you know it, but you did what no one else could have done. If we had continued there would have been thousands of more losses to our forces. Yes, we lost friends, but we could have lost so much more."

I looked at her for a moment. Perhaps she is right. I don't know. I suppose the future will tell if I am the monster or the messiah. Or maybe I'm just a guy who is stuck in the middle, doing the best I can just to be Human.

***

We stood at the front rail of the cargo ship that was slowing to enter the harbor at Greymouth, New Zealand. Two soul weary Soullords. Lyrica was nestled in at my side. She had been so quiet after everything was out in the open. We had lost friends in both of our conflicts and she took it even harder than I had. I had to wonder if it was all worth it. We had killed more Kresh in Australia than all the other places they had come. But what had we accomplished?

"Stop it." She said, squeezing my waist. "I can hear what you're thinking now."

Her head came up as we rounded the edge of the harbor.

"What did we accomplish?" she asked. "Look."

Ahead of us, packed on the shore at the docks was an enormous crowd of people. My enhanced vision let me look closer. A smaller group stood out on the docks awaiting the ship. I saw Paige Turner and seven children. In the front stood a little girl whose head bobbed around as she tried to see the ship better. Her aura rolled with anticipation. When she saw the two of us on the prow of the huge ship, it glowed with a joy that had us both in tears.

What had we accomplished? Three hundred thousand people awaited us on the shore that could attest to what we had accomplished.

Epilogue

The squeal of Rachel woke me from a dead sleep. Two small forms charged into the bedroom.

"Sam pulled my hair," Rachel complained in her Australian accent.

"You called my mate a turd," Sam returned.

"That's because he is a turd!"

I pointed at Lyrica, "Do you guys really want to wake her up?"

They stopped and ran from the room. I heard her snicker from under the covers.

"Who taught her the term, 'turd'?"

"I don't know where she would get somethin' like that."

"Mmm hmm," she said. "Sure you don't."

She slid from under the covers and stood in front of the mirror over the dresser. Her hand rubbed her abdomen, gently. It had begun to bulge the smallest bit in the last month.

My admiration was interrupted as I felt the Gate open. I was on my feet in an instant and reaching for my uniform. Lyrica was across the room and pulling her pants on. As I exited the bedroom, Lydia Doresti, met us.

"Sorry those two got past me…"

"Sorry, Lydia," I interrupted. "The Gate just opened. We have to get to work. Can you pack a go bag for the kids in case this gets out of hand? I'll need you to get down in the shelter until the clear signal."

She nodded and rushed toward the group of kids we could hear squealing in the Den.

It only took us a few minutes to get to the Headquarters from the house we were using as quarters for us, Lydia, and seven kids. Lydia was one of the Romanians who had been marked when I learned what the Mark was. She had come to help with the kids until we could prepare something for them in Oklahoma. It had stretched on for a lot longer than we had planned due to the fact that we both enjoyed having them there.

"Sir," the National Guard at the door greeted us, "The Gate opened, but nothing has come through."

Another voice yelled from behind him, "Someone came through! Two! Both are Human."

"I'm goin' out to see."

"We are," Lyrica agreed.

I rounded the building and passed the guns. I could see the distant forms. I focused my eyesight as I recognized the one on the left.

"Holy shit," I muttered and launched myself forward.

Lyrica caught up with me as I embraced my friend.

He pushed me out to arm's length and looked at me, "Boy, what have you done to yourself?"

I was looking at the blinding power rolling inside of his Soul, "Perhaps I need to ask you the same thing."

He grinned, "It's kind of a long story, Boss."

"Then, by all means, let's go somewhere and you can tell me."

"I'll start by telling you Hub is completely under your command. And I would like to introduce you to my wife, Sibine."

We walked out, past the guns, toward the HQ building.

"Love what you've done with the place."

I heard comments from around us.

"Who is…?"

"…came out of the gate."

"…thought he was dead."

"Welcome home, Ric," I said.

This Fallen World
By Christopher Woods

Chapter 1

I walked down the dreary street. Smoke hung in the air from the fires burning in the alleys that led back into dark corners filled with those less fortunate than the people who resided in the buildings alongside J Street.

Before the Fall, those in the street would have been rounded up and hauled away in vehicles to be incarcerated. Now, twenty years later, you'd find a better grade of people living in the alleys than the ones inside the buildings. Hell, maybe it wasn't so different, then.

Those, that had inhabited the city twenty years ago, were pretty despicable. I know this because I was one of the bastards. How things change.

"Fresh fruit, Mister?" a voice came from my right.

I glanced toward the young girl with an apron full of apples. Then pulled one of the apples from her apron. As I polished the apple on the lapel of my long coat, I listened for the telltale buzz from my rad marker. There was no buzz so I handed the girl a coin.

"Wow," she said, "is that an Old World coin?"

"They called 'em quarters," I answered. "Worth twenty Scripts. Take that and hide it well. There's a grocery store over on K Street. He'll change it for ya. He's good people."

She pulled a bag from her pocket and dropped the rest of the apples into it. She handed it to me.

"Mister, that's ten times the worth of the whole bunch," she said. "Thank you."

She slipped the quarter into a pocket and disappeared into the crowd.

I continued my trek down J Street. I couldn't spread too many of the coins I had found around too quickly. I had many more where that one had come from, but if word got out I was spending a lot of Old World coins, one of the Warlords would surely come down on me.

It didn't hurt to help the people around me when I could, as well. Most of the good will I had around the city had come from similar acts. Those on the street didn't have much, and when I helped them, they would remember. There will be a time I'll need help, and there are quite a few people who will remember.

J Street crossed Third Avenue ahead of me and my destination wasn't far down Third. There was a bar called the Strike Zone there. My contact had said he had a man who wanted to meet with me about a job. I tended to use the

Strike Zone as a meeting place for potential customers.

I had helped the owner find his kidnapped wife eight years ago, and he kept a booth unoccupied for me to use at any time. Good will is a priceless commodity in a Fallen world.

I came within view of the bar and there were crowds of people waiting to enter. Some things never change. People search for escape from reality in any world, Fallen or not.

The doorman nodded as I strode past the line of waiting patrons, some of which yelled in anger.

"Kade," he said as I reached him, "welcome, as always. You're booth is clear, and there is a guest awaiting your arrival."

"Thanks Sam," I said and walked into the noisy, smoke-filled room.

I made my way across the large room full of dancing men and women. The music pounded some sort of digital created music from the Old World. I had found a stash several years back of several kinds of Old World music discs. I traded most of the discs for a player to Jared Mcknight, the owner of Strike Zone. I had kept a small collection of a style of music called Blues. I liked the Old World Blues music. Most of the rest had been dance music of some sort or another. Some digital, some of what they had called Country, R&B, Hip-Hop. I didn't care for most of those.

The Old World music had brought crowds of people into Strike Zone, and Jared had been making money hand over fist. Then the local Warlord had stepped in and began taxing Jared to keep his bar open. Now Jared made enough to get by but not much more.

"Kade!" Jared's voice boomed across the room.

I looked to my right to see Jared waving at me. He was pushing through the crowd toward me.

"Mathew Kade," He said with a huge smile, "a sight for sore eyes!"

"How are ya, Jared?" I asked.

"Could be better, but I'm still here."

"How's Jenny?"

"Pregnant."

"Really?" I said with a smile. "Congratulations, my friend!"

"Thanks, Kade," he said. "It never woulda happened without you."

"I'm pretty sure I didn't have anything to do with that."

His laugh boomed across the room again.

"True enough," he said. "But you found her for me, Kade. I can never thank you enough for that. And now I'm about to be a father."

"You deserve it, man," I said. "Take good care of 'em."

"Will do," he said. "I'll be by your table in a few. Had a little episode we have to deal with. Someone didn't like my reservation policy."

"I'll talk to ya then," I said and made my way to the booth in the back that was conspicuously empty.

As I slid into the booth, I could see two people with an interest in me. One was an older gentleman in an old suit. The other was a young man who had a perpetual snarl on his face.

I motioned to the older gentleman, and he made his way toward my booth.

"Mathew Kade," I said with my hand outstretched. "I understand you have a job for me?"

"Yes I do," he said. "My name is Cedric Hale. I need you to find my daughter for me. She disappeared three days ago, and I haven't been able to find a single clue as to where she has gone."

I motioned for him to have a seat

"What made you search me out for this job?"

"I worked for a company called Obsidian," he said.

My eyes narrowed.

"I'm not here to let your secret out, Mr. Kade," he said. "I know what you were. I know what happened to you. It's amazing that you were able to rebuild your psyche into something more than a drooling vegetable. Yet you did. You have the skills to find my daughter, no matter where she is."

"You know a lot about me, Hale," I said, "and I'm not very comfortable with that."

"When the end came, I know you were still in the Imprinter and it scrambled your brain," he said. "I also know, you spent three years inside the Obsidian building, under treatment for serious mental illness. No one even knows how you did it, Mr. Kade. Treatment did nothing and then one day you just stood up and became Mathew Kade."

"I'm not here to blackmail you or any such nonsense," he said. "I just know what you were capable of before the Fall. If you have a fraction of that capability, you can find my daughter."

A commotion on the floor caught my eye, and a bottle was hurled across the room. I was on my feet and caught the bottle in my left hand.

For just a second, I was someone else. The young man with the perpetual snarl was staring into the cold dead eyes of someone entirely different from the man that had sat at the table. His eyes widened in fear and he ran into the crowd.

In a moment I sat back down.

Hale was smiling, "A fraction."

I stared at him in silence.

He placed a coin in front of me. I looked at it in surprise. It was a solid gold coin from the Old World. Probably worth ten thousand script now.

"This is a down payment," Hale said. "You find her, you get another. Return her to me unharmed, you get three."

"I'll see what I can do."

"Thank you, Agent," he said softly.

I nodded.

He passed me a folder and I opened it to see a picture of a pretty young red-haired woman. She appeared to be late teens or early twenties and that could be bad. This Fallen world is hard on young beautiful people.

Warlords could swoop in with their troops and steal people at will. They were Warlords because the held the weapons or tech that gave them control over those around them.

There had been incidents for years. I had a great disdain for the term, Warlord. They were the ones who had found some advantage and abused it, for the most part.

There were a few good men, such as Wilderman, who held the reigns of fourteen city blocks. He provided protection to those who lived in his domain. He taxed his people but he also provided true protection.

Miles to the East, there was Joanna Kathrop. She held sixteen blocks and ruled with an iron fist. She had found a cache of weapons and provisions in her area several decades back. Her cadre of loyal soldiers backed her and she established her rule of that area.

There were others, both good and bad. The majority of them were bad. They ran single and double blocks. The Warlord that controlled the area where strike Zone was located wasn't the worst, but he was far from the best.

I turned the page and found the sector that Hale and his daughter had lived.

"You were under Yamato?" I asked.

"Yes," he said, "he took down the Bishop a decade ago."

"Yamato's always been fair," I said. "Did you take this to him?"

"He couldn't help me," he said. "She was traveling across the city."

"What the hell was she doin' travelin'?" I asked. "Was she in a caravan?"

The Caravans were the only semi-safe way to travel the city. You paid for your ticket, and the Caravans paid their tax to run through the Zones.

"She was going to the new College, set up by Kathrop, in a small Caravan," he said, "run by a man named Drekk. He claims she never showed up for the last leg of the trip."

"Drekk," I spat the word out. "I've heard of Drekk. If you want to travel anywhere, you have to use the Accredited Caravans. You can't use people like Drekk."

His face fell, "We didn't know about this until it was too late. We aren't rich people, Mister Kade."

I looked down at the coin still in my hand, and looked back to him with one eyebrow raised.

"The life savings of both my family and the family of Seran Yoto, her fiancée."

"Poor would not be what I would call this, Hale," I said. "There are people right in this room who won't see this much wealth in ten lifetimes. You dwell inside the Scraper. You have running water and electricity. Don't you ever try to pass yourself off as the poor. It's insulting."

He nodded

"Who set up the Caravan?"

"I set it up through a man in the Scraper. His name is Denton. He owns a supply store on the bottom floor."

"Ok," I said. "That's where I'll need to start. I'll be there first thing in the morning."

"But the Caravans don't run at night..."

"Some people, it's safer to leave alone, Hale. When you get back to the Scraper, tomorrow, I'll have some answers for you."

"How will you cross three zones tonight?"

"I'll walk, Hale," I said. "Corporate Agents can take care of themselves."

"You haven't been an Agent for twenty years."

"You're right, there," I said, "I'm something else, now. I'll see you tomorrow night at your Scraper."

I stood and walked away from the booth. Jared was beside the bar, talking to several suits.

"Yo Jared," I said, "I'm on a job for a few days. Ya can fill the table if ya need to."

"Be careful, Matt," he said. "Last time Jenny took a week to get you patched up.

"I'll try, buddy."

I had a feeling about this one. Things looked bad for Maddy Hale. Drekk wasn't known to be trustworthy.

Life can be dangerous in this Fallen World.

This is a sample chapter in This Fallen World, the beginning of a series of novellas. If this peaks your interest, it and the second in the series are available on Amazon.

www.ingramcontent.com/pod-product-compliance
Lightning Source LLC
Chambersburg PA
CBHW022033120726
47899CB00001BB/151